I0747282

HEMLOCK

AND

HOMICIDE

A SMILEY AND McBLYTHE MYSTERY

HEMLOCK

AND

HOMICIDE

A SMILEY AND McBLYTHE MYSTERY

BRUCE
HAMMACK

1

Heather heaved a sigh of impatience as Steve leaned on his white cane and said, "Say the victim's name again."

"Michelle Le Blanc."

Steve shuddered like he'd caught a chill.

Leo, Steve's former partner at Houston Homicide, took a full breath and recited the demographic data without inflection in his words. "Pharmacist. Female. Age, thirty-two. Divorced. Former husband lives in Paris." He paused. "That's Paris, France, not Paris, Texas." He continued. "No children. Immigrated eight years ago. Both parents also live in France. Ms. Le Blanc's last address is a condo in The Woodlands, a few miles from Heather's office."

Heather stood with arms crossed, rolling her fingertips on the sleeve of her silk blouse. "Well, is it a homicide or not?" She looked around the banquet room of an upscale hotel in North Houston. The hotel staff hadn't bussed the table that was marked off with crime scene tape. Otherwise, no furniture remained in the massive room.

Instead of directly answering her question, Steve faced Leo. "Have you notified The Woodands P.D. or Montgomery County Sheriff's office?"

"Not yet. The initial tox report shows she ingested poison. I wanted you to do your trick to make sure it wasn't an accident or self-inflicted."

Steve spoke in a flat voice. "I'm seeing red."

Heather knew what this meant, and it didn't please her. Steve had discovered early in his homicide career that he possessed a gift called associative chromesthesia. When he was at a homicide scene, and he heard the victim's name, he would see a red film over the scene if the victim had been murdered. Even after losing his sight a few years ago, he still had an impression of seeing red at murder scenes. But gift or no gift, she had all she could handle right now with her businesses. "Steve, if you're thinking about me and you working this case, I'm sorry, but I can't help you this time."

The last word escaped her lips a split second before her phone rang. She retrieved the device from her purse, glanced at the caller ID, and put the phone to her ear. Quick steps took her away from Steve and Leo as she spoke and walked at the same time. The conversation was short and sour instead of short and sweet.

"I hate to break up the party, but the wheels have officially fallen off my construction schedule. I need to get back to the office." She then mumbled, "I told you I didn't have time to play private detective with you until the first phase of homes is ready for occupancy. The entire project will be dead in the water if families aren't in before Christmas."

She knew she was breaking the agreement she'd made with Steve, and it grieved her to go back on her word. Theirs wasn't a binding written contract; they hadn't even sealed it with a handshake. But she'd given her word that she'd drop whatever she was doing to be his eyes and business partner in solving the occasional murder that came their way. Trust was something they both took seriously.

She'd painted herself into a corner by investing so much of her personal money in this project, not counting the loans she'd secured. The scope of the lakeside housing development with two golf courses, homes, condominiums, apartments, multiple swimming pools, a massive recreation center, and retail shops was daunting, but with monumental risks come tremendous rewards. It would go a long way toward matching her father's wealth if she could pull it off. Deadlines loomed with significant consequences if she didn't meet them.

Once again, Steve directed his attention to Leo. "What does the rest of your day look like?"

Leo shot Heather a glance that, of course, Steve couldn't see. "I'm teaching a class at the training academy. Why don't you come with me? Heather can put the fires out at her office, and you can tell me how you and Heather solved the last case on that private island in the Caribbean."

"Are you sure you have time to take me home afterwards?" asked Steve.

"No problem. I'll call my new partner and tell her to wear out her computer doing background information on Ms. Le Blanc."

Steve faced Heather. "You heard the senior homicide detective. You're excused."

Heather stiffened. "I don't appreciate your tone or the perfunctory dismissal."

"And I don't appreciate you trying to kill yourself on this project, or assuming I have any interest in helping Leo with this case. He hasn't asked for anything but to help determine if it was a homicide or a suicide."

Steve wasn't finished. "And while we're clearing the air, when was the last time you slept for over four hours?" He didn't wait for an answer. "I'll tell you. It was when we were on the private island. You ate well, exercised, and allowed other people to do their jobs without you interfering."

Heather's hands moved to her hips. "And when we got home, it took me three weeks to put things back together."

"That's not true. You trusted the people you left in charge, and they stayed on schedule. What you can't stand is not being around to micro-manage this project."

Leo held up his hands, even though Steve couldn't see him. "That's enough, you two. Steve is right about one thing. I haven't asked either of you to help me solve this case. From where I'm standing, both of you need to get a prescription for chill-pills and take them until you're halfway human again." He directed his next words to Steve. "Do you want to come with me to the academy or fight with Heather all the way back to Montgomery County?"

"I'm going with you."

"Good," said Heather. "Don't forget to feed Max when you finish playing cops and killers."

"That reminds me, when was the last time *you* fed that overgrown ball of fur?"

She shot back, "What else do you have to do with your time?"

Heather bit her lip. It was a cruel thing to say to the man whose career ended when he lost his sight, and his wife, to street thugs.

Leo gave her a stare that said she'd crossed a line. He followed the stare with a stinging command. "Like Steve said, you're excused."

Heather's eyes clouded as she left the building. The dam burst on her emotions as soon as she closed the door to her SUV. Sobbing, she dug in her purse for a tissue. She'd sworn to herself that she'd never again attempt to complete such a massive project, no matter how much money the build would yield. Yet, here she was in the middle of a deal that had taken over her life.

Red-rimmed eyes stared back at her in the mirror. Who does she think she's kidding? It's in her DNA to select projects that challenge her beyond the limits of her mental and physical ability.

On the way to her office, she thought of her father. How could he run a multi-billion-dollar empire and make it look so effortless? Even though their relationship was much improved from when she was in her teens and twenties, she couldn't help but feel she didn't live up to his expectations. She certainly didn't live up to his performance. Someday she'd ask him how he did it. Someday, but not today.

Her thoughts swirled as she drove north on I-45. Despite her protestations of not having time to think about the homicide, the crime scene and Leo's description of the victim stuck in her brain like the words of an old nursery rhyme. When exactly was Michelle Le Blanc killed? Where was she sitting at the table? Who else was at the table? No blood on the tablecloth or the floor. That made it unlikely there was another contributing cause of death, but Leo wouldn't know that until he received the results of the autopsy.

"Poison," she repeated out loud. "That's significant. Criminologists used to say to look for a woman in cases of poison." She chuckled. "They used to say a lot of things."

From past experience, she knew Steve would allow Leo to solve the case on his own—at least until he got stuck.

Miles ticked by while her thoughts rested solely on the murder. She'd never worked a homicide by poisoning case before. It might be interesting.

A firm shake of her head brought her back to reality. Interesting or not, she had a crisis to handle that required her full attention.

2

———

S teve placed his hand on Leo's arm as they walked in silence toward the door of the banquet room. He barely heard the footsteps of someone approaching before Leo slowed and stopped. A woman's voice cut through the stillness of the cavernous room. "Detective Vega?"

"Yes."

"I'm Ms. Patino, the hotel manager. I wanted to let you know another convention begins tomorrow that will require this room. I hope your people have completed their work."

Leo sounded stern. "There wasn't much they could do after your staff removed all the crime scene tape from the secondary area, cleared all the dishes, removed all the tables but one, and vacuumed the carpet."

She cleared her throat. "I apologize. The person responsible for the banquets in this room thought only the one table needed to remain untouched."

He pointed. "That doesn't explain why they cleared the table of dishes where the victim was sitting before officers arrived."

"Only the first two courses. It was a hectic scene. Three hundred guests attended the banquet. That doesn't count a small army of servers and first responders. Mistakes and chaos go hand in hand in such situations. Again, I apologize, and my heartfelt sympathy goes out to the young woman and her family. My staff believed she choked on a piece of meat." She hesitated. "That's what happened, wasn't it?"

"I'm waiting on the autopsy before I can answer that question. For now, we're treating her passing as a suspicious death."

"Oh, dear."

Leo answered her concern with, "What's done is done. I'm releasing the room to you. I'll remove the crime scene tape from around the table and take it with me."

"Thank you, Detective Vega."

Steve stayed where he was as he heard the soles of Ms. Patino's shoes brush against the short pile of the commercial carpet. Leo soon returned. "Do you want a souvenir from a crime I don't have a prayer of solving?"

"That's not a very optimistic attitude."

"Admit it; even you would have trouble with this one. Clearing the table compromised any physical evidence that might have been there. The potential suspects include three hundred pharmacists, all familiar with more poisons than you or I have heard of. Add cooks and servers to the list of suspects and it would take a dozen detectives six months to put a dent in a thorough investigation. Whoever killed her couldn't have picked a better place."

"Don't forget," said Steve. "Many of the servers for hotel banquets are temporary hires. They may or may not be in the country legally." He teased Leo with his next question. "By the way, how much is a fake Social Security card going for these days?"

Leo issued a sarcastic, "They're a dime-a-dozen and thanks for the reminder."

Steve gave Leo what he hoped was a ray of hope in a seemingly hopeless situation. "Start with the victim, move to any romantic interests, try the money angle, and work out from there. Shake the trees and see what falls out. There's always a reason people kill each other. Also, get the names of the people at the table and pinpoint the server."

Leo let out a long sigh as they encountered a blast of warm, sticky, September air that told Steve they were approaching the hotel's entrance.

They remained silent until they were inside Leo's car. Steve noted the familiar smell of the vehicle. "Have you ever noticed that airplanes and cop cars both have distinct odors?"

Leo started the engine and said, "I never gave it much thought, except patrol cars sometimes smell like vomit and urine. I rarely transport suspects or people detained or arrested. This car is new. What does it smell like?"

"Plastic. Your back seat must be hard plastic. Also, the radios have a unique smell all their own."

"Interesting," said Leo. "That snoz of yours picks up on things I don't think about. Did you notice any unusual smells at the table where Michelle Le Blanc died?"

"I believe I did, but I'd need to go to a fancy French restaurant to confirm it."

"You're joking," said Leo.

"No, it smelled like *pate de fois gras.*"

"Goose liver?"

"Either duck or goose liver. It had a real metallic smell to it. They cleared the dishes, but there must have been some spilled on the table. Was there a stain on the tablecloth?"

"Yeah, there was. A report said the victim flipped her plate over when the poison hit her."

A touch of mirth seasoned Leo's next words. "When did you become a connoisseur of French cuisine? You were a chicken-fried steak and hamburger kind of guy when we worked together."

"Still am. Heather eats all kinds of fancy stuff. Sometimes she gives Max a treat. It reinforces his snooty attitude."

"That's one spoiled cat."

The rest of the trip passed with Leo filling the time with the exploits of his six children. Most were in their teens, which meant one or more were in a crisis-du-jour at any given time. Steve listened, laughed, and offered a silent prayer of thanks that he wasn't navigating parenting through such turbulent waters. The world of modern teens wasn't totally unfamiliar to him, but it had been a while since he spoke with Briann, Heather's boyfriend's daughter, and the only teenager he knew these days.

They arrived at Houston's police academy near Bush International Airport. After gaining admittance, they walked down a hallway. Steve heard a door open, and the sound of a dog's toenails tapping against the hard vinyl floor. Leo exchanged hellos with a man named Hank and his K-9.

"No need going in yet," said Hank. "They're about to take a fifteen-minute break."

Steve held out the back of his hand for the dog to smell. "Is this a German shepherd?"

"Sure is. Most of the dogs on the force are shepherds, but not all."

Leo interrupted. "This is Steve Smiley. He was my supervisor and the best homicide detective in Houston before he had to take medical retirement."

"I remember hearing about you, Mr. Smiley. They say you were something else."

"He still is," said Leo. "He and his new partner still help solve homicides."

"Only part-time," said Steve. "We're consultants who work with local, state, and federal agencies. Sometimes we travel to foreign locations, but most of the time we stay close to home."

"Perhaps I could get a gig like that after I retire."

Leo spoke in a tongue-in-cheek manner. "I doubt you'd find one like Steve's. His gig includes flying in a private jet to exotic locations with a rich, beautiful business partner."

Steve interrupted. "I never judge a woman by her looks. They all look the same to me. It's what's between the ears that matters."

Leo scoffed. "Heather's in a class by herself. Money, looks, an Ivy League education, and a former detective in Boston, Mass."

"Sounds like you got the one-in-a-million partner," said Hank.

Steve changed the subject. "How do I go about getting a dog that will protect me? My partner's father is supposed to be looking for something special, but I haven't heard from him in a couple of months."

The door to the classroom flew open, forcing the three men and the dog to move down the hall. Once they were away from the noisy cadets, Leo explained. "There's a former cop named Bucky Franklin, who assaulted Steve. Did you hear about it?"

"Yeah. He was in the fraud division. Didn't he torch your homes?"

Steve nodded. "Arson along with a few other crimes against me and several others. There's a long list of crimes he needs to answer for. He swore he'd get back at me for getting him fired. I believe he's a sociopath and capable of anything. Coming out of fraud means he knows all the tricks to take on new identities. There's no telling where he is or when he might come looking for me."

Steve took a full breath. "I need a dog who's a combination service dog for someone who can't see and has the instincts to keep me safe from Bucky." He held up a single index finger. "The dog will probably be around children someday, too. He'll need to protect them and their parents."

Hank took his time. "That's going to take a very special dog. I have one in mind that I'd like you to meet." He paused. "What's your home like?"

"Right now, I live in a lock-off mother-in-law apartment in a five-bedroom home with a fenced backyard. My business partner, Heather McBlythe, and her snooty Maine Coon cat claim a huge master bedroom. We share the common areas and Max has run of the entire house."

"Did you say the cat is snooty?"

"Snooty, snitty, aristocratic, entitled... take your pick."

"I don't want you to get your hopes up, but there's a dog that sounds like a bookend to the cat you're describing. His name is Roi. The Texas pronunciation is R-O-Y, but spelled Roi."

"Isn't that French for King?"

"He prefers to be called *Le Roi*, The King. He also likes the French pronunciation, which is two syllables and sounds like Ro-ah." Hank chuckled. "Of course, here in Houston, he doesn't get too much French."

Steve chuckled. "I'm not sure there would be room for two kings under the same roof, but it's worth meeting him. What breed?"

"Giant schnauzer. He's full-grown and weighs a hundred pounds."

Steve tilted his head. "What's wrong with him?"

"Nothing, other than he's picky about what he eats. All our dogs come to us fully trained by a company that finds them in Europe. Why don't you meet him first? The trainers can show you his strengths and tell you more about his one little weakness."

"This sounds ominous, but I'm willing to check him out."

"I'll call and see if he's still available. Let me warn you, trained police dogs don't come cheap."

Leo spoke up. "Money is no object for this guy. He still has fifty cents out of the first dollar he ever earned."

Steve and Leo waited as Hank made the call, which didn't last long. "He's available whenever you want to see him."

"I'll go tomorrow," said Steve. "I took French in high school and two semesters in college. Heather speaks it like she grew up in Paris. The idea of having a dog that only responds to us if we give commands in a foreign language appeals to me."

3

Heather stumbled into the kitchen after dragging herself out of bed at four-thirty in the morning. She wasn't expecting to see Steve sitting on a barstool, sipping coffee.

"Good morning," said Steve. "Coffee's ready."

She tried blinking crusty residue from her eyes and croaked a question. "What are you doing up so early?"

"I couldn't sleep. I have an appointment in Houston this morning that I'm excited about."

"Oh." she said around a yawn.

Steve chuckled. "Put half a cup of mud in you and I'll tell you about my appointment."

She moved to the coffeepot and poured herself a full serving of steaming black stimulant. Instead of listening to Steve's plans, she launched into a soliloquy of her own.

"If I face another day like yesterday, you'll need to put me in a monastery, or some other place where they prohibit talking. Every person I spoke to had an excuse for not being able to meet their schedule. First, it was my plumbing contractor. Then the electrical contractor phoned with supply chain problems. Next in line was a civil engineer who discovered a street that would need to be raised three inches to drain properly.

The coup-de-grâce was a lame-brain county inspector who said a support beam in the recreation center didn't meet specifications and would need to be replaced. That beam passed inspection three months ago, and he issued a certificate of occupancy. It turns out he misplaced his original paperwork." She let out a huff. "He had the nerve to accuse me of forging his signature on my copies. I had to call two county commissioners to pressure the inspector and his people to search their files. I raised such a stink his clerk had to work three hours overtime. As expected, someone in his office misfiled it. Now he's furious with me because he missed Monday night football. Mark my words. He'll drag his feet on future inspections and be super-picky."

She lifted her coffee cup to her lips but didn't take a sip. "Did I tell you there was another accident on the jobsite yesterday? That makes three in the last thirty days." Heather glanced at the clock. "I'm already late." Quick-stepping to her bedroom, she spoke over her shoulder. "Make sure you feed Max. Was there something else you needed to tell me?"

"I'll send you an email."

"Don't expect me home before ten tonight. You're on your own for supper."

She thought Steve mumbled, "And breakfast, and lunch," but she couldn't be sure of his exact words. A full day awaited her.

Steve received a text from the Uber driver announcing his arrival. With cane in hand, he tapped his way to the garage and located the button that raised the door. Whirls, creaks, and groans sounded as the door retracted and fresh air flooded the empty triple garage. Heather and her Mercedes SUV had long since left.

Once outside, Steve located the number pad beside the door's frame and punched in a four-digit code and the ENTER button beneath the others. More mechanical sounds and a thud told him the door had returned to seal the garage.

"Do you need help?" asked the driver in a heavy Middle Eastern accent.

"No, thanks. Do you mind if I ride up front with you?"

"It's your choice, sir. We can talk or refrain from conversation, as you wish."

Steve appreciated the driver's attitude and wanted to know more about him. He located the passenger door, entered and sat on a comfortable cloth seat. "I like the new car smell, even though I believe it's an older model."

"God be praised," said the driver. "I'm in the presence of a prophet."

Steve laughed. "I'm neither a prophet nor the son of a prophet. This feels like a ten-year-old Toyota Sienna minivan. My wife had one, but hers always smelled like paint. She was an artist."

"Ah. You use past tense. I conclude you've suffered misfortune."

"Am I the one in the presence of a prophet?"

A hearty laugh came from the driver as he backed the vehicle out of the driveway. It came to a complete stop before the transmission clicked into drive. The man proved himself a smooth, cautious driver who used turn signals in plenty of time and didn't wear out the brakes making sudden stops.

"My name is Rasheed, Mr. Smiley. Your destination intrigues me. I've never been to a dog training business before. No such thing exists in my home country."

"And where was that?"

"If you don't mind, I'd rather speak in generalities about the country of my fathers. The name ends with the letters S-T-A-N and is not on favorable terms with this country. I fell out of favor with some of its leaders and lost my position at the university."

"What did you teach?"

"Philosophy. I had to flee with only the clothes on my back.

My transcripts, diplomas, and history of employment were all destroyed in a purge of academics. That's why I'm driving a glorified taxi."

The tone of his voice and his next words spoke of hope instead of self-pity. "A bad day of driving in Houston traffic is better than any day would be if I was in the country of my birth."

"Your words remind me to be thankful for this country. It's so easy to get caught up in our troubles."

After a mile of sitting in traffic that barely moved, Rasheed said, "If I may be so bold, tell me about this place we're going."

"It's a facility for specialized training of police and service dogs. The dog I'm going to see has completed training for police service, but I need him to be more than that. He must undergo additional training to become a service dog for me, since I'm blind."

"Ah," said Rasheed. "You need a dog with an advanced degree."

"That's a good way of explaining it."

"Dogs frighten me. Soldiers used them extensively. They came frequently to the university. I hate to say it, but they often reacted to the scent of explosives on students. Detentions for questioning were common."

"They're amazing animals," said Steve. "I'm hoping to find one that can combine many different skills and still be a companion."

The traffic started moving. "It's a good thing the training facility is on the north side of Houston," said Rasheed.

Steve shifted in his seat. "If today's meeting goes well, I may need to hire you for regular trips to and from the training facility. Would you be open to that?"

It took Rasheed several seconds too long to respond. "Would it involve transporting the dog, too?"

"Yes." Steve quickly added, "Police and service dogs are the safest dogs to be around. They're trained not to react to adverse stimuli."

"My initial inclination is to reject your proposal. Besides my experience with the military, a dog mauled me as a child. I bear the scars on my legs. Other scars are in my mind." A sigh followed. "On second thought, it would be good for me to overcome my fears. I've always wanted to explore the topic of fear but haven't had the courage to do so. Perhaps I could write an essay on the subject."

"The irony of our situations isn't lost on me," said Steve. "You'd prefer to not be around dogs and I'm actively seeking one to protect me. Perhaps we both could overcome some fears."

"I sense adventure in our future, my friend."

"The prophet speaks again."

4

A mechanical voice announced, "You've arrived at your destination." Rasheed asked, "Will you need further assistance?"

"Please," said Steve. "Unknown places keep me humble. It rarely takes me long to memorize floor plans, but I play human bumper cars the first time or two."

"It is said that humility is a favored dish of those who truly excel, but I've found it tastes like dung."

Steve's laugh filled the vehicle as he reached for the door handle. "I have much to learn from you."

"And I, you," replied Rasheed as they set out across the parking lot. "My fears are rising with each sound the dogs are making. How do you recommend I take you inside, when I can feel teeth tearing my skin?"

"My grandfather was a devout believer in God. He memorized large portions of the Bible, but he spoke to me with words I could understand. He said if I was afraid of anything, to pretend the strongest person who ever lived was standing between me and that thing or person."

"Your grandfather was a wise man. I'll try to follow his words, but fear is gnawing at my insides."

"He once told me to imagine a dog without teeth."

Three seconds passed before Rasheed asked, "Did he really say that?"

"No, but you'll not be able to erase the image of a toothless dog when we go inside."

It was the driver's turn to laugh, which he did until they reached the building's door. Rasheed opened it and took a single step inside before stiffening, frozen in place. Steve had his hand on the driver's arm, squeezed it, and whispered, "One step at a time. Every dog here is wearing dentures that come out if it tries to bite you."

A chuckle sounded, and Rasheed stepped forward with newfound confidence.

"Good morning. You must be Steve Smiley. Welcome to K9 University. I'm Emile Dubois, co-owner."

Steve extended a hand for the man to shake. "This is Rasheed, my driver and new friend."

"Let's go to my office, where we can discuss your needs."

Emile's shoes squeaked as Rasheed and Steve walked behind the man whose French accent was barely perceptible. He spoke as Rasheed closed the door behind them. "Yesterday's phone calls came as a shock. Of all the dogs we've trained for the police department, Le Roi was one of the best, if not the best. I knew they preferred German shepherds, but they also accept Labs for narcotics detection and the occasional hound for tracking."

Emile took a breath. "Forgive me for talking so much. My partner says it's because I'm from France. My mouth and hands work in unison." His chair let out a squeak as he sat.

Rasheed directed Steve to a wooden office chair. "I appreciate you making time to meet with me."

"Instead of me making assumptions, tell me why you want a police dog."

Steve expected the question and launched into an explanation. "I not only want a trained police dog, but also one that realizes I'm blind and have limitations."

"We train service dogs for the visually impaired but have never combined the two types of training in one animal."

"Is it possible?"

"There's a lot of overlap in skills. Just because we've never tried it doesn't mean it can't be done."

"What would be required of me?"

"Time is the main thing. The initial training would mean coming to this facility five days a week for three to six months. Also, the dog would become a family member and would require regular refresher courses to keep up his skills."

"Can I do those at home?"

"Yes, but you'll need training as much as your dog. We strongly recommend you both return here for periodic evaluations."

"What else?"

"I'd like to come to your home and evaluate the residence to make sure it's appropriate to provide adequate exercise for the dog."

"I'm having a home built on a spacious lakeside property. Could you give recommendations for modifications to the plans to best accommodate my potential new roommate?"

"Certainly. The chief priority will be adequate yard space. Police dogs thrive on exercise."

Steve searched his mind for other things to ask. While he was thinking, Emile brought up another issue. "There's one more thing I need to cover before I introduce you to Le Roi. As distasteful as it is, there's the issue of money. We offer a money-back guarantee on all the dogs we train. In cases of returns, we pass on as much of the financial loss incurred as we can to the next customer. I'm willing to offer Le Roi at a reduced price, but the additional three months to become a fully certified support dog will bring the cost back to full."

Steve rubbed his cheek. "That's acceptable. In fact, it's very generous."

"I was hoping you'd see the value of such an arrangement."

Steve leaned forward and lowered his voice. "I understand Le Roi has the personality of an aristocrat. Perhaps we shouldn't mention he's being offered at a discount. Kings don't like that sort of thing."

Emile chuckled. "Mr. Smiley, I believe you and Le Roi will make an excellent team. You understand that psychology has a place in the world of animals every bit as much as with humans. Are you ready to meet Le Roi?"

"That's why I came."

Rasheed's chair scraped on the floor as he stood. "Mr. Smiley, I'll wait for you in the parking lot. Take all the time you need."

Steve asked, "Are your fears growing teeth again?"

"Sharp, long teeth."

Emile's next words showed he understood Rasheed's desire to leave. "Did a dog bite you when you were a child?"

"It took over forty stitches to close the wounds."

"Dogs can smell fear. It's best if you go to the car today. I can refer you to a professional counselor who specializes in helping people who've had traumatic experiences with dogs. Are you interested?"

"Yes, but not today. I must flee to the safety of my car."

The breeze from the opening and slamming office door blew across Steve. "He wasn't kidding when he told me about his fear of dogs."

"And you, Mr. Smiley? Your desire for a police dog tells me you have fears of your own. Hank told me a former cop assaulted you. Is that true?"

"Yes. I'm attempting to become a writer. The cop who assaulted me pretended to be a writing coach and publisher. He stole my work and published it under his name. I fought back legally, and he didn't like it. He then set fire to my condo, which spread to the adjoining one owned by my business partner. Heather bought a large home in an upper-middle-class neighborhood of The Woodlands. We'll move as soon as our new homes are finished, hopefully before Christmas."

"I'm confused. Is your partner a publisher?"

"That's probably the only thing she's not. Her name is Heather McBlythe. She's an entrepreneur with a Boston pedigree. We're both former detectives. Every so often we help solve homicides."

"That's intriguing. How often do you take cases?"

"So far, it's varied between two and four times a year."

"Are you currently working on a case?"

"Not yet, but we went to a crime scene yesterday. It involved a homicide by poison."

"Is that unusual?"

"Not in British detective stories, but intentional poisonings rank near the bottom in US statistics."

Steve leaned forward. "A question just came to me. I know dogs have an amazing sense of smell. Can you train them to identify and alert to poisons?"

Emile hesitated. "Our best sniffer dogs have around one million sensory receptors in their nose and muzzle. They are one hundred thousand times more sensitive to smells than humans. I don't see why we couldn't train one to alert on a poison if we had a sample."

Steve leaned back. "You'll have to excuse me. Yesterday's crime scene has my brain working overtime on novel ways to solve a poisoning case. My former partner at Houston Police is leading the investigation. I'm sure he'll solve the case by traditional means and won't need help from a dog."

Emile's chair squeaked, meaning he'd leaned back. "Now, you've piqued my imagination. I wonder if there's a market for dogs trained to alert on poisons."

"It beats the old way of protecting royalty by having servants taste all their food."

The wheels on Emile's chair let out a squeal as he pushed away from his desk. "Are you ready to meet Le Roi?"

"More than ready."

"I'll lead you to his kennel and describe him to you. We'll take him to the obstacle course. He likes to show off."

"I hope he realizes I can't see him. Showing off won't impress me."

"That may work to our advantage. He's a natural-born learner. Challenges make him try harder."

After turning right and left down several corridors, they left the building and walked along a concrete sidewalk. "We're passing a row of kennels. Le Roi is in the last one."

"It seems like I'm going to conduct a job interview," said Steve.

"You are."

"But who's being interviewed, me or Le Roi?"

"Both. I'll be watching how he reacts to you. Being rejected yesterday didn't please him."

They came to a stop and Steve took his hand off of Emile's arm. He also placed his cane on the ground beside himself.

Emile whispered, "Good thinking. We trained Le Roi to be extra vigilant around people carrying anything that could harm his partner. Stand here while I attach his leash and bring him to you."

The sound of a latch being thrown on a metal gate preceded Emile issuing a greeting in French.

Shoes scuffed and toenails clicked on concrete, which gave away the dog and handler's position. Emile and Le Roi stood facing Steve, who improved his posture with a straight back and chin slightly raised.

"Le Roi," said Emile, "this is Mr. Steve Smiley."

The dog made no sound.

Steve gave a slight bow. "Bonjour, Le Roi."

Emile gave a firm command. "*S'asseoir.*"

The Frenchman's voice softened. "I told him to sit."

"I must have skipped the day we covered sitting in college. Let me try something else. *Poser, s'il vous plait.*"

"Very good, Steve. He's lying on his stomach with his head up, waiting for the next command."

"Would you describe him to me?"

"Of course."

"First," said Steve, "I'll get him to stand so he can look more kingly. *Debout, Roi.*"

"He's on his feet and looks stately, striking a pose like a show dog. He's angled his hind legs outward from his rump and is giving us a full view of his profile. His whiskered chin is up, and his ears are at attention. Le Roi is black as a lump of coal. His coat shines like a pair of highly polished shoes. He's truly a magnificent animal, and he knows it."

"Can I run my hand over him?"

"Go ahead. You've made a friend by speaking his native language, albeit with a Texas accent. He appreciates your effort. He always responds well to respect."

Steve held out a hand. After feeling a cool nose, the dog moved forward so Steve's hand could feel the top of its black head. "He's taller than I thought he would be."

"Just his head," said Emile. "His back is much lower."

Steve took his time as his hands took mental photos of the dog, including his Van Dyke beard and the long hair on his legs. Steve returned to Le Roi's head and gave it a last stroke. He directed his next words to the dog. "You're worthy of your name, Le Roi."

The dog's head lifted a little higher.

Steve asked, "When can we begin training?"

"Let's go back to the office and complete the details. I'll email a contract to you this afternoon."

By the end of the meeting, Steve was convinced he'd hit the proverbial jackpot. Le Roi would be dual certified, and in a few months they'd be living in a new lakeside duplex next door to Heather. For the first time since losing Maggie, he didn't hate the thought of Christmas.

On the trip back to The Woodlands, Steve remembered he

hadn't told Heather about his potential new companion. He explained the dilemma to Rasheed and asked for his advice.

"You ask too much of me. I cannot imagine being in the same room with a dog, let alone paying money to obtain one. As for knowing the thoughts and ways of a woman, that is a well without a bottom." He paused. "I suggest you grovel."

"You might be right, but that's not the way we communicate." He took off his sunglasses and rubbed his eyes. "I may have to pull a rabbit out of my hat if I'm going to get out of this doghouse."

"Those are two American sayings that make no sense to my Eastern ear. I still believe groveling is your best course of action."

Steve spent the rest of the day wondering how he should tell Heather about Le Roi. He explained the situation to Max, Heather's portly Main Coon cat, but he seemed more interested in sleeping and preening.

It was approaching ten-thirty when the creaking and squeaking of the garage door signaled Heather's arrival. He knew she'd be ready to fall into bed, but this was a conversation he couldn't delay.

5

The sound of the garage door closing behind her car was music to Heather's ears. The day was marginally better than the previous one, but not by much. Supply chain issues still plagued the project, but she'd at least secured new assurances of arrival dates for many of the products. It remained to be seen whether the suppliers could live up to their commitments and contracts. If not, they'd incur monetary penalties.

She grabbed her phone from the cupholder in the console, retrieved the valise holding her laptop from the passenger's seat, and swung open the driver's door. Once inside, she walked past the door leading to Steve's suite of rooms and made her way to the kitchen.

Steve sat on a barstool facing the refrigerator. "Rough day?" he asked.

"I give it a C minus. Another day, another set of problems. One minor victory was the delivery of the jetted tubs for another fifty homes, including our duplex. They came in a week ahead of schedule."

"Doesn't that count as a modern-day miracle?"

"I'm not celebrating until the sinks and plumbing supplies are on site. Coordinating supplies and labor is like nailing Jello to the wall. You look away for a few seconds and there's a mess on the floor."

"Good analogy." Steve paused. "I know you're tired, but there's something I need to tell you."

The tone of Steve's voice was one he reserved for serious conversations. She placed her valise and phone on the bar and sat on the barstool next to him. "I'm listening."

"I'll be traveling to Houston and back five days a week for the next three months."

"Oh? Did Leo talk you into helping him with the poisoning case?"

"That's a good guess, but you're off the mark. As you know, Leo and I went to the police academy yesterday."

"I remember. Do they want you to teach again?"

"Another good guess, but no. We ran into an officer with his K9 partner, teaching a class on narcotics detection."

"Those dogs are amazing. I love to watch them work."

"That's good. You'll get your chance."

She sat up straight. "What have you done?"

"I found a dog that's already been through police training. We'll need to go through three more months of training to certify him as a guide dog. Tomorrow, the owner of the company that trains dogs will be here to look at our home and collect the contract. I'd like for you to look it over, if you have time."

Heather held up her palms. "Hold on. Are you telling me you've found your own dog when you knew my father wanted to find the perfect dog for you?" She sucked in a quick breath and slid off the barstool. "Why didn't you discuss this with me before you committed to a home visit?"

"If you can hit the rewind button and look at last night, you'll find I couldn't get a word in before you launched into a tale of woe about your construction issues."

"There's nothing wrong with my email or text messages. I always respond to you at my first opportunity. You've crossed the line this time, Steve."

"Knock it off," said Steve. "I may be blind, but I'm not a child. You have no right to scold me or make me feel guilty for making an important decision. I made adjustments to my life when you and Max moved into my condo. I expect you to do the same when Le Roi comes tomorrow."

His words stung like a red wasp had popped her on the top lip. She fought off the moisture coming to her eyes and regrouped. "That doesn't negate how insensitive this is to my father. You've cheated him out of doing something important for you, something that you agreed to. For your information, the dog he's looking for was going to be your Christmas present."

"I know," said Steve in a softer tone. "I called your father today and explained the situation. He accepted my apology and said the dog I described to him was superior to anything he'd located."

Heather realized she needed time alone to get past the shock. She then noticed a small stack of papers. "If that's the contract in front of you, let me have it."

Steve pushed it toward her.

She took them and retreated to the table in the breakfast nook. It didn't take her long to read the contract. "How will you and your dog get to Houston five days a week?"

Steve joined her at the table. "I've hired an Uber driver. His name is Rasheed. He was a philosophy professor before radicals took over his country."

"Tell me about the dog."

"He's a giant schnauzer. They tell me he's black, just as black as Max."

"If he's such a perfect dog, why didn't the police accept him?"

"Did you catch his name?"

"Of course. It's Le Roi, The King."

"He lives up to his name with rather a snobbish nature. Same as Max."

"Max is a cat. It's their natural disposition. I thought dogs were supposed to specialize in obedience."

"Le Roi likes it when people give him commands in French. You'll enjoy talking to him."

"You're joking."

Steve smiled. "You'll see. Emile found him as a pup in a kennel outside of Paris. All the dogs they train come from Europe."

"Emile?"

"The training facility's co-owner. He's from France, too."

Heather folded her hands on the papers before her. "I'm back to my previous question. Why did Houston P.D. reject this dog?"

Steve swallowed before answering. "Like I said, he's particular, especially with his food. They feed the dogs raw meat, but Le Roi has standards with what cuts he'll accept. Anything less than sirloin stays in his dish. Emile understood this and made allowances during training. So did the officer, who was going to be his partner, but not the officer's supervisor. He insisted on a diet approved by the vet, which included cuts of meat that didn't meet Le Roi's standards."

Heather didn't know how to react to this information, so she sat silently, staring at Steve.

"It worked out better than I imagined," said Steve in an upbeat manner. "As you read in the contract, Emile threw in guide dog training at no cost."

She looked down at the contract. "I can see there's no talking you out of this. The contract seems adequate, and you're obviously not open to further discussion on this matter. I'll add one thing before I take three Tylenol and go to bed. If that mutt in any way harms Max, our relationship will be seriously compromised."

Steve nodded but closed the conversation by saying, "I believe the chances of Max slicing Le Roi's nose are much greater than my dog eating your cat. He prefers steak."

Heather escaped to her inner sanctum, the jetted bathtub of the en suite bathroom off her bedroom. With two doors between her and the rest of the house, she allowed hot water and candlelight to ease her frayed emotions. She'd hunted behind hounds in bloodless fox hunts, but she'd always preferred cats because they fit her busy lifestyle so much better than dogs that thrived on human contact. Except for their litter box, cats were virtually odor free. They bathed themselves and were usually content with their own company.

In her imagination, she pictured a black mound of fur whose head reached well north of her waist, with drool dripping onto the carpet. The regular exercise that Steve mentioned would cause their home to smell of dog. She'd need to find the most effective deodorizers available. It then occurred to her that their homes were being built on a peninsula that jutted out into Lake Conroe. The dog would, no doubt, spend a considerable amount of time in the water. She could almost smell the odor of wet dog and moved a scented candle closer to her. At least Steve and his dog would have their own home then.

She wasn't expecting the sense of betrayal by Steve that settled over her. Also, how disappointed was her father? Steve had violated an unspoken agreement. He should have consulted her.

She awoke in water that felt as cold as a glacier-fed stream. A single candle cast a ghostly shadow, and she shivered like she'd camped in the Alps without a tent or sleeping bag. The fluffy towel brought only limited relief. She spoke through chattering teeth, "I need to get warm."

Sliding beneath the sheet and duvet gave her no immediate relief. As if sensing her need, Max shifted from his side of the bed and lay like a spoon in the contour of her body.

She didn't wake up until a knock sounded on her door. A glance at the window told her the sun was well up and she'd missed at least one meeting and no telling how many phone calls. She reached for her phone, but it was no help as she'd failed to charge it.

Another knock sounded, followed by Steve's voice. "Emile and Le Roi are here. Get dressed and meet them."

"Holy smoke," whispered Heather to herself. "I'm three hours behind schedule already. If there's one thing I don't need, it's wasting time with a stinking dog."

"Heather? Are you all right?"

"Give me five minutes."

"Take your time and make yourself presentable for Le Roi."

She mumbled, "Steve's lost his mind if he thinks I'm dressing to impress a drool factory."

6

———

Ten minutes later, Heather emerged from her bedroom dressed for the day, but without makeup. She'd apply the modest amount she normally wore on the way to the office. The smell of coffee lured her into the kitchen where she filled her travel cup almost to the brim. Voices sounded from the living room.

"There you are," said Steve as she crossed from porcelain tile onto carpet. "Heather McBlythe, this is Emile Dubois."

"Bonjour, Mademoiselle McBlythe."

"Bonjour, Monsieur Dubois. *Comment allez-vous?*"

"*Tres bien, merci.*

Heather noted the man's appearance and silently rattled off a description like a radio broadcast for a wanted fugitive: White male, five foot ten, black hair, one-hundred-sixty-five pounds, last seen wearing designer jeans, a blue and white striped shirt, and tennis shoes. Tattoo of German shepherd on right forearm.

She shifted her gaze. "*Bon matin, Le Roi.*"

The dog was already standing at attention. He dipped his chin after she bid him good morning.

Emile smiled. "Steve told me you are fluent in French. Le Roi appreciates your effort to make him feel welcome."

"Do you believe he understands both French and English?"

Emile gave an exaggerated shoulder shrug, so common among men from France. "Perhaps he understands both, like you and I do. Who can say? I know he responds better to French."

Despite being late to begin her day, Heather's training as a detective and an attorney teamed up with her natural curiosity. "Steve tells me you intend to train Le Roi to be a guide dog. That seems to clash with his prior training. Do you believe he can do both?"

"He already handles crowds, sudden noises, and high-stress situations very well. I see no reason why he can't master the skills needed to be a guide dog."

"I'm still confused about why the police department rejected him."

Emile ran a hand across the back of his neck. "To be honest, I am also confused. His first partner had only good things to say about him."

"Do you believe the problem lay with the second partner?"

"I must be very careful how I answer you. My livelihood is based on maintaining a good relationship with the Houston Police Department. All I can say is, get to know Le Roi and form your own opinions."

Heather rewarded his answer with a tight smile and said, "That was a very diplomatic non-answer."

Steve interjected, "I know the man who rejected him. He expects complete obedience from the dogs and officers he super-vises. I did some checking; German shepherds and Labrador Retrievers are the only dogs in his section."

"Isn't total obedience required for guide dogs?"

Emile had the answer. "Not necessarily. The last and hardest part of training a service dog is teaching them intelligent disobedience."

"That sounds like an oxymoron," said Heather.

"I should explain the three stages of training for service dogs. The first is proper placement. Mr. Smiley is right-handed, and he uses a cane. Le Roi will need to stand on his left side. I'll also fit him with a vest and harness. Until now, all he's known is a collar and leash. Part of his training for crowd control, pursuit, and attack involves baring teeth, barking, and straining on the leash. The challenge in training him for service will be retaining enough aggression to protect Steve while teaching Le Roi not to jerk the harness out of Steve's hand."

"Is that even possible?"

"I'm convinced Le Roi will show himself worthy of the challenge. If any dog can do it, he can."

Heather wondered if this was part of a sales pitch, but didn't challenge Emile's words, at least not verbally. Instead, she asked, "What happens in phase two of the training?"

"Acclimation to different environments and more training in leading Steve through them. He'll lead Steve down known and unknown streets, sidewalks, dirt paths, around holes, obstacles, hills, mud, slick surfaces, low branches, walls, puddles, and many more. Le Roi will have to see for Steve and guide him safely through them all."

Emile kept talking. "That leads us to the final and most difficult phase of training, intelligent disobedience. This occurs when Le Roi detects danger and disobeys Steve's command. Let me give you an example. Let's say Steve and Le Roi are walking along a city street and come to an intersection that Steve needs to cross. This intersection has no light or crosswalk. An electric car approaches. Steve doesn't hear it coming, but Le Roi sees and hears it. The instruction comes from Steve for them to cross the street. We will train Le Roi to ignore the command and block Steve's path."

"That's amazing," said Heather. "You've convinced me that Steve could benefit from such a dog." She took a breath. "However, I'm a firm believer in having more than one candidate when I have a position to fill. I'd hate for Steve to spend so much time and money, only to be disappointed by a dog that's already labeled substandard."

Le Roi let out a snort.

"Baloney," said Steve. "You and I both know why you don't want me to get Le Roi. It has nothing to do with his ability to protect me."

Heather stiffened. "I'm trying to apply professional business practices to a decision that will affect both of us for years to come."

"Double baloney. You're so used to micromanaging everyone and everything that you've brought your obsession for control home with you."

"That's not fair!"

"Fair? I'll tell you what's not fair. It's you interfering in a decision I've already made."

Without her realizing it, Max had entered the room and stood looking up at Le Roi. The giant schnauzer lowered his muzzle for a sniff and received a right cross to his nose with Max's rapier-like claws fully extended.

Instead of reacting with a yelp or a growl, Le Roi raised his chin and allowed drops of blood to fall on Max's head and the back of his neck.

The insult of having dog blood on him sent Max tearing from the room.

"What's happening?" asked Steve.

Emile had the answer. "The dog and cat are deciding who will rule the home. Le Roi has a bloody nose but retained his dignity. The cat retreated to rethink his strategy."

"Not a bad idea," said Steve.

"What's that supposed to mean?" demanded Heather.

"It means I wish Bucky hadn't burned our duplex. You and I need to clarify our boundaries." He straightened his shoulders. "It also means I'm too old to be told what dog I can have. I'm glad I'll be going to Houston five days a week for the next three months. That will give us both time to establish a new normal."

Heather let out a huff of exasperation. "I still don't appreciate the way you're dismissing my father's feelings and generosity."

"You're making assumptions," said Steve in a firm voice.

"And you're insulting my father." She stood. "This much I know for sure, neither of us will have homes we can call our own if I don't get to work and make it happen."

She looked at Emile. "I apologize for airing our dirty laundry in front of you." She glanced at Steve who stood rigidly beside Le Roi. "If you'll excuse me, I need to get to work."

Heather mumbled unkind and accusatory words all the way to her destination. She made it to the parking lot of her office building before regret covered her like a cold, wet blanket. It was a silly fight, and to her way of thinking, there was enough blame for each of them to take a share.

Her thoughts shifted to the statuesque dog that would soon inhabit part of what Max considered his domain. Would Max feel betrayed by Steve having a new roommate and confidant? She sighed. "He's a magnificent dog. I may not admit it to Steve, but it gives me peace of mind knowing Le Roi's trained to protect him." A smile tugged at her lips. "And it might be fun speaking French to a dog."

It occurred to her that she didn't know Steve's plans for the day. Was he going to Houston with Emile and Le Roi to train? Would the dog stay nights and weekends there until training was complete? She should have asked more questions last night and this morning. Between her emotions over Steve's decision and the housing development demanding her time, she didn't have the capacity to think like she should.

She fought off a desire to call Steve. Instead, she took out her phone and hit the speed dial icon for her father. Six rings before he answered told her she'd interrupted something he considered important. She began the conversation with an apology. "Sorry, Father. You can call me back if you're in the middle of something."

"I was, but not anymore. Is something wrong?"

"No. Well, not exactly. I wanted to apologize to you for Steve ruining the surprise you planned for his Christmas present. He's found a dog in Houston that he believes will be perfect."

"I know. He called me yesterday and explained the situation. Have you seen the dog?"

"I met him this morning."

"Isn't he the most stunning creature you've ever seen? He reminds me of bygone German kings. It wouldn't surprise me if he came from the bloodline of dogs owned by royalty. His bearing is superb."

"But you told me you thought you'd located a dog for him."

"I followed your advice and increased the pool of candidates. They were all German shepherds who don't compare to Le Roi. I can tell by watching the video Steve sent me that this is the perfect dog for him."

"What video?"

"The one taken at the training facility yesterday. The owner, Emile, took it as Le Roi was put through his paces on the obstacle course. He also went through attack and release on command. Most impressive." He paused. "I take it you haven't seen the video yet."

She closed her eyes and mumbled, "Not yet, but I'll make a point to view it tonight."

"You must not have opened your email. Steve sent it to both of us."

Heather wasn't usually one who engaged in mental self-loathing, but she made an exception on this bright September morning. Her eyes narrowed, and she asked, "What else have you and Steve been discussing?"

Her father spoke in a lower register. "Heather, we talk about many things. You should know better than anyone how sharp his mind is. He's a veritable warehouse of obscure information. You'd do well to not limit him to solving crimes."

"I'll take that under advisement. For now, I'm hours late arriving at work and I have a housing development to finish."

"Say hello to Jack for me."

Heather rolled her eyes as she spoke. "I will. Got to go."

"Slow down, Heather. Life is short. Try not to speed through it."

"I'll try. Goodbye."

The phone clicked off, and she tried to remember the last time she had spoken to her former fiancé and current boyfriend. She'd call Jack at lunch. At least, that's what she told herself.

7

———

Heather exited the elevator and wasted no time walking to her office where her personal assistant sat at the conference table speaking on the phone. She looked up and said, "She just walked in. I'll tell her that I've rescheduled your meeting for two o'clock this afternoon."

Raised eyebrows sufficed for Heather asking for the identity of the caller.

"That was your eight o'clock appointment calling to apologize. She spent most of the night in the emergency room with her three-year-old. Nothing serious. It turns out eating crayons is a relatively harmless thing to do."

"What else did I miss?"

"The roof trusses for the next set of homes are ready for delivery and the special order of Italian marble is being unloaded at the Port of Houston."

"That wasn't supposed to be here until next week. I'll need to find a place to store it."

"Already taken care of. The distributor has plenty of room in their warehouse."

Heather received the news with a nod as she sat behind her desk. "What else?"

Her assistant sat in a chair in front of her desk. "Nothing else. It's one of those days that comes along like the extra day in February every four years. The suppliers are supplying, the contractors are busy as beavers, and the phones aren't ringing."

The timing of Heather's phone ringing caused Heather to groan. "You spoke too soon." She looked at the caller ID and saw Jack's picture and name.

"Hello, handsome," she said.

"Hello, beautiful. Say yes."

Heather wondered what he was up to. "Yes, to what?"

"Lunch. I called earlier, and you weren't in. Your girl Friday told me it was the first slow day you've had in over a month. If it's slow enough for you to be late to work, it's slow enough for us to have lunch."

She spoke before thinking. "You're right. Believe it or not, I was going to call you today and set a date for us to reintroduce ourselves."

"Noon at Dominic's," said Jack. "I've already made reservations. No excuses."

"All right." She put a sultry tone to her next question. "Is there something interesting you'd like to discuss?"

"As a matter of fact, there is. Steve sent me a video of his new dog. What an amazing animal."

All the air went out of her emotional balloon. She'd wasted a perfectly good flirt on a man who loved to hunt with his retriever. All she could say was, "Yeah, the dog is something else."

<hr>

WITH THEIR DIM LIGHTING, SOFT MUSIC, AND ESCARGOT ON the menu, Heather couldn't decide if she enjoyed the intimacy of Dominic's more than the quality of the cuisine, or vice versa. Regardless, Jack's choice suited her down to the soles of her black Stuart Weitzman shoes. The choice of a charcoal gray skirt and blazer over a pure white blouse had been fortuitous. In reality, it was the first ensemble she came to after Steve banged on her door that morning.

The morning had gone smoothly, with only a few matters to attend to. This gave her plenty of time to apply more makeup than her usual bare minimum. Unlike the stab-and-smear method she used on the way to work, she stood before a real bathroom mirror and took her time. The results pleased her. By Jack's one-word reaction, it pleased him, too.

"Wow!"

They embraced. She intended it to be a discreet kiss. He had other ideas. Jack got his way, and she didn't mind.

The maître d' cleared his throat, and they broke the clench.

"Bonjour, Mademoiselle McBlythe et Monsieur Blackstock. It has been much too long since you graced one of our tables."

Jack answered for them. "I couldn't agree more, Jean Claude."

Heather broke in and explained in French that it was entirely her fault and promised to come more often.

"All that matters is that you are here today." He gave a nod to a server who took two steps forward. "Monique will take extra good care of you today, but if you have any special desire, I am but a wave of the hand away."

Heather thanked him and launched into a discussion with Monique about the chef's recommendations for the day. As usual, Jack chose a salad, steak, and what he called safe vegetables. She, however, instructed the server to tell the chef to imagine her sitting at a table on the *Champs-Élysées* and craft her a typical Parisian lunch.

Monique gave a nod of approval and promised to send the sommelier to take their order for wine to match their meals.

Jack leaned into her. "That took you a long time to order. What are you getting?"

"I left it up to the chef. The French eat smaller portions at lunch and save the largest meal of the day for the evening."

As was her custom, Heather discussed wine selections with the sommelier and made selections for both herself and Jack. He was content with not selecting wines because her knowledge was encyclopedic and she never considered the price. His upbringing was middle class, which imprinted the habit of looking at the right column of prices before considering the offerings. Old habits were hard to break.

As they were waiting for their wines to arrive, Jack asked a question that she wasn't expecting. "Why aren't you and Steve helping Leo with his latest murder case?"

"Are you talking about the poisoning of the pharmacist?"

"Of course. Steve said you two went to the crime scene. That's usually all it takes to put you on a trail like two hounds."

She partially suppressed her desire to overreact. "Can we omit the references to dogs? Steve and I had an argument this morning over the unexpected news of him selecting a dog. There was a confrontation that led to bloodshed."

"You hit Steve?"

"Of course not. How could you think such a thing?"

She mentally regrouped. "Max didn't appreciate Le Roi invading his space, so he sliced his nose."

"Is Max still alive? All it would take is one bite from that beast and you'd be catless."

"He's fine physically but confused and feeling sorry for himself. The dog acted like a true warrior-king and didn't whimper. Instead, Le Roi sat on his haunches and lifted his regal chin so blood could drip onto Max's head. I know he did it to show Max that he was the superior animal."

Jack tried to muffle a laugh but did a very poor job of it. Heather kicked him in the shin. "It wasn't funny when it happened, and it still isn't."

Jack's laugh reduced to a chuckle. Heather had to fight the slow burn of anger that his reaction ignited. To do so, she changed the subject. "How is Briann coping with the new school year?"

"Better than last year. Putting her in the private prep school with other high achievers made all the difference. She found a tight circle of friends who challenge each other for grades and everything else, including trivia. I feel like my job as a dad is little more than providing food, shelter, transportation, and a wallet shaped like a cornucopia. Instead of fruit and things to eat, it never runs out of cash."

Heather nodded in agreement as she considered her own teen years. "That's how I treated my parents, especially my father. He got his revenge by giving me his gene that compels me to overachieve."

"Speaking of," said Jack, "how is the housing development progressing?"

"I don't want to jinx it, but we're ahead of schedule on almost everything."

"Does that include the homes for you and Steve?"

"We poured the slabs last week and framing starts today. I learned this morning that the roof trusses are ready for delivery. Barring a hurricane, a tornado, or the start of World War III, Steve and I should celebrate Christmas in our new homes. Steve and Le Roi in theirs and Max and me in ours."

The wine arrived, which meant they had to take a break in the conversation to allow the sommelier to perform the ritual of uncorking the bottles and allowing them to sniff, taste and approve the selections. With the formalities out of the way, Jack offered a toast to their relationship. They drank and lowered their glasses.

Jack tilted his head. "You never answered my question about you and Steve helping Leo with his latest murder. Are you doing anything?"

"Not me. I made it clear to Steve that I'm not available until we're in our new homes." She took another sip of wine. "I can't speak for Steve, but I know he'll be busy for the next three months training with man's best friend. I don't think he'll want the distraction of working a case that has such a low probability of being solved."

"You don't think he and Leo could solve it?"

"I don't believe Leo, Steve, me, and Sherlock Holmes could solve it."

"What if Sherlock brought along Toby, the dog he sometimes used to track down the bad guys?"

It was Heather's turn to let loose with a hearty laugh. "That might do it, but I'm not interested unless Sherlock and Toby come back from the grave."

8

Days melted into weeks, as an Indian Summer morphed into November. Heather looked at the progress made on her and Steve's new homes. They occupied the best view in the development, the tip of a peninsula jutting out into Lake Conroe.

Heather wasn't smiling. There was a law among contractors and construction workers that emphatically stated that building anything always took longer than projected. It was a corollary to Murphy's law that claimed anything that could go wrong always did.

She wondered if an evil witch had placed a curse on her spreadsheets of timetables by hearing her tease fate. Why had she mentioned a hurricane to Jack almost two months ago? A late season category one hurricane had indeed hit the Gulf Coast, traveled inland, and chose Lake Conroe as a nice place to stop. The forecast called for it to dump six months' worth of pounding rain during the next week.

Windshield wipers slapped at the fat drops assaulting her car but did nothing to slow the downpour. Her phone rang. Grudgingly, she looked at the screen.

"Hello, Jack." She knew her voice sounded as flat as her wet hair, but it was the best she could muster.

"I need your help," he said in a tone that was all business.

"With what?"

"Saving someone from a life sentence."

She spoke before thinking. "Not interested."

"You should be."

"Why?"

"Because I don't believe he did it, and you can't do anything about the weather."

"I'm still not interested."

"Steve is, and so is Leo."

"Good. They can work it."

"It's another poisoning, almost a carbon copy of the one in Houston, but this one happened in Conroe. Steve's taking a week off from training with Le Roi. He wants you to do the same."

A bolt of lightning struck the pine tree next to her SUV. Concern filled Jack's voice. "Are you all right?"

"I'll let you know after I pull my heart out of my throat." She settled her nerves and said, "I'm not superstitious, but that bolt of lightning tried to get in the car with me. It seems there's a conspiracy between heaven and mortals to steal a week where I can't work on my development." She paused. "One week. That's all I'll give you."

"Great. Come to my office. Steve and Leo are already here."

The trip from Lake Conroe to Jack's office in the city of Conroe took much longer than it should have. Twice she had to take an alternate route to avoid high water. She finally made it and checked the condition of her hair in the rearview mirror. "Hopeless," she whispered. "Just like trying to build in this monsoon."

She grabbed an inadequately sized umbrella and opened her door. A sudden gust jerked the door from her hand while the umbrella popped open of its own volition. The next thing she knew, the umbrella turned inside out and became completely useless. She wrestled the door shut, but not before the driver's seat looked like someone had sprayed it with a garden hose.

A mad dash to the front door of the converted 1960s ranch-style home on one of the major streets leading into the city did nothing but soak her hair even more. Jack had converted the former rambling homestead into a law office with room enough for at least four attorneys, support staff, and a client waiting room. Heather had talked him into hiring one attorney but had made little progress in convincing him to add another. He preferred to keep things simple.

After bursting through the front door, Heather restricted her movements to a limited area of floor tiles. "Lose your umbrella?" asked Briann, Jack's fourteen-year-old daughter who came to her aid by handing Heather a towel. "I thought it only rained like this back in Louisiana."

"The wind took it to Oz. I'm fairly dry from the neck down. I can't say the same for my hair. Can you help me off with my Wellies?"

Briann chuckled. "If you mean your rubber boots, take a seat and I'll pull them off. Did you go to the lake?"

"I did, and located some low spots that aren't draining the way I'd like, but so far there's no flooding in the development. I can't say the same for the roads leading to the lake."

"That's why I'm here and not in school. Their disaster plan calls for classes to be held online whenever it's too dangerous to drive. I'd rather be at school, but coming here is second best."

"Hey," said a lady in a raspy voice as she looked up from a magazine. "I've been waiting for over an hour to talk to Mr. Blackstock. Find out what's taking so long."

Briann issued a cherubic smile and turned so the woman couldn't see the roll of her eyes. "Of course, Mrs. Bains."

A plastic chair soon became a depository for Heather's rain gear, which included waterproof pants, a jacket, and the Wellies she'd picked up on a soggy trip to Scotland. With practiced efficiency, she corralled her long, auburn hair in the towel on top of her head. Jack and Leo would have to take her looking like she'd walked out of the sauna. Steve and Le Roi didn't count. One couldn't see and the other didn't care.

She passed Briann in the hall leading to Jack's office. Heather took note that Briann's sweater showed more feminine curves than last winter's. Once the braces came off, Jack would face a problem he'd never encountered. She wondered how successful he'd be at keeping suitors at bay. That was assuming he wasn't already on high alert.

She opened the door and strode into Jack's office. With a turban on her head, she looked more like a reader of fortunes than an attorney. Jack and Leo rose from their chairs. Steve and Le Roi stayed seated but lifted their chins. The dog tilted his head slightly. He wasn't used to seeing her with hair wrapped in a towel.

"*C'est moi, Le Roi.*" She walked to where the dog sat beside Steve's chair and held out her hand. He stood, gave it an obligatory sniff, and wagged his tail. They'd long since made amends, as had she and Steve. Max was another story. Cats have long memories.

Jack had rounded his desk and greeted her with a peck on the cheek and a question. "How is your development holding up to all this rain?"

"Good, so far. As long as they keep letting water flow out of the dam, all streets and homes should survive with minimal damage. Completion and move-in dates will need to be adjusted, but that's a temporary inconvenience."

"I thought you'd be more upset," said Steve.

"The drive here gave me time to think. My sales team reported flooding in other developments. This storm is the acid test for drainage and everything is looking good on my property. Other places aren't faring as well. If we come out of this unscathed, I'll emphasize how we lost zero homes when other developments were literally under water."

Steve formed his hands into a church with steeple. "I listened to a documentary a couple of nights ago about how much more valuable land and houses are that don't fall within the boundaries of a flood plain. I did a quick analysis of your homes. If I'm right, and none of your development floods, you could sell your homes for substantially more than you're currently asking."

Heather couldn't help but smile. "I'd never considered how a hurricane could have a silver lining. I'll get my sales team to prepare new advertising."

Leo said, "Do you mind if we talk about a couple of homicides first?"

Jack nodded. "Good idea. There's a mother waiting to see us whose son is in jail. She's hired me to defend him. I'm almost convinced he didn't do it, but I could be wrong. Even if I am, she's paying me to defend him."

Steve broke in. "Before you ask her to come in, why don't you and Leo bring Heather and me up to speed?"

The dog let out a snort. "And Le Roi," said Steve. "He needs to hear this, too."

Heather opened her mouth to give Steve a cutting remark about treating Le Roi like he could comprehend the complexities of human conversations. The word hypocrite flashed into her mind. She spoke the same way to Max.

9

J ack and Leo looked at each other, each one waiting for the other to take the lead in the discussion. Jack broke the silence. "Leo, you go first. Tell them what progress you made with the first murder."

"Progress is too strong of a word." Leo shifted in his chair and took a full breath. "The first thing I did was establish the identities of everyone at the table. Five pharmacists, all from Conroe or The Woodlands, were present when Michelle Le Blanc died. The coroner confirmed it was hemlock that killed her."

"That stuff grows wild. It wouldn't take a pharmacist to find some," said Steve.

Heather interrupted. "I remember counting eight chairs at the table. Were three of them empty?"

"You and Steve both have memories like elephants. They set the table for eight, but only seven pharmacists should have been there. A pharmacist's wife from Philadelphia went into labor early and he flew home that morning. The second pharmacist who missed the banquet received a better offer on how to spend her evening."

Steve's mouth twitched upward. "I have a feeling Leo has an interesting story to tell us."

"It's a repeat of a story we've all heard before. People get away from their high-pressure lives and do things they normally wouldn't do at home. This time it involved a pharmaceutical rep and a pharmacist from Indiana whose husband recently left her. Room service confirmed they delivered a bottle of champagne and chocolate-covered strawberries before the banquet and two complete meals of oysters Rockefeller about the time first responders arrived at the banquet."

Steve said, "Leo, you've changed. I remember a time when you'd give all the details to a story like that."

"It must be the onset of old age," said Leo. "Besides, strawberries make me break out in hives and oysters are nasty, slimy creatures that should be left in the water."

Heather shifted the conversation back to suspects and victims. "That means five pharmacists were at the table when the banquet started. Someone poisoned Michelle Le Blanc. That leaves four potential suspects. Who are they?"

Leo used his left hand to count off names. "Constance Petrovitch is the first."

Jack added, "The victim of the second poisoning."

"Right," said Leo. "She Americanized her first name to Connie."

Heather nodded. "Who else?"

"Claude and Marjorie Hicks, a husband-and-wife team of pharmacists from the Conroe area, Erin Stoops and Luke Bains."

"Here's where it gets sticky." Leo turned his head to look at Jack. "Why don't you tell them about Luke Bains?"

"Luke is my client, who is now charged with murdering Connie Petrovitch. He was alone with Connie in his apartment when she died. They'd been seeing each other for three months. According to Luke, they had a strong, intimate relationship. He claims the subject of marriage had already come up, but Connie wanted to wait to make sure. Agreeing on how to raise children was a sticking point because they weren't of the same faith. He claims a willingness to compromise, but she was inflexible."

Jack took a breath and shook his head. "Luke made the mistake of talking to the police. He admitted to a recent argument. Now he's in jail hoping for a bond reduction hearing."

Steve summarized. "Looking at it from a detective's point of view, Luke had motive, means, and opportunity to kill her. He also was present when Michelle Le Blanc died. No wonder they arrested him."

"True," said Jack. "However, he wasn't the only person with a motive to kill Connie."

"Who else?" asked Heather.

"Erin Stoops. She was Luke's main squeeze until Connie came along. Luke describes her as his former placeholder girlfriend. He dated her until the true love of his life came along."

Heather rolled her eyes. "I'm not sure I like Luke."

Steve jumped in. "It's not our job to like or dislike anyone. We find truth and follow it wherever it leads us."

"Duly noted," said Heather.

Steve moved on. "What about the Hickses?"

"They're not the most cooperative people I've ever encountered," said Leo. "They refused to say anything about the first murder without a lawyer present. He told me they had nothing to hide, but nothing to say, either. The assistant district attorney said she'd subpoena them for a deposition if I could convince her there was a reason for their silence. I'm in a Catch-22. Without their cooperation, I haven't been able to discover a link between Michelle Le Blanc and them, and without that, the assistant district attorney won't demand a deposition."

Leo took a deep breath and continued. "One interesting tidbit. Their financial statements tell me they'll be working for many years to come."

"Are you saying they're broke?" asked Heather.

"Not completely, but they're not anywhere near where you'd expect them to be."

"Do you know why?"

Steve shifted in his seat. "This sounds like a job for Heather."

"Why me?" asked Heather.

"You're the money expert in our partnership. You'll think of a way to get them talking."

Sarcasm peppered her response. "Thanks a lot for the vote of confidence."

Leo offered a ray of hope. "There's one thing that might help. Luke told Jack that he used to work with Claude and Marjorie."

Jack added, "It was a long time ago, when Luke was fresh out of pharmacy school. He said Claude and Marjorie were terrible money managers. Naturally, their business suffered."

While Heather considered how she might approach Claude and Marjorie Hicks, Steve uncrossed his legs. "Jack, I don't think I need to say this, but I'm going to, anyway. You're obligated to defend Luke by all legal means. Heather and I intend to follow the evidence we uncover."

"I'm convinced he didn't kill Connie Petrovitch. As for Michelle Le Blanc, I don't have a dog in that fight," said Jack.

Le Roi's ears picked up. Steve patted the dog's head. "Easy, boy. There's not a dog to fight." Steve explained. "He understands the words dog and fight. Hearing them together caught his attention."

Leo asked, "Does he understand any other languages?"

Steve wagged his head. "He's partial to anything said in French or with a French accent."

Jack interrupted. "As interesting as this conversation is, my client's mother is waiting. Mary Jo Bains hired me to defend her son."

Leo added, "My primary interest is in the murder that occurred in Houston. I find it a strange coincidence that there's been a second murder by the same poison, and it took place one county north of my patch."

A knock sounded, followed by Briann entering and closing

the door behind her. "That lady is going to have a stroke if you don't get her in here. I'm surprised you haven't heard her."

"I have," said Steve.

Le Roi gave his head a nod that looked like he agreed with Steve.

Leo stood. "Explaining why a Houston homicide detective is here discussing a murder case with a defense attorney will be a tough sell to the woman footing the bill. I'll sneak out and hide in the bathroom while Mrs. Bains chews you out for making her wait."

"Coward," said Jack. "The best chewers in the world have chewed me out. One more shouldn't do too much damage." He smiled at his daughter. "Please show Mrs. Bains in after Detective Vega hides from a harmless, senior citizen."

Briann shook her head. "She may be short and older, but if her bite is anything like her bark, she's not harmless."

It wasn't long before a loud voice sounded in the hall. "You go back to playing on your phone. I know where his office is."

10

———

The door flew open, and Mary Jo Baines strode into the room. She might as well have had a steam whistle sticking out of her head, as she plowed forward like a locomotive until she stood with thighs touching Jack's desk. She spoke while wagging a finger at him. "Listen to me, you hot-shot ambulance chaser. If you keep me waiting like that again, I'll take my money and go somewhere else."

Jack leaned back in his chair. "That's your prerogative."

The raised voice of the woman brought Le Roi to his feet. Steve had already hooked his left hand around the handle attached to the dog's harness. He whispered, "En garde."

Le Roi took a step forward, bared his teeth, and let out three barks that put a chill down Heather's spine. They also worked to still Mrs. Bain's tongue, at least for the moment.

Steve gave Le Roi a second command. *"Allongez-vous."*

The dog went to his stomach, but kept his ears pitched forward, black eyes fixed on Mrs. Baines.

Steve spoke in a calm voice. "Sorry if he scared you, Mrs. Baines. Le Roi is a trained police dog, as well as a service dog. He's trained to detect aggression. But there's nothing to worry about. I don't think he'll attack unless I tell him to. Please have a seat so I can take my hand away from his harness."

She needed no further convincing.

Heather used the relative calm to make mental notes of the woman that she could relay to Steve later. Mary Jo might top out at five two, including her inexpensive tennis shoes. She guessed her age to be around forty-five, but from the looks of her face, they had been hard years. Hands were red and rough with uneven, unpolished nails. She was a pear-shaped woman with thick calves, her ankles poking out from the bottom of rolled-up jeans. No makeup. An unbuttoned, buff-colored, cable-weave cardigan hung loosely over an almost shapeless top that covered wide hips.

Jack took over. "Mrs. Baines, let me introduce you to Steve Smiley and Heather McBlythe. They are top private detectives who will gather information that will hopefully prove your son's innocence." He paused. "You've already seen Le Roi in action."

Mrs. Baines found her voice. "Do you mean I'm paying for a blind man, a woman who doesn't have sense enough to get in out of the rain, and a rabid dog to do your work for you?"

Heather knew the best defense was a strong offense. "Who said we're doing this for money? Sometimes we do it for fun. We haven't discussed money with Mr. Blackstock yet."

Jack took his turn. "Steve was the top homicide detective in Houston before he lost his sight. Heather spent ten years as a cop and detective in Boston. She's also a practicing attorney. I asked them to help because they're the absolute best in the business."

Steve didn't wait for another objection. "Tell us, Mrs. Baines. Other than your motherly instinct, what makes you so sure your son didn't kill Constance Petrovitch?"

Heather detected confusion in Mrs. Baines's expression. The woman faced Jack, but her eyes cut to look at Steve. "Whose side are they on?"

"You needn't worry about that unless Luke is guilty," said Steve.

She gave Steve her full attention. "He's not guilty. I know he's not. Luke could never kill anyone. He's a licensed pharmacist. That's like a doctor. Luke even had to take an oath."

Heather knew the pharmacist's oath wasn't the same as a doctor's, but she refrained from correcting Mrs. Bains.

Steve jumped back in. "Let's assume Luke is innocent. Do you suspect anyone else?"

She searched the corner of the ceiling for answers before lowering her gaze. "I'd start with Erin Stoops. I didn't particularly like her, but she was better than that Petrovitch girl. At least she didn't speak with a funny accent."

"How long did Luke and Erin date?" asked Steve.

"Too long."

"Why do you say that?"

"Anyone with eyes could see she wasn't right for my Luke."

Heather cringed. The woman had no sensitivity to Steve's blindness.

Steve was unfazed and asked, "Can you be more specific?"

"Money. She spent a ton every month on hair, nails, clothes, and especially shoes. I know for a fact she had to throw away a pair every week to make room for a new pair. I think she had some sort of mental problem that made her a compulsive spender. I raised Luke to be frugal and invest for the future."

Steve spoke up. "That's a very prudent thing to teach your children. Do you have other children?"

"Oh, no. Luke's my one and only."

As was his habit, Steve moved on quickly. "We understand Luke used to work for Claude and Marjorie Hicks."

Mary Jo let out a huff of disgust. "Talk about people who can't manage money. They had no business trying to own a pharmacy. It's no wonder they went bankrupt."

Heather made a note to check the records at the courthouse.

If the Hickses had declared bankruptcy, it would be easy to verify.

Steve continued. "How long has it been since Luke worked for the Hickses?"

She shrugged. "About eight years, and they still owe him the money he loaned them."

Jack interrupted. "Luke told me the ten thousand dollars was a misunderstanding. He thought it was a loan, but the Hickses believed it was a gift. Either way, there was no contract."

Mary Jo lifted her chin. "Loaned, gave, what's the difference? If two pharmacists talked my Luke into forking over ten grand, there's no telling how much they conned out of a foreigner like that Petrovich girl."

Steve had a last question. "Did the police ask you where you were the night Ms. Petrovitch died?"

Mary Jo stiffened. "Yeah, you were a cop. You all ask the same stupid questions, looking for anyone but the guilty to accuse."

Jack broke in. "Mrs. Bains is a member of a bowling league. She was throwing strikes and spares the night Connie Petrovitch died."

Steve turned on the charm. "I bet you don't leave many pins standing."

The wide smile on the short woman told Heather he'd found the woman's pride point. With shoulders squared, Mary Jo said, "They know better than to bet against me. I may be little, but I can chunk that ball with the best of them."

"Can you make it hook?"

"Of course."

"Do you mainly rely on the ball's speed or hooking it into the head pin?"

"Both," said Mary Jo with self-satisfaction. "You can always tell a novice. It takes years of practice to control rolling it hard, smooth, and making it hook right into the pocket."

"How did you develop such arm strength?"

Mary Jo didn't hesitate. "Hard work, and I've always been strong for my size. After Luke's father left us, I had to do whatever it took to make enough for him to get through college and pharmacy school."

"What kind of work did you do?"

"Mostly working in a tire shop by day and temp work at night. Luke's job was to get good grades, mine was to make money. I still had to take out loans, but they're all whittled down now."

"Is Luke helping you pay them back?"

"He didn't take out the loans, I did. His job is to work, save, and invest. He's going to have a better life than me."

Heather was wondering if Steve would get back on track. The next words showed he hadn't lost his place. "You're a bright woman and a generous mother. I'm sure you know that the best way for us to set Luke free is to find the person who killed Connie Petrovitch. You've already told us Erin wasn't a good match for your son. Is that correct?"

She gave her head a firm nod.

Heather had to give a soft instruction. "You need to speak. He can't see you nodding."

The woman's bluster died down as her cheeks pinked. "I never thought she was right for him."

Steve asked, "What about Connie?"

"She was looking for a husband to help her pay off student loans. Also, Luke was years older than her."

Steve picked up where he left off. "We're starting this investigation with the assumption that Luke didn't kill Connie. Logic and experience tell me that almost everyone makes enemies in their life. I suspect Connie did too. I want you to go home and search your memory for the names of anyone who might have had a reason to kill Connie. Can you do that for me?"

Excitement came into Mary Jo's voice. "Sure. I'll do that as soon as I get home."

"Heather will give you a business card with our email

addresses on it. Get that list to us as soon as you can. You may have the name of the person who killed Connie, and you don't realize it."

Steve asked Jack, "Do you have anything else for Mary Jo?"

"Only that I'll file for a bond reduction hearing as soon we can give the judge at least one other person with motive, means, and opportunity."

"Does that mean Luke might come home for Thanksgiving?"

Jack shook his head. "I warned you that things move slowly after the initial bond hearing. Even with a subsequent hearing that reduces the bond down to a manageable figure, Luke will be lucky if he's home for Christmas."

Mary Jo turned to Heather. "I expect you and your partner to earn your keep, and I want my Luke home for Christmas."

She slid to the front of her chair, but Steve's next words stopped her motion. "We're in complete agreement that we should get started on discovering who killed Connie Petrovitch. You know your son better than anyone. I want a complete list of people who might have reason to kill Connie or bring harm to your son. I worked a case once where a suspect tried to kill a man's wife instead of the guy who owed him money."

Mary Joe's forehead wrinkled. "Why'd he do that?"

"To inflict maximum pain." The words hung in the air before Steve said, "Don't limit your list to people who might have something against Connie. Who hates your son enough to want to hurt him by killing his girlfriend?"

Mary Jo stood and was out the door without another word.

Heather looked at Steve. "You know what she's going to do, don't you?" She didn't wait for an answer. "She's going to go home and develop a list of suspects that's longer than Santa's wish list from a classroom of first graders. Why did you do that?"

Steve had already tuned her out, or so she thought. He and Le Roi rose to their feet. "I had my reason."

"Do you mind telling me what it is?"

"I'll tell you on the way to your office. You need to put

someone else in charge of your project until we solve this case. I'll give you one hour a day to check on progress and give instructions."

The negotiations began. "Ten days, max, plus two hours a day to check in with the office."

"Twelve," said Steve. "Christmas is coming up and we need to move. You'll help me for twelve days to match the song. After that, we renegotiate."

"You hate that song."

Steve ignored the comment and sealed the agreement by saying, "I'm glad we got that settled. Le Roi needs to see his workplace. I ordered a bed for him."

Sarcasm filled Heather's next question. "Orthopedic or stuffed with cedar shavings?"

"Orthopedic. It's five feet long and four feet wide. It's a good thing our office is extra-large, because he's an extra-large dog."

"Do you want to stay there for the rest of the day?"

"Leo scanned and sent everything to me concerning the homicide in Houston. Reading all that, making a murder board, and scheduling interviews will keep us busy the rest of the day. We'll need to call in something for lunch."

Steve was on a roll, and his focus was absolute. He had a reason for everything, including putting his dog in a new bed by his desk.

Heather asked, "Are you sure the two murders are linked?"

"No, but..." Steve sat again without finishing his thought.

"But what?" asked Heather.

"How many homicide cases involving poison did you work in Boston?"

"Only one, and it turned out to be an accident."

Frustration crept into Steve's voice. "Part of me says there has to be a link between the two cases and another part says we don't need to assume anything."

Heather stood. "We're not getting any closer to solving either by staying here. Le Roi looks like he's ready to go catch some bad guys."

"He's always ready for that." Steve hooked his hand around the handle of Le Roi's harness. "Jack, can you set up a jail interview for tomorrow with Luke?"

"I already have." Jack looked at Heather and winked. "They approved me, you, Le Roi, and Heather for tomorrow morning."

"Two questions," said Heather. "What time, and why did I get last billing on your list of attendees?"

"I refuse to answer the second part of that question on the grounds that it may interfere with our date Saturday night."

"What date?"

"The one I'm going to tell you about tomorrow morning when I meet you at nine-thirty."

11

―――――――

Heather didn't arrive in the kitchen until four minutes before nine the morning after committing to help with the investigations. Steve sat perched on a barstool while Le Roi sat on his haunches in his normal regal pose. Max was already on top of the kitchen cabinets, looking down. Both four-legged creatures were still competing for the title of king of the castle. No further assaults had taken place since their initial encounter, but they weren't cuddling together by the fireplace, either.

She poured coffee into a travel mug. "Do you want a cup to go?"

"No, thanks," said Steve. "You sound more chipper this morning."

"It must have been the rain pouring down all night. It relaxed me better than three sleeping pills."

"I'm guessing it has more to do with you focusing on something besides deliveries and deadlines. Sometimes the faster we try to go, the behinder we get."

"I don't believe *behinder* is in the dictionary."

"It should be. They add all kinds of words every year to dictionaries that I've never heard. Who are *they* and why can't I add one or two? What qualifies them to say what's right or wrong? Are they paid by the hour? Is it a government job?"

Heather tuned him out as he continued to rattle off questions. To anyone else, Steve's questions would seem like rambling without purpose. Heather had been around him long enough to know he was activating his brain and mouth to ask lots of questions after long periods of silence in his dark world.

She made sure the lid to her travel mug was on securely and grabbed her valise. "Let's go before we miss our appointment."

Jack was waiting for them when Heather pulled her SUV into the county detention center's parking lot. She pushed a button and the rear door yawned upward. Wire mesh divided the luggage compartment from the back seat. She didn't want muddy paws and rock-hard nails from the hundred-pound dog damaging the leather in the back seat. Le Roi bounded from what Steve called the dog's jail cell and went to the passenger door.

Raincoats with hoods covered both humans, while only a service dog's vest protected Le Roi from the steady rain. He had a good shake under the building's covered entry and held his head high when he led Steve inside. His nose worked overtime to take in the unfamiliar scents.

Steve did the same and spoke to his dog. "I wish you could tell me everything you smell. I'm picking up burned bread, laundry detergent, and floor wax."

Heather noticed a jail trustee with a mop, bucket, and towels. She realized he'd overheard Steve when he said, "The bread was this morning's biscuits. That new cook made the kitchen look like someone threw in a canister of tear gas." He added, "The reason I know what that looks like is when I was young and dumb, me and about a thousand other fools thought it was time for a little prison riot. That didn't turn out well for us."

The man leaned on his mop. "Today's biscuits weren't too

bad after you cut away the black bottoms, covered them with gravy, and hit them hard with salt and black pepper."

The man kept talking. "That's a fine dog you got there. I don't reckon I've ever seen a dog like that."

A voice interrupted. "Johnson, if you want to keep your trustee status, quit talking and start drying the floor."

"Yes, sir, Boss Hadley." The gray-haired man with ebony skin slung a mostly dry mop onto the water the four had tracked in.

After showing identification to the officer, another man wearing sergeant's chevrons on his sleeves took them through a metal door that clicked open as they approached. A camera hung from the ceiling. Heather knew somewhere in the building sat an officer controlling many different doors from a single bank of screens.

The sergeant must have weighed close to two-hundred fifty pounds. Fat accounted for little of it. Even though the weather called for long sleeves, his short-sleeved shirt showed off his biceps and trim waist. Surprisingly, he spoke in a high, soft voice. "Baines is on his way. Everyone but the dog has been here before, so I don't need to tell you what you can and can't do. Because this is an attorney-client visit, no one will listen to or record what you say."

Steve asked, "Any trouble since he's been here?"

"Nothing from Baines. Others pester him to make something to get them high with whatever's available here. He tells them all he could make from what he has access to is something that would make them vomit."

"Smart man," said Steve. "I'd think twice before asking to ingest anything from a man accused of killing someone with poison."

The three were settled on metal chairs when Luke Baines shuffled in wearing an orange jumpsuit, white socks, and dingy cotton slippers. Without a hard sole or toe post, there was no chance of a shoe becoming a weapon. His brown hair looked like he'd just stepped out of the shower. The smell of prison made soap and bleach permeated the air.

Luke's thin lips made a straight slash across his face, not giving any clue as to his disposition. He nodded a greeting to Jack and sat in a metal chair on the other side of the table that was bolted to the floor.

Jack began the interview with introductions. "These are the private detectives I told you I'd bring. Steve Smiley and Heather McBlythe."

"I recognize Ms. McBlythe. She's building that massive development on Lake Conroe. I hope it's not washing away."

"It's holding up well. Thank you for asking."

Jack finished what he started. "The handsome one between them is Steve's new dog, Le Roi. He's a certified police and service dog."

Steve wasted no time. "I know you've already told Jack and the police your version of what happened the nights Michelle Le Blanc and Connie Petrovitch died. We're going to take these one at a time and hear your version again, starting with Michelle. Let's start with your arrival at the hotel."

"Wait," said Luke. "I thought Mom hired Jack to defend me in this county. The Houston Cops haven't arrested me for Michelle's death."

"Not yet," said Steve.

Heather jumped into the discussion. "It's likely they soon will. The same poison was used in both deaths, and because you knew both victims, they may jump to conclusions. District attorneys love to clear crimes off their books."

"I don't understand. I didn't poison either one of them."

Jack took his turn. "Right now, the strongest case against you is here in Montgomery County. Houston isn't in a rush to file charges because they don't need to be. Unless Steve and Heather can find who killed both women, the D.A.s will get together and use both charges to pressure you into accepting a guilty plea for a reduced sentence."

"What about being presumed innocent, or fair treatment, or justice?"

Steve leaned forward. "Innocent is a word you need to take out of your vocabulary. Almost every person serving time says they're innocent. Also, your idea of fair treatment is a pipe dream. As for justice, you'll get it if Heather, Le Roi, and I can discover who killed two women and we give that person to the police gift-wrapped for Christmas. That's why it's important we miss nothing in our investigation."

Heather took her turn. "It's also true that time and hard thinking sometimes helps people remember little things stored in their brain. Therefore, put on your thinking cap and start with your arrival at the hotel in Houston for the pharmacists' convention. I'll record everything you say. Allow your speech to flow and give no thought to what you think is important or unimportant. Many times, it's the smallest detail that makes all the difference."

Luke inhaled deeply and released it. "Here goes. Connie and I arrived at the hotel too late to attend the meet-and-greet. It was almost nine in the evening. Neither of us were in a great mood."

Steve asked, "Why not?"

"Claude and Marjorie Hicks work in the same pharmacy as Connie." He swallowed hard. "In the same pharmacy she used to work in. They asked to attend the conference *after* Connie put in her request. The supervisor said she could juggle schedules so all three could attend, but someone would need to work late. Connie had already arranged her schedule to work the early shift."

Luke shifted his gaze to focus on everyone on the other side of the table, one at a time. "You'd have to be around Claude and Marjorie to understand how manipulative and entitled they are. There was no question in their minds who should change their schedule and work the late shift on the day the conference started. They talked for months about how the meet-and-greet was more like a family reunion to them. So many friends from all over the country were coming in to see them and it would ruin the entire conference if they weren't there to play host and hostess, as they always did. I'd never been to a conference put on by this pharmaceutical company, so I didn't know if they were blowing hot air or not."

"It sounds like a big bag of hot air to me," said Steve.

"We had our suspicions, but Connie relented and put her name down to work late. It turned out the joke was on us. Plenty of people at the conference were talking about Claude and Marjorie, but no one had anything good to say about them. I later learned they arrived around three in the afternoon, checked in, and Claude was first in line for hors d'oeuvres and the open bar. He ate and drank until he stumbled into Marjorie, who fell into a table topped with glasses of champagne. People asked Marjorie to take Claude to their room, but he became belligerent. They kept on until a group of attendees and hotel staff half-dragged Claude to their room."

"That must have made you furious," said Steve.

"I was mad long before that."

"What else had you wound up?"

"My mother!"

"Oh?"

The single word had enough inflection to it that Heather asked Luke to explain slowly. By this time, he was already leaning forward.

"My interfering, overbearing mother." He paused. "Don't get me wrong, I love my mother, and she sacrificed so much to get me through college and pharmacy school, but she hasn't accepted that I'm not a little boy anymore. We had a terrible fight the day I moved out and got an apartment of my own. Do you know what she did?"

It was a question that didn't get an answer because he didn't give a chance for a response.

"She sold her home and moved into an apartment with a view

of mine so she could spy on me. She justified it by saying she needed to downsize since she was all alone and getting older."

Steve shook his head in sympathy. "That sounds awkward."

Luke scooted farther to the front of his chair. "I pretended she hadn't followed me and tried to ignore her, but that didn't work. Every time I brought a girl to my apartment, Mom knew about it and invented some sort of lame excuse to come see me. Do you have any idea how embarrassing it is to have your mother pounding on your door when things are getting interesting?"

Steve asked, "Did your mother do that with every woman you dated, or just Connie?"

"There weren't that many, but Mom always ran them off. Like I said, I love her, but she has definite ideas about how my life should be."

"Give us an example of what your mom would do," said Heather.

Luke pursed his lips. "Erin Stoops is also a pharmacist. We were dating, and she came up with a plan to get around Mom that worked for a while. We agreed that she'd only come to my apartment once a week. She'd dress conservatively and sit in a chair while I took the couch. When Mom came calling, we were across the room from each other watching Hallmark movies. Erin always left by nine o'clock."

For the first time since the interview began, Luke grinned. "What Mom didn't know was our work schedules. One of my days off coincided with one of Erin's. I'd go to her apartment. That worked until the day Mom followed me."

Heather bit the inside of her mouth to stifle a catty remark. Steve maintained a calm demeanor. "How did Erin react?"

"Mom's timing couldn't have been worse. I'd just finished telling Erin that I wanted to see other women. It had been building a long time inside of me to break off the relationship, while Erin was making wedding plans."

Heather asked, "Had you already started seeing Connie?"

"Yes, and no. It's sort of complicated."

Steve tapped on the desk. "Let's get back to how Erin reacted to your mother."

"She was already upset with me for telling her I wanted to see other women, but Mom coming to her apartment lit the fuse to dynamite. After calling my mother every name in the book and a couple I'd never heard, she ran to the bedroom and came back with a pistol. She was shaking so bad; I wasn't sure who she'd shoot first. Luckily, the pistol wasn't loaded."

"Who was the pistol pointed at when the gun clicked?"

Luke's shoulders raised. "Like I said, the barrel of the pistol was bouncing around so much, she couldn't have hit anything smaller than an elephant."

After taking in the story, Steve said, "Let's get back to the day you and Connie arrived at the hotel. Claude and Marjorie Hicks are in their room, and you're at a meet-and-greet. Did anything else happen?"

12

A knock on the door preceded the sergeant entering and asking if anyone wanted coffee and cookies.

Three heads shook at the same time. Jack acted as the group's spokesman. "No thanks. I'm still getting a whiff of burned biscuits."

"You're not smelling the charcoal biscuits. That's the first batch of Old Testament cookies."

"Burnt offerings?" asked Steve.

The sergeant let out a snicker. "You've been around jails. That's half of an old joke."

Steve completed the saying. "And undercooked meats are blood sacrifices. There's nothing like biting into a chicken thigh that's crispy brown on the outside and raw in the middle."

"Yuk," said Heather. Le Roi sneezed, seemingly in agreement.

The door closed behind the sergeant and Jack got the conversation back on track. "Luke, we're still on the first day of the conference. You and Connie checked in and went to a happy hour of sorts. Claude and Marjorie Hicks are in their rooms, sleeping off a food coma and way too many glasses of champagne."

"From what we heard, especially the beverages," said Luke.

Steve broke in before Luke could expand. "Before we go on, the Hickses interest me. Did you have words with them about pulling a fast one over on Connie, forcing you two to be late?"

"I shot a few eye daggers their way at the banquet, but they're immune to anything verbal. I found when I worked with them that the only thing that penetrated their thick skin was a formal complaint."

Heather took down a note to find out if there was reciprocation, even before Luke said, "Of course they retaliated with their own complaints about me."

Heather could tell that Steve wanted to pick up the pace when he didn't delve deeper. "Did anything else happen the first night of the conference?"

"Some guy from out of state got a phone call saying his wife was going into labor. I heard later that he left the hotel that night and caught a flight back to Philadelphia, or Pittsburg, or somewhere like that. The only reason I remember him is because he started hollering, 'She's going to kill me for coming here.' He kept saying it over and over. It turns out he was supposed to sit at our table the next evening."

Luke tilted his head. "I've been thinking. There was one other person missing from our table. It would have been easy for someone to switch the place cards. The plates or drinks might have gone to the wrong person."

Steve almost spoke over Luke's last words. "We're considering all possibilities, and we'll talk about that later. For now, let's account for your actions, minute by minute. I guarantee the police are doing the same. How long did you and Connie stay at the meet-and-greet?"

"Our night was ruined by then. We might have waited five minutes before taking the elevator up to our room. I could tell she wasn't in the mood for romance, so I turned on the television and found a movie to watch. She was asleep long before I was."

"Did you leave the room for any reason?"

"Not until the next morning."

"What about Connie?" asked Steve. "Did she leave the room at any time during the night?"

"Nope. She slept like a baby until just before dawn. We dressed for our morning workouts and went to the hotel's gym."

The narrative of the day's activities continued. Heather noted nothing that stood out to her as unusual. She'd been to so many vendor conventions in upscale hotels that she could have told Steve what would happen next.

Her ears picked up when Luke spoke about arriving at the Saturday night banquet.

"It was a full day of hearing about the latest and greatest drugs, but that's the price you pay for staying at the top of your game."

Steve said, "I've always wondered how many drugs pharmacists have to track. It seems there's something new coming on the market every week."

"The lazy ones wait until they're approved. I track them when they're in stage three of clinical trials."

"Can't they look them up on the computer if they have questions?"

"Of course, but that takes time. You should know as well as I do that time is money."

"Don't remind me," said Heather.

Steve brought the focus back to the murder. "What can you tell us about your relationship with Michelle Le Blanc?"

"There was no relationship, other than I knew she was a pharmacist. I learned a little about her by listening to the conversation between Connie and her earlier in the day."

"Did they sit next to each other at the banquet?"

"Connie sat next to me while Michelle sat on the other side of the table next to Claude. He kept leaning close to her; most of the time we couldn't hear them. Claude was a foodie and I'm sure he was asking her about French cuisine."

"What did you learn about Michelle?"

"Mainly what Connie told me. She was born and raised in France."

Le Roi's ears twitched.

Luke continued. "She went through a messy divorce, no kids, and her ex-husband is still in Paris. She was forty-two years old, liked to sky dive and thought the pastries they served at breakfast tasted like cardboard."

Heather nodded her head at the last statement but said nothing.

Steve kept on. "What did she eat and drink at the banquet?"

"Don't you already know?"

"An investigation involves gathering facts, then double-checking to make sure they're accurate." Steve raised his chin. "Do you need me to repeat the question?"

Luke shot back, "Of course I don't. She had a glass of white wine. Next, they served a spring salad that she said shouldn't come until after the main course."

Heather nodded her head in agreement. "It's also considered a major faux pas to use a knife with your salad."

"She told us that, too," said Luke. "Then they brought out the main dishes. She had chicken confit with au gratin potatoes."

Heather asked, "Who was sitting on the other side of Michelle?"

The response came peppered with frustration. "No one. It should have been the man who was missing the birth of a child."

Steve asked, "What did you and Connie eat?"

"All the breads and salads were the same. Connie had the same main course as Michelle, chicken confit. My main course was boeuf bourguignon."

Steve had a habit of lightening the mood after he'd tested someone's patience. He grinned and asked, "How was the fancy version of beef stew?"

"Better than anything they serve in here." He took a deep breath and released it. "I'm sorry I snapped at you. This place isn't what I'm used to. I've never had to go through anything like this before. Have you heard anything that can help me get out of here?"

Steve tilted his head toward Jack. "I'll defer to your attorney."

Jack had said little up to now, and Heather was wondering if he'd heard something that might convince a judge to lower the bond.

"Up to now," said Jack with hands folded and resting on the table, "we've concentrated on the murder in Houston. You're being held for the murder in this county. Once Heather and Steve finish asking you about Michelle Le Blanc's death, we can move on to what happened to Connie."

Steve had his own agenda and was quick to get Luke to refocus on the murder in Houston. "When did Michelle develop signs of poisoning?"

"They began shortly after the servers took away all the plates. I'd say she started convulsing twenty minutes after she finished the main course."

Steve leaned back in his chair and rubbed his chin. "You're a smart guy and you've already brought up the possibility that Michelle wasn't the target of the poisoning. Did you accidentally kill her?"

Luke shot up so fast his chair fell over backward. "What kind of stupid question is that? Of course, I didn't kill Michelle. I didn't even know her."

Le Roi sprang to his feet, baring his teeth. Heather held her hands straight out in front of her and lowered them in a slow motion for Luke to sit down. She spoke in a soft tone. "Pick up your chair and sit with your hands flat on the table. The guard behind the glass will have you in cuffs if you do anything like that again. Steve was testing you to see how you'd react. You failed."

Steve added, "You're smart, but you've never played a game like the one you're playing now. The judge will consider your behavior in jail when Jack files for a reduction in bail."

Luke retrieved the chair and settled into it.

Heather expected the sergeant to come storming through the door, but that didn't happen. She shot a glance at Jack. He shook his head. "That was close. The officer on the other side of the glass was looking at his phone."

Steve waited a few more seconds and said, "Answer my question in a way that would convince a judge you didn't kill Michelle or Connie."

Luke sat up straight and spoke in a clear tone. "Michelle and I worked for the same company. I had no reason to kill her."

His voice cracked. "I loved Connie. We planned to spend our lives together. Our marriage would last forever and a day. She was the light and sunshine in my life. I could never harm her. It would be impossible."

Heather shook her head and explained, "That's way too much. It would sound like a soap opera to the judge. The less you say the better."

Jack said, "I'll make it easier for you. Say nothing. The only exceptions are if you're speaking to me, Steve, or Heather." He looked past Steve to Heather. "Can we trust Le Roi?"

Steve answered, "Absolutely. Now that we've got that out of the way, let's move on to questions about the second murder."

13

Heather noticed that some of the bravado had gone out of Luke. His shoulders came down a fraction of an inch and his gaze didn't stay locked on the person he was addressing. Steve had orchestrated all this as some sort of test. Perhaps it was to see what it took to make Luke lose control. She thought it was more likely to get Luke to see the seriousness of his situation.

All these thoughts raced through her mind as Steve said, "Tell us about the first time you met Connie." It was a benign question, one designed to take Luke's mind away from the seriousness of his present situation.

Heather was quick to recognize Steve's interview technique. He called it poke-and-stroke. Hit a suspect with a hard question and wait for a reaction, which in this case was an overreaction. Then, he would come back and ask an emotionally neutral question. It was a way for the person to redeem themselves, at least in their own minds. Also, it kept them talking.

Luke's eyes seemed to brighten. "It started with a phone call. As you know, we work at different pharmacies, but in the same parent company. A customer came in looking for a specific item that we had run out of. Everyone else was busy, so I called our sister store to check if they had that specific brand in stock. Connie answered. Her accent intrigued me. I couldn't get her voice out of my mind, so I sort of stalked her."

Heather shot him a glance. "How do you *sort of* stalk someone?"

"That was an awful choice of words, but it's what we both used once we got to know each other. We made an ongoing joke about it. I got her full name before the call ended. The world of pharmacists is like lawyers or doctors. All it took was one phone call, and I found a pharmacist who knew Connie. He said she was smart, gorgeous, and, as far as he knew, available."

Heather noticed the pace of Luke's words increased the longer he spoke about Connie.

"My next step was to find out for myself if she was all that my friend advertised her to be. I intentionally bumped into her after I found out what grocery store she went to. We hit it off right away."

Heather asked, "Weren't you *sort of* engaged to Erin Stoops when you *sort of* stalked Connie?"

"Never engaged," said Luke. He tried to keep the bite out of his quick reply, but it seeped through.

Heather kept on. "How long did you carry on with both women?"

"Not long."

"Can you be more specific?"

"I don't really remember."

"Yes, you do. Someone who knows the scientific names of drugs before release dates knows how long he dated two women at the same time."

"Two months," said Luke, in a way that reminded her of the dismissive way her father would answer her until she reached her thirtieth birthday.

"Wrong," snapped Heather.

"I'm never..."

The unfinished sentence hung in the air.

Steve intervened by using his calm voice. "Luke, we already know how long you dated both women. In fact, we have the answers to most of the questions we're asking. We're looking for diamonds of information buried in an enormous hill of small rocks."

Jack added, "Let's continue."

"Good idea," said Luke. "Mom's billed for every fifteen minutes."

"That reminds me," said Steve. "Where's the money coming from to pay for Jack's services?"

"What does it matter?"

Dead air met his question until Luke realized how contentious his answer sounded. "Sorry. It slipped my mind that you already know Mom has access to all my accounts. She's paying, but out of my savings."

"That's better," said Heather.

"Moving on," said Steve. "Did Erin and Connie know about each other?"

"Not for months."

"How many months?" asked Heather.

Luke spoke in an even tone. "I'm not trying to dodge the question, but I'm honestly not sure. I was seeing both of them, but it wasn't as bad as it sounds. Things between Erin and me started off slowly and never gained much speed. Conversely, my feelings for Connie burned hot from the first. I'm not the type of guy who rushes into or out of relationships, but with Connie it was different. Erin asked me what was wrong, but I didn't have the guts to tell her about Connie. Things between us cooled quickly. She might have followed me to Connie's place or seen us together somewhere in Houston. Looking back on it, I hated deceiving Erin, but I also didn't have the guts to tell her we were through."

Luke kept talking. "Everything crashed and burned when I came clean with Erin. Mom happened to pick that night to butt into my business."

A note of sympathy came into Steve's words. "Disappointing people is tough at any age, even if the person you're disappointing the most is yourself."

Luke hung his head. "It sounds like you have first-hand experience. Am I right?"

Heather burst in. "Everyone who's over four years old knows that feeling." She hoped to attempt to minimize the effect of Luke's question on Steve. It was too late. He seemed to withdraw into himself. She couldn't help but believe Steve had skipped back in time to a balmy night in Houston. He and Maggie were going through a dimly lit parking lot when four drug-addled street thugs attacked with clubs from behind. They took his gun, money, badge, and his sight. Most importantly, they took his wife's life.

Jack shot Heather a quick gaze that asked, *What now?*

She had the answer. "I've been here enough times to know they serve lunch early. After that lousy breakfast you had, I'm sure you're starving. You've given enough for us to start our investigation. We'll be back with other questions. In the meantime, try to think of anyone besides Erin who might have had something against Connie."

Luke looked at Jack. "Why won't Erin do? Isn't one crazy woman holding a grudge enough to get me a bond hearing?"

Jack took his turn. "Steve and Heather still need to verify her alibi."

Luke jutted his face forward. "What is her alibi?"

"We don't know yet," said Heather. "Remember what Jack said about things going slow with judicial proceedings? There are a lot of things going on beneath the surface that you can't see."

"And they're all costing me money."

Heather had heard enough for one day. She motioned to the guard behind the glass. It wasn't long before he entered the room and said, "The sergeant will be here soon to escort you out of the building. The rain is still pouring down."

Jack thanked him. Steve remained silent until the sound of

footfalls and a door closing echoed in the room. He turned to Heather. "Why did you cut the interview short?"

The question took her by surprise, but she made a quick recovery. "I thought you needed a break after that question he asked."

"Do you mean the one where he tried to guilt me about not protecting Maggie?"

"Yes. I sensed you shut down."

"That's what I wanted him to think. For a guy like Luke who's so full of himself, I wanted to make him think he got under my skin." Steve reached and patted Le Roi on the head. "I didn't fool you, did I *mon ami*?"

The dog responded to the question with a soft woof.

"Wait," said Heather. "Are you saying Le Roi knew you were only pretending to be upset?"

"He would have nudged my hand or brushed up against me looking for affection if he had sensed I was distraught. He raced through the guide training so fast that I added another module, one in emotional support."

Jack let out a laugh. "Le Roi has more diplomas than any of us."

Heather cast her gaze at Le Roi and said, "Since you're so smart, what's our next step?"

Steve said, "I'm his spokesman. He wants you to interview Erin Stoops. Find out how much of what Luke told us checks out. Was she head-over-heels in love with Luke or just a rainy-day friend?"

"Anything else?"

"You made me hungry when you mentioned lunch. Jack must have missed breakfast. His stomach began sounding like a garbage disposal twenty minutes ago."

"That's true," said Jack. "A Pop Tart isn't my idea of break-fast, but it was all I had time for today. Where do you want to go?"

Steve rose from the table. "The sergeant is about to open the door. Let's go somewhere that serves steak. Le Roi deserves a nice, thick slab of meat."

Heather's breakneck schedule had prevented her from dining out with Le Roi. She didn't know exactly what to expect. Bringing a little levity into the jail's interview room seemed the thing to do. "How will Le Roi join us at the table if he doesn't have a throne to sit on?"

"Don't be silly," said Steve. "The king always eats before the peasants. You'll need to take him out to your car and feed him in his cell."

"Why me?"

"You two need to bond, and he loves it when you speak French."

Jack's snickering caused her to shift her gaze. "Just for that, you get to feed him."

"Don't look at me. I don't speak French."

14

Halfway across the parking lot, Jack received a phone call and had to get back to his office. It seemed strange to Heather that he was the one with an excuse to decline an invitation to lunch and not her.

As things turned out, Steve took care of Le Roi's need for food without them getting soaked to the skin. Instead of going to a restaurant, Steve came up with a better plan. "I'm calling the meat market you use and have them do a rush delivery of steaks to your office. There's always room in your refrigerator. We can call out for our lunch."

With a plan in place, Heather drove through the steady rain until they reached her office building. Le Roi performed his duty as a guide to absolute perfection. This was his first time entering the four-story office building and everyone who saw him had something to say. It was as if people had never seen a one-hundred-pound giant schnauzer wearing a service vest and leading a blind private detective before.

Heather kept a straight face and walked into the elevator with Le Roi and Steve right behind her. Word of Steve's new companion traveled through the building at the speed of light.

By the time the trio reached the fourth floor, the offices had emptied and a gallery of admirers stood in the hall waiting to welcome The King.

She walked past her employees and made her way to the sanctuary of her office. It took Steve and Le Roi ten more minutes before the celebrities *du jour* came through the door.

A knock sounded on the door. Heather's personal assistant entered. "Are you expecting a delivery of steak?"

Heather pointed to Steve. "Ask the prime minister where to put the prime rib." She hadn't intended to make a joke, but that didn't stop Steve from releasing a loud guffaw, followed by, "Leave it on my desk. I'll put it in the refrigerator in Heather's miniature apartment."

Her personal assistant had other ideas. "Is it for Le Roi?"

"Yes."

"I'll be glad to take care of it. How much do you want him to have?"

"About a pound, cut into one-inch-by-one-inch cubes."

Heather shook her head at the sight. "Never accuse me of spoiling Max again."

Steve directed Le Roi to follow Heather's right-hand helper. Both disappeared into the tiny apartment.

Heather had been at her desk long enough to have her laptop fully operational. "Another sandwich for lunch?"

"Yeah, the usual. A po'boy for me, and I'm guessing you'll have another salad."

"I'll call it in this time," said Heather as she thought about how the rain was wreaking havoc on her construction schedule.

Steve spoke from behind his desk on the other side of the room. "Stop worrying about it. The rain comes and then it goes. There's nothing you can do about it."

She asked, "Was I drumming my desk with my pen again?"

"Yeah. Regular beats. It always signals you're worrying." He asked, "Did you call Erin Stoops and set up an appointment?"

"Not yet."

Steve said nothing else. He didn't have to. Their agreement called for her to devote herself completely to the cases they took on. Steve didn't hold her completely to that, but he expected results. This meant she needed to stop using her mental energy on something she couldn't control and interview someone who could be a viable suspect.

She manipulated her computer until she found Erin's phone number.

Meanwhile, her assistant and Le Roi exited the apartment. The dog walked a straight path to his new bed beside Steve's desk. Her PA asked Steve, "Does he always inhale his food?"

"Only if it's excellent meat. He'll eat other cuts if he has to, but he prefers prime rib."

Heather dialed Erin's number and waited for her to answer. She said her name and reason for calling when someone in the background screamed. Both Steve and Le Roi raised their heads.

"Are you all right?" asked Heather, as she punched the speaker option.

The volume of response decreased. "Take a deep cleansing breath, Patty... that's good... now take short, shallow breaths."

The volume increased. "I don't know what this is about, but you couldn't have called at a worse time. My sister is having a baby, and the midwife is taking her sweet time getting here."

"I'm an attorney. It's important that I speak with you in regard to an ongoing investigation, but it can wait."

"I have your number. If I don't call you back by this time tomorrow, call me again." The call cut off.

Le Roi walked in a tight circle on his bed and resettled. Steve said, "That's a first. I never worked a case where I had to delay an interview because a baby was coming into the world." He paused. "I delivered a baby, in the back of my patrol car once. You should have seen the mom-to-be trying to run from me. She was past due and selling drugs to buy a fancy bed for the baby. It made one heck of a mess in the back seat."

Heather's phone rang, keeping her from asking for details on another of Steve's stories. Her first thought was flooding in her development as she picked up her phone. She breathed a sigh of relief when her father's name appeared on the screen.

85

15

———

Heather pushed away from her desk as she took the call from her father. "Are you where you can talk?" he asked. It was a bit out of character for him to ask. Normally, he launched into what he had to say. Perhaps their improved relationship was taking some of his rough edges away. Then again, perhaps not. She never knew with her father.

"Steve, Le Roi, and I are at my office. I'm going into my apartment, so I won't disturb Steve's concentration or the dog's nap."

Her father spoke as she walked to her apartment. "I wanted to thank you for the photos you sent of Le Roi. He's a magnificent beast. Have he and Max settled their differences?"

"They've called a truce and pretend the other doesn't exist."

Chit chat wasn't her father's norm. A slight sense of dread settled in as she closed the apartment door behind her.

"I'm keeping up with the weather in the Houston area. The prophets of doom are saying flooding is widespread and will only get worse. How is your development holding up?"

"I haven't checked today, but as of last night, the drainage is doing its job better than I expected. The heavy rain comes and goes."

"I'm sure you realize this may work out for you if the flooding continues and you're left on wet, but solid ground."

She sensed there was more to the conversation than a father's concern. "Have you and Steve been talking again?"

Her father seldom laughed, but her question caused him to release a deep chuckle. "It serves me right for trying to get something past my daughter, the detective. He told me about your new marketing plan. Brilliant. Absolutely brilliant."

Heather had to bite her bottom lip to keep from blubbering. She'd never heard a double expression of praise from her father. He followed it with another surprise. "The reason I called is to ask if you'd mind if I came to see you at Christmas. I don't want to interfere if you already have plans."

She had to clear her throat before she could reply. "Uh... no. I mean, I have no plans other than to be in my new home. What I mean is, Steve and I will both be in our new homes."

"Don't forget Max and Le Roi."

"How could I?"

A few seconds of awkward silence passed. Her father broke it by confessing. "Really, the main reason I called was to tell you that you're at the point with your project where you should consider backing away. The hardest work is behind you. You have a competent staff who will finish the project with minimal supervision."

"Now I'm sure you and Steve have been talking. Did he tell you we're working on another murder case?"

"Two cases. He says you're slowly turning into a human being again. I'll never understand how solving crimes settles your mind, but I can't deny the results."

"You're right and thank you. It was very nice of you to call."

"One more thing before I let you go. I understand you're dead set on being in your new home by Christmas, but remember the first rule about construction. It always takes longer than it should. You don't have to prove anything to me. If it reduces some of your stress, we can celebrate Christmas in your present home. I'll think no less of you."

Something came alive in her that caused her to flinch. "I hear what you're saying, and I appreciate it, but being in my new home is a goal with a deadline that I can't ignore. You'll have a fantastic view of the lake from your room."

"Always striving to reach the elusive end of the rainbow. Like father, like daughter. A room with a view of the lake will be nice." He added, "Nice, but not essential."

The call ended and Heather returned to her desk. Steve pulled off his noise-canceling headphones. "How's your father today?"

She spoke as she settled into her chair. "You should know."

"I asked how he was doing today. I haven't spoken to him since yesterday."

"I stand corrected."

"You're sitting."

She huffed to let him know she didn't appreciate his attempt at humor. "What's with you today?"

"I'm catching up on months of corny things to say to you. I'm also reminding you to stay focused on these cases. Leo and Jack are both counting on us to make progress. That means we need to pay attention to details. I have a feeling we're dealing with people who are very smart, clever, or both."

"That reminds me, what stood out to you in the interview with Luke?"

"He threw everyone he could under the bus."

With that simple reply, Steve showed her again why he was such a good detective. He took an hour's worth of information gained in an interview and boiled it down to one sentence. Not only could he focus on the tiny threads, but he saw in his mind the whole sweater. Except it wasn't an article of clothing, it was a murder. Or, in this case, two murders.

She came away from her thoughts when Steve said, "Your father and I also talked about Christmas. I told him about the cases we're working, and that he should be prepared to stay in one of the upstairs guest rooms of our current home."

Heather bristled. "If there's one thing I don't need, it's negative thinking coming from you. I don't care if it rains from now until Christmas Eve. My father and I will drink hot chocolate and look at the lake through the windows of my new home on Christmas morning. It's a present to myself."

Steve gave a slight nod in acknowledgement. "In the meantime, let's give Leo and Jack a present by solving these cases. Who do you plan on interviewing next?"

"I planned on speaking to Erin Stoops, but she's delivering a baby somewhere. I guess I'll stay here and listen to the recording I made of our interview with Luke."

"You can do that tonight. We're meeting with Marjorie Hicks after lunch. She agreed to come here."

"That was fast. What about her husband?"

"He's working, and I got the impression she didn't want him to come. I'll try to interview him after Marjorie tells us his work schedule."

She glanced out the window to check the rain; it had slowed to a drizzle. "You sound sure that Marjorie will tell us when Claude works."

"I believe she'll tell us more than that. She impressed me as being a tad chatty."

Steve changed the subject. "By the way, I ordered lunch while you were on the phone with your father. It should be here before too long."

"You're assuming the delivery driver's car can make it here. Many of the streets aren't draining very well."

"It's likely this guy will. The sandwich shop I called is one I'm familiar with. The driver has a jacked-up fifteen-year-old pickup truck. He can go places your SUV can't. He knows we both give good tips, so it stands to reason he'll make our delivery one of his first."

Heather shook her head. Steve was a natural problem solver.

He could connect so many things in his mind that seemed to be random bits of information. Somehow, he rejected and selected the bits as if they were letters in a game of Scrabble. Similarly, he'd arrange and rearrange things until they made sense. He wasn't clairvoyant, but exceptionally gifted in linking seemingly unrelated things until a clear picture emerged.

They each went back to their computers, but didn't have long to wait until a knock sounded on the door. Le Roi bolted up from his slumber.

"There's lunch," said Steve. "He's earlier than I expected."

Heather hated to admit it, but there was something comforting about knowing she didn't have to be the best detective in the room. She'd settled that issue by the time they solved their third case. Perhaps that's why she always felt rested after they solved a case.

A skinny teen wearing camouflaged hunting gear and tall rubber boots came through the door. He carried rain-speckled paper bags of food. Steve was right again.

Heather dug in her purse and pulled out a hundred-dollar bill. The young man put the bags on the table and stared at the bill. "You don't have to do that. He already paid for it and added a nice tip."

"That truck of yours must drink gas like a camel takes on water. You earned it by coming to work in this weather."

"You're right about Old Betsy. That's what I call her. She may be old, but I've never been stuck. Believe me, I've been hunting in places where water almost came into the cab. Betsy always came through and got me out of trouble."

"Don't sell her," said Steve. "A good truck is hard to find. The same goes for a good woman."

"I don't know about the woman part, but that sure is a fine dog. Does he retrieve?"

"He specializes in retrieving people. He's a trained police dog."

"I don't have much use for that, unless he could fetch me a

cute girlfriend." He chuckled. "Got to go. I'm the only one from our shop who can make deliveries anywhere in town."

Heather retrieved drinks from the refrigerator in her apartment. By the time she returned, Steve had his sandwich and chips laid out in front of him. Le Roi let out a soft whimper. Steve responded with a sharp reply.

"Allez a votre lit."

Le Roi raised his head and marched to his bed.

"I'm impressed," said Heather. "There are other ways of saying go to your bed, but he got the message loud and clear."

The meal progressed slowly. The few words of French reminded Heather of how the people in France ate their meals at an unhurried pace. Perhaps she should slow down. She looked at her fingernails and couldn't remember how long it had been since her last manicure.

Steve returned to his desk without the aid of his cane or dog. Normally, Le Roi would rush to his side as soon as he stood. It seemed as if the king didn't appreciate the words of correction and needed to regain his dignity.

A sentence in broken French from Steve brought Le Roi to his feet and had his tail wagging. A loose translation equated to Steve asking his dog if he needed to go outside and attend to personal business.

"Did you put plastic bags in the pocket of his vest?"

"We don't leave home without them."

"Do you want me to come with you?"

"No need. He takes care of the serious stuff first thing in the morning. This is a tinkle and sniff break."

Steve put on a hooded raincoat, grasped the handle attached to the harness, and started walking. The two returned about fifteen minutes later, both in good spirits.

It wasn't long before both man and beast raised their heads. Steve said, "That should be Marjorie Hicks."

Three knocks sounded on the door.

16

———

Heather crossed the room to meet Mrs. Hicks while Steve instructed Le Roi to come with him. Marjorie took one look at the dog and gasped. "What a stunning schnauzer. May I pet him?"

"Let me tell him you're a friend first. He won't bite, but he's trained to be cautious of affection from strangers." Steve spoke a single word, "*Ami.*" That's all it took for Le Roi to step towards Marjorie and receive not only pats on the head but scratches behind the ears. Her admiration was obvious as she ran her hands down the dog's back and sides, then looked at his eyes and even checked his gums."

Heather asked, "Do you judge competitions?"

Her gaze remained on Le Roi. "I used to. That was a long time ago, before I married Claude."

Heather noted that Marjorie said it in a way that hinted at resentment, or perhaps anger.

Marjorie gave an explanation without further prompting. "Claude developed an allergy to dogs, so I had to back away from competitions. I miss not being around dogs."

"I hope being around Le Roi won't adversely affect your husband."

"I'll wash my hands and change clothes as soon as I return home. Claude is working the afternoon shift, so he'll never know, as long as I take precautions."

Steve continued to regale the visitor with Le Roi's pedigree and qualities while Heather made mental notes of Marjorie's physical appearance. Petite was the first word that came to mind. She was not over five feet tall, from her tiny shoes to her perfectly coiffed gray hair. Heather guessed the woman to be in her mid-fifties.

Marjorie unzipped and slipped out of what appeared to be a Mackage rain jacket, that had mostly covered a stunning aqua-colored business suit. A Louis Vuitton purse hung from her arm.

"Let me take your Mackage and hang it up," said Heather.

Marjorie's pride seemed to bloom. As Heather took the jacket, it was obvious to her that its look and feel weren't right; it was a knock-off. She had one like it in her closet, but hers was genuine and came with a price tag of a thousand dollars. Upon closer inspection, the business suit's cuffs showed wear and slight discoloration where someone had tried too hard to remove a stain.

The three took seats at one end of the conference table that could seat twelve. Steve took the leather chair at the end while Heather and Marjorie faced each other. He began with small talk about the weather while Heather concluded that Marjorie's income didn't align with her desire for status. Luke had described her with less than glowing words, but her eyes were clear, and her speech was precise.

Steve proceeded at an unhurried pace. He finished his discourse on how the torrential rain had its origin from tiny particles of African dust that drifted westward in a slowly turning ball of low barometric pressure. It finally developed into a tropical storm after it entered the Gulf of Mexico and slowly tracked to the west-northwest. Instead of veering off to the east, as most storms do, the category one hurricane came ashore between Beaumont and Galveston. It settled over Conroe because of a shift in the jet stream.

It was a long, complicated explanation filled with technical terms but served the purpose of making Marjorie focus on something other than the grim subject of murder. Many people rehearse what they'll say in an interview. This was one of Steve's tricks to occupy their minds with something completely different. His goal was to make their responses more extemporaneous.

The mood took a turn when Steve said, "As I told you on the phone, Heather and I are both former police detectives. Leo Vega, my former partner in Houston, asked us to review the unfortunate death of Michelle Le Blanc. My physical limitations make it almost impossible for me to be of much help, but I agreed to give him as much as I could."

Heather took her turn. "Look around. Does this look like a police station? I'm up to my ears in running this company and stretched so thin with a housing project that Steve's doing almost everything."

Marjorie straightened the position of her wedding set. "I read about your housing development. Most impressive."

"It's the biggest challenge and headache of my life, and this rain isn't helping. But, with enormous risks come big rewards."

Marjorie let out a huff of air. "That's what my husband says."

Steve pressed on. "What we're saying is, this conversation is a favor for a friend. We want to ask you about the conference you and your husband attended."

"I already gave a statement to Detective Vega."

"True, but I have to listen to an AI-generated text-to-speech reading of the report. Only by listening in person can I come close to hearing what someone is really saying. I never realized until I lost my sight how important the inflection of words and seeing physical reactions are. The latter is no longer possible for me, so I must settle for listening to personal interviews."

Steve took a deep breath. "Heather has a mountain of other things to do. Let's get started so she can get back to her work."

He snapped his fingers, and Le Roi came to Steve's side of the table and sat looking at Marjorie. Heather realized this could work in Steve's favor with this and future interviews, especially if a suspect became belligerent. All Steve had to say was en garde, and Le Roi would transform into a growling, snarling monster.

Steve didn't tell Marjorie about the tiny devices that were capturing everything she said and every expression. Heather would send the video and audio to Leo and Jack after making copies for herself and Steve. Texas was a one-party consent state, so they didn't need Marjorie's permission to record her.

"Tell us about your first day at the conference. I believe there was a meet-and-greet. Is that correct?"

"Yes. As usual, we arrived early."

Heather issued an opinion. "That's difficult in Houston's traffic."

"There's always horrible traffic, and Claude drives like a maniac. He believes if you're on time, you're already thirty minutes late, especially for food."

Steve tapped his index finger on the table, but not loud enough to make an aggravating noise. "How many pharmacists from your store attended the conference?"

"Three, but Connie Petrovitch and her date, Luke Bains, didn't arrive until much later."

"Any idea why?"

"I can only guess that the two of them had a tiff."

"Ah," said Heather. "I'm sure that's what it was." She paused a tick and asked, "Did you know Ms. Petrovitch well?"

"Only slightly. Claude knew her better than me."

Heather and Steve remained silent. A skilled interviewer knows how to wait as long as it takes for silence to become too uncomfortable for most people.

Marjorie broke at the twenty-second mark. She looked down at her nails. "You might as well hear it from me. Claude doesn't think much of people from the former Soviet Union. His father was a serious doomsday prepper during the Cold War. He drilled xenophobic attitudes into my husband. Try as he may, they still rise to the surface."

"How do they manifest?" asked Steve.

"Don't get me wrong. Claude's much better than he used to be. Still, he'll make cutting remarks if he's watching television, especially when he watches the news. I think it's the accent that sets his teeth on edge."

Steve lifted his voice half a step and said, "Let's get back to the meet-and-greet. Did Ms. Petrovitch attend?"

"Not that I remember." She closed her eyes. "Wait. Yes, she did. She arrived late."

"Did your husband have a confrontation with her? We heard something about a minor disturbance."

"There wasn't a disturbance that I was aware of."

Heather provided the answer. "It had to do with someone falling into a table topped with glasses of champagne."

"That happened much earlier. My husband is a large man and not as light on his feet as he once was. Mr. Smiley, I know you can't see me, but my dress size is extra small. Claude must have tripped and ran into me, sending me up against a table. It was an unfortunate accident. He'd do nothing to harm me, and certainly wouldn't want to spill champagne. It was most embarrassing for both of us."

"How did he trip?" asked Heather.

"I don't know, but he blamed it 'on that Petrovitch woman,' as he called her."

"It's a shame," said Steve.

Heather played along. "What's a shame?"

"She's not around to question. Someone poisoned her."

Marjorie maintained a poker face and said nothing.

Heather spent the next several minutes asking Marjorie about the presentations they had attended the next day and if she noticed anyone acting suspiciously. It came as no surprise that nothing of value came from this part of the interview.

Steve came back into the conversation. "I'm confused about

some things that took place at the banquet where Michelle Le Blanc died. The first is when people arrived at your table. Who was present when you arrived?"

"Like I said, Claude always arrives early. We were sitting at the table for ten minutes before Michelle Le Blanc arrived. She sat beside Claude."

"Did that upset him?" asked Heather.

"Oh, no. It's the Eastern Europeans he doesn't like. He's fine with the French, especially when Ms. Le Blanc brought up the subject of French cuisine. My husband is quite the epicurean. He loves to cook."

"Can you remember the seating arrangement?" asked Steve.

"Do you mean the original arrangement or where everyone wound up sitting?"

"I wasn't aware there was a difference."

"I'm afraid Claude is to blame for moving the place cards. One reason he arrives early for banquets is so he can face the stage without having to crane his neck. It doesn't turn like it used to. Another is so he can put people he doesn't like as far away from him as possible."

"I know the feeling," said Steve. "I never moved place cards, but it's not a bad idea."

Marjorie gave her head a hearty nod. "The first thing he did was move the name cards of the two out-of-state people to where they had their backs to the stage. We took their places."

"He didn't move Michelle's card next to him so they could discuss food?"

"Oh, yes. He moved her card, too."

Heather clarified her statement. "There were eight place settings. Is that correct?"

"Yes. The tables seated eight, but there were only seven place cards. Two people never showed. The servers cleared all the dinner plates after the main course."

"Can you draw us a sketch of the table, the chairs, and where everyone sat?"

"Certainly. All I need is paper and a pen."

Heather tore a page from the legal pad and took an extra pen from her valise. Marjorie began by drawing a circle, then boxes to represent chairs. Next to each chair, she drew a line outward and wrote the names of everyone present."

Heather examined the sketch. "If the table were a clock, the stage would be some distance away at twelve o'clock."

"Correct. Claude likes to sit near the rear at banquets or the theater. He's at the age when being able to get to the restroom quickly outweighs other desires. We no longer get good seats for performances."

Heather moved on. "You and Claude are sitting at approximately five and seven o'clock. Following clockwise, we come to Connie Petrovitch at about nine o'clock, with Luke Bains between Connie and you. Then we have three empty seats. Two for the out-of-town attendees and one with no place card. Correct?"

"That's right. Those are the ones Claude calls the neck-breaker seats."

"Finally, moving around the clock," said Heather. "Michelle Le Blanc is at about three o'clock beside Claude."

Heather knew Steve had the table and attendees locked in his mind, but she'd double check with him after Marjorie left.

Steve said, "I think that's enough questions for one day. We may need to speak to you again, Marjorie. Will that be all right?"

"Certainly. Anything to help."

"By the way," said Heather. "Claude is supposed to stop by tomorrow. Could you remind him of our appointment at nine in the morning?"

"Just send him a text around eight. I'll be working tomorrow morning."

Heather dipped her chin. "Of course."

Marjorie rose and spent more time with Le Roi on her way out. Once she retrieved her rain jacket, Heather saw her to the door and closed it behind her.

She returned to the conference table and asked, "What did you think of her?"

"She doesn't like her husband, and she's a pretentious fake. The moving of the name cards complicates things. The interview with her husband should be interesting."

17

It came as a double surprise to Heather when Jack called the next morning before she left for her office. Jack's idea of early morning differed from hers unless he had a hunting or fishing trip planned. His office hours were nine to five. He rarely deviated from his schedule and liked to ease into his workday. He reminded her that the next day was Thanksgiving and made sure she hadn't forgotten that she and Steve were to arrive at his house by eleven.

How could she be so forgetful? Truth be told, she'd lost track of the days, probably because she hadn't taken a day off in months. Both the holiday and the invitation had completely slipped her mind. "I'm such a dunce," she said. "I'll bring the wine. Your poor mother. I should have called and asked what I could bring. Tell me she's not cooking the entire meal by herself."

"Of course not. Briann will help her, and I'll do my part by stopping by the bakery and picking up two or three pies. Does Steve have a favorite?"

"Any, and all. Wait. Now that I think about it, he likes pecan and pumpkin pie around the holidays. He says pies and turkey leftovers are the only good things about late November and December."

"I thought he only hated Christmas."

"Maggie started decorating for Christmas as soon as she and Steve had Thanksgiving dishes put away. They'd skip breakfast and eat an enormous meal around eleven. She let him nap for only one hour. After that, it was full steam ahead with hauling artificial trees and decorations from the garage. To hear Steve tell it, the house transformed into something from a Hallmark movie with all the lights and glitter you could imagine."

"Trees? As in more than one?"

"An artificial tree for every room but the living room. She believed it was bad luck to put presents under a plastic tree, so she insisted on a real one there."

Heather could imagine Jack shaking his head as he asked, "Don't they make doctors that can help people with that type of obsession?"

"The doctor would have had two patients. Steve won't hardly talk about it, but he loved Christmas as much as Maggie. He'd pretend not to, but he saved up overtime so he could be home with her as much as possible over the holidays."

With plans for Thanksgiving solidified, Heather dressed for another soggy day and found Steve sitting at the bar, nursing a cup of coffee. Le Roi sat at his side, looking regal, bright-eyed, and alert.

The trip to the office teased her with a two-mile stretch where she didn't need to use her windshield wipers. "Perhaps it's going to clear up," she said in a hopeful tone.

"It's the equivalent of fool's gold," said Steve with hope-crushing finality. "It's still pulling moisture up from the gulf. Relief won't come until the jet stream swings south from the center of the country and blows everything east."

Heather let out a puff of air. "Oh well, I guess it doesn't matter. Contractors are all off work for the long Thanksgiving weekend."

Steve kept facing forward, looking as if he could see out of the windshield. "Do you have questions ready for Claude Hicks?"

Heather put on her blinker before turning into the parking lot. "I have my doubts about the strength of their marriage. From the background information we received from Leo, it seems the only thing they have in common is their profession."

The SUV came to a stop in Heather's reserved spot. Steve located and pushed the red button that freed him from the seat belt. "Don't underestimate love. It comes in all different shapes and sizes. There's validity to the old saying about how opposites attract." He wiggled his eyebrows. "Then again, sometimes people tire of living with each other, and try to pin a murder on their spouse to get away from them."

Because they arrived earlier than normal office hours, Le Roi's adoring crowd was not there to fawn over him. His ears dropped a little, but not enough for anyone who didn't know him well to notice. Heather was learning the dog's little idiosyncrasies and how to read his moods. Like Steve, Le Roi could appear simple and compliant, almost lazy. Then, out of the blue, they both could astound with their abilities.

The two detectives and the dog went to their respective workstations and began their day. Heather zipped through the highlights of the *Wall Street Journal's* news stories, checked a fistful of stock prices, and made phone calls to her construction supervisor and personal assistant.

Steve raised his head after her second call ended. "Any disasters?"

"Nothing major local, national, or abroad. Everyone seems to have started the holiday season a day early."

Steve responded with a grunt. She guessed he was gearing up for his holiday funk.

At precisely eight o'clock, Heather left the office to check on the arriving workers and wish them a happy Thanksgiving. Many had taken the day off and even more were working only half a day. An idea struck her as she returned to her office.

She stopped in front of Steve's desk. "You're right."

He leaned back. "Of course, I am. What am I right about?"

"I need to act more like a human being and take some time off."

"Can you wait until after our interview with Claude Hicks?"

"That depends on whether I can get into the salon this afternoon. If all they have is this morning, you'll be on your own."

Steve clapped his hands four or five times. "Bravo. Spoken like a person ready to rejoin the rest of us mortals. Make the call."

Heather did and scored an early afternoon appointment. It didn't surprise her that they worked her in. Her tip alone would go a long way to buying Christmas presents for several of the salon's employees. Her afternoon would include a sauna, whirlpool, cold plunge, manicure, pedicure, haircut with styling, and facial.

It wasn't long before her gatekeeper buzzed. "Mr. Hicks is here for his nine o'clock appointment."

"Send him in."

Steve said, "It's showtime."

The door opened and Claude made his grand appearance. He walked confidently into the room, his jowls jiggling with every step. When Marjorie said he was a big man, she wasn't kidding. Not overly tall at approximately six feet, his excess girth gave him the appearance of a balloon with stubby arms and legs haphazardly attached. He possessed a larger-than-necessary head that bobbed like a fishing cork when he walked.

The mental picture of Claude and Marjorie in bathing suits flashed into Heather's mind. She cursed her active imagination and extended her hand to greet him. "Heather McBlythe, and my business partner, Steve Smiley. Thank you for taking time out of your day."

"Not a problem. The turkey is soaking in a special brine I developed and I don't start baking pies until after noon. Tomorrow's the busy day."

"Did Marjorie give you a full report of our meeting with her yesterday?"

"She said you and Mr. Smiley are consultants for the police, and you discussed the death of Michelle Le Blanc."

Claude's gaze shifted to Le Roi. "She talked about your dog more than anything else. Marjorie is obsessed with dogs."

Heather couldn't believe she and Steve had been so forgetful. "I'm so sorry he's here. Marjorie told us you're allergic to dogs."

Claude flipped a meaty hand as if to shoo away an insect. "It's a very slight allergy. I take an antihistamine daily to ward off the symptoms of pet dander and the many pollens in this part of the country. He won't bother me as long as I don't pet him."

"That's a relief," said Heather. "Let's gather at the conference table."

The chairs had arms, and she wondered if Claude could squeeze into it. He did, but folds of his midsection protruded above and below the chair's arms.

Steve told Le Roi to return to his bed. He obeyed but gave a snort of disapproval.

"Such a handsome and well-trained schnauzer," said Claude. He continued explaining, "If Marjorie would keep dogs out of the kitchen and dining room, I wouldn't object to her having one."

"Only one?" asked Steve.

"Yes. That's one of my pet peeves. I believe one pet per home is sufficient, and proper training is a must. Marjorie would have a pack of hounds doing as they please if I'd let her. In fact, that describes the first five years of our marriage. Dog hair in our bed, on the furniture, and even in our food. Luckily, they all died by our fifth anniversary. That gave me the opportunity to put my foot down concerning replacements."

As the man rambled on, Heather's thoughts had shifted to the indulgent way she'd spend the afternoon. She needed to refocus, so she looked at the questions she'd written on a yellow legal pad. "Marjorie described you as an epicurean. Do you grow your own herbs and spices?"

"Of course. I also have a greenhouse with raised beds where I grow a large variety of vegetables. It's impossible to serve the best meals without superior ingredients."

"Marjorie didn't mention your green thumb."

"She wouldn't. Her idea of horticulture is hiring a lawn service to cut and trim the grass. I don't allow incompetent foreigners to prune the fruit trees."

Steve changed the direction of the questions. "How well did you know Michelle Le Blanc?"

"Not well. By that I mean I knew her name and that she was a native of France. I looked forward to meeting her to see if we shared an appreciation of well-prepared food. It turned out we did. We had a delightful conversation about trends in French cooking. It surprised her that I was more up-to-date than her, but we were in complete agreement about taking time to appreciate the flavors and textures of a well-crafted meal. I invited her to the weekly suppers I prepare for a small group of fellow epicureans."

"That explains why you rearranged the seating arrangement."

"Of that I plead guilty." He grimaced. "Oh dear. That didn't come out the way I intended."

It was Steve's turn to flip away the comment and move on with another statement that held a hidden question. "Marjorie indicated she does her share of the cooking. I suppose that's a passion you two share."

This brought on a belly-shaking laugh. "You're misinformed. It's unorthodox, but we cook for ourselves." He paused. "That's not true. Marjorie doesn't exactly cook. She survives on half a bagel for breakfast and reheated leftovers from chain restaurants. Sometimes there are leftovers from my meals that she reheats. I must admit she's a big help with cleaning the kitchen. I've always appreciated her high level of energy."

Heather was tiring of all the talk of food and said, "It's confirmed that Michelle ingested poison. It's possible that someone seated at your table is responsible. Do you suspect anyone in particular?"

Claude interlaced pudgy fingers and rested his hands on his protruding midsection. "I've given this a considerable amount of thought. There were two people from out of town that should have been at the table. I'm wondering if one of them is responsible."

Steve took over. "It takes motive, means, and opportunity to explain a homicide. Satisfy each of those requirements."

"I'll try, but I'm working with limited information. Means and opportunity go together. One of them could have paid someone to slip the poison into Michelle's wine or food. She mentioned that her chicken confit wasn't cooked slow enough and they'd used olive oil instead of fat."

"Did she drink all her wine?" asked Steve.

"Yes. I believe she did." Claude's eyes opened wider. "I see what you're getting at. With her sensitive palate, she would have detected a poison. The killer must have put the substance in the chicken confit."

"How do you think this out-of-town pharmacist delivered the poison?"

"He could have put on the white shirt and black pants of a server and made sure he served Michelle her main course. No one pays attention to servers. Of course, he'd have checked out of the hotel earlier and had a cab take him to the airport. Then, he took a cab back to the hotel and did the deed."

"And the motive?" asked Heather.

Claude held up his palms. "I can't speculate about that. Not enough background information." He took a full breath. "There is another possibility."

"Oh? What's that?"

"If I were you, I'd make sure Michelle's ex-husband wasn't in the States. She didn't discuss details, but I had the impression that she left France to avoid further abuse. I've seen the fear in the eyes of so many abused women over the years. Doctors habitually prescribe antidepressants and psychotropics to help them cope."

Steve asked, "What about the people at the table? Do you suspect any of them?"

"I considered them and came up empty except for Luke Bains."

"Why Luke?" asked Heather.

"He's in jail for murder, isn't he? Perhaps he finally snapped."

"Finally?"

"He has issues."

"Can you explain?"

"Let's just say that he doesn't mind twisting the truth to get what he wants. He cost me a promotion many years ago. I changed jobs and had to take a significant reduction in pay."

Steve pushed back from the table. "Thank you for your time. We'll tell the police to take a hard look at the two people from out of town."

"Yes, but don't dismiss Luke too quickly. He may be a serial killer."

"That possibility has occurred to us."

Everyone stood, and Heather walked out with Claude. When she returned, Steve was on his phone. "I'll be waiting for you under the awning at the front door. You can't miss me. I'll be the only man with a white cane and an extra-large black dog."

"Are you leaving?" asked Heather.

"Yep. I called Uber."

"I could take you home."

"You haven't had a decent workout or spa day in months. Your vacation starts now."

"But—"

"No buts. You've already checked out mentally. Let's walk downstairs together. We'll discuss Claude on Sunday. Until then, it's turkey and dressing, turkey sandwiches, and football." He paused. "And pies."

18

Heather took Steve's advice and settled into a vacation routine. The workout in the gym tore down muscles that weren't accustomed to being told to perform. Promise to self number one was to return to her prior regimen of four workouts a week, no matter what.

Thanksgiving Day turned into an all day, and into the night, marathon of overeating. This resulted in the second promise to self. She committed to a strict diet until Christmas, and moderation on that day. Dressing, mashed potatoes with gravy and all pies were on the list of prohibited items.

Friday morning came with a special surprise, no rain. She glanced out a window into the backyard. Steve sat in a lawn chair, throwing a tennis ball all the way to the eight-foot-tall wooden fence that formed a barrier around three sides of the backyard.

She exited the sliding patio door wearing a robe with house shoes and stepped into sunlight so bright it caused her to squint. Her heart soared. "What did you do with the rain?"

Steve threw the ball again. "I told it you'd learned your lessons, and it was time to leave. The rain apologized and said it would go to Louisiana. There's nothing but blue skies in the forecast."

"You said I learned my lesson. What was it?"

"Lessons. Two of them. The first is patience."

"I never liked that one. What's the second?"

"There are a lot of things beyond your control. When life doesn't play fair, learn to roll with the punches"

"I prefer to punch back. Let's take a ride out to our new homes this afternoon. I want to envision a Christmas tree, lights, and a sea of poinsettias. With decent weather, we'll still be in by Christmas."

"Don't forget the mistletoe. You never know when Jack might come over."

Le Roi covered the ground like a greyhound. He returned the ball to his master's hand. Excitement filled Steve's voice. "Tell him we're going to the lake today to show him our new homes."

She translated Steve's sentence into French. The dog's tail looked like windshield wipers on high speed.

Heather caught a full dose of the excitement. "Let's go to the lake now. I'll need to throw on some jeans, an old work shirt, and stick a baseball cap on this mop of hair." She looked at Steve. "You're already dressed in jeans and a flannel shirt."

"Le Roi and I are ready to go."

Heather couldn't help smiling. "As a reward for your patience, we'll stop on the way home and get lunch. How does a plate of smoked ribs sound?"

"That takes the pressure off. I wasn't sure if I could talk you into a decent meal after you put us both on a strict diet."

"Which you'll break by sneaking leftovers."

"It's still Thanksgiving weekend. Calories don't count until after midnight on Sunday."

Heather beat a path to her bedroom, where she changed in near-record time, told Max the house was all his for several hours, and slipped on boots. Steve had already raised the overhead garage door and put Le Roi in the back.

Heather only made it half a block before she pulled the car to the curb.

"What's wrong?" asked Steve.

"I'm looking for my sunglasses. It's so bright I'm squinting like a mole in a theater spotlight."

"Nice word picture."

"There they are. Right where I left them... in the center console."

Easy banter filled the car for the first few miles. The streets were drying quickly, and it seemed everyone wanted to escape the confinement of their homes.

Steve had an interesting take on people being stuck inside for over a week. "Alcohol-related crimes rise dramatically when the weather forces people inside for extended periods. I have an unproven theory that the rains we experienced doubled police calls for domestic disputes."

"You're probably right, especially in places used to hit-and-run rains. Back in Boston we learned to cope. I believe people can tolerate almost anything if they know it's coming well ahead of time and prepare for it mentally."

"That's very insightful. Let's apply it to the two murders. Was there an unexpected event that happened to any of the suspects?"

Heather tapped on the steering wheel with her index finger as she considered the question. "We still haven't interviewed Erin Stoops. According to Luke, he blindsided her by suddenly ending their relationship."

Steve nodded and mumbled an agreement. "When did you say she'll be back from her sister's?"

"The screams from the contractions were so loud, either I missed it or she didn't say. I got the impression that it wouldn't be long. She's supposed to call me. If I don't hear from her by Monday morning, I'll call her."

Heather took a quick glance to her right. "What about you?

Did you pick up on anyone who had an unexpected major change in their life?"

"Michelle Le Blanc and Connie Petrovitch certainly did. They weren't expecting to die." Steve's response proved he was in a good mood by his use of gallows humor.

"Let's stick with the living," said Heather.

Steve massaged the back of his neck, and his tone changed to one of regret. "I did a lousy job during our first round of interviews. It only takes a few well-timed questions to discover points of pain. Take Claude and Marjorie Hicks. They're both miserable in their marriage."

Heather added, "Being deep in debt doesn't help, but I can't link a lousy marriage to either of them having a reason to kill either Connie or Michelle. Besides, their financial problems are nothing new."

"What about Luke?" asked Steve. "Can you think of any extra pressure in his life?"

"Nothing comes to mind prior to him being arrested for killing Connie."

Steve puffed out his cheeks and blew out a full breath. "Let's allow our subconscious to percolate today and tomorrow. Call Jack and have him schedule us for another attorney-client visit Monday morning."

"He won't be back from trying to kill Bambi until tomorrow evening."

"Then make it for Monday afternoon. That will fit your schedule better."

"What do you mean?"

"You'll hit the ground running on Monday morning, making sure your contractors make up for lost time."

She wheeled onto the hairpin-shaped driveway leading to their new homes. "Thanks for understanding. Be sure Le Roi stays on the driveway. The yards are a muddy mess."

"How's the drainage?"

"The yards will require more topsoil and leveling. Otherwise, everything looks good. Let's go inside and check for leaks."

"How does the lake look?"

"Higher than normal, but the water would have to rise about five or six more feet before it came into the yard."

Steve went to the back of her car and released Le Roi, making sure his four-legged companion didn't stray off the concrete. Heather waited for them to join her and described the finished exterior of the home.

"Describe the lake to me," said Steve.

"There's not a trace of wind, so it looks like a giant mirror."

"Nice."

"More than nice," said Heather. "It's perfect. I can't wait to see what this place looks like with a thick lawn. I plan on spending a lot of time before and after work enjoying the view of the lake."

"Not if you go to work and return home in the dark like you usually do."

"That's changing, too."

"Jack will be glad to hear that." Steve lifted his chin. "It smells so fresh, like the rain washed the sky."

"A clean restart," said Heather.

"What's your estimate on finishing?" asked Steve.

"All the sheet rock is up, taped, floated, and painted. The flooring and cabinets aren't in yet. I'd say there's two weeks of work to do before the final inspection."

They walked in silence until reaching the front door of Heather's half of the duplex. "I hope this isn't a bad omen," said Heather.

"What's wrong?"

"The contractor forgot to lock my front door."

"That's not unusual," said Steve. "Didn't you tell me the painters were coming back to finish?"

"Yes, but it grates on me when people make silly mistakes like this."

Steve waved off the comment. "This gives us a chance to put Le Roi to the test. He's trained to go into vacant buildings and search for intruders. I'll give him the command to search."

Heather pushed the door open as Steve said, *"Cherche!"* and dropped the handle of the harness. Le Roi exploded through the doorway. She watched as the dog went around the perimeter of the rooms, with head down, sniffing as he went.

They listened for excited barking, but none came. It didn't take long before Le Roi returned to Steve's side. He gave the dog a treat and congratulated him for a job well done.

Heather made a careful examination of every room and the garage. There were no signs of anything amiss, until she looked in the master bathroom. The double-paned window high above the shower looked cloudy. A closer examination revealed moisture between the two panes of glass. It was then she noticed the electrical socket next to the sink was standard, not one with a ground fault interrupter.

She locked all doors when they left. It was too nice a day to waste her time worrying about a contractor's simple mistake. Still, the imperfections gnawed on her as she checked the same window and bathroom electrical socket in Steve's home. Neither home would pass the final inspection. She wondered what other things the contractors had missed. Her stomach churned and she belched yesterday's sage dressing.

Steve and Le Roi waited for her on the front sidewalk. "Come on," she commanded in a stern voice. "I need to check all the homes that are almost ready for occupancy."

"All of them?"

"Every one. Moisture infiltrated the bathroom windows in both of our homes. They're custom made and took months to manufacture. The electrical work is also substandard."

"Why didn't you get a standard size window?" Steve realized it might be the right question, but he couldn't have spoken it at a worse time. "Sorry. Forget I said anything."

Heather didn't count, but she estimated that she checked a

hundred homes before concluding all bathroom windows in the showers needed to be replaced. She tried to call her construction foreman but received a recording telling her to leave a message. The gobble of a turkey preceded and followed the instructions.

Frustration rose when her personal assistant didn't answer her calls. Neither did her procurement officer, nor the electrical contractor.

The sun dipped low in the western sky when the door to the last home slammed behind her. She'd found infiltration in every custom window and a long list of other imperfections in materials and workmanship. Her carefully laid plan of breezing through final inspections on the first tranche of homes lay in ashes and she blamed herself. She should have known better than try to coast to the end. Speaking to herself, she said, "It's what I deserve for taking my eye off the prize."

Steve sat in the passenger seat of her car. She climbed in and slammed the door. "Before you ask, not a single home is where it should be, and I'm not talking about needing a little caulk or a dab or paint."

"What are you going to do about it?"

"Whatever it takes, even if I do it all myself, every one of these homes will be ready for occupancy before Christmas. That includes ours." She gulped a breath. "I'm taking you home, then going to the office."

"Uh-huh," said Steve in a flat voice while he fastened his seat belt.

"Keep your 'Uh-huhs' and your 'Take some time offs' to yourself. I did what you said and look where it got me. I don't care if it's Thanksgiving weekend or not, I'm going to find out who hasn't been doing their job and make them wish they had."

Days and nights no longer meant anything to her. Saturday had come and gone.

The phone call came at three-fifteen on Sunday morning. Sirens wailed in the background.

19

———

Heather brought her car to an abrupt stop when she encountered a sheriff's department car blocking the entrance to her subdivision. The SUV had so many emergency lights flashing and blinking that it looked like an overly ambitious Christmas tree. The officer took his time approaching her window. She hollered, "I need to get through!"

A flashlight's beam blinded her. "No, you don't. What you need to do is slow down and not approach a police vehicle the way you did. That's a good way to get shot."

"You don't understand. I own—"

"No! You don't understand. You're going to jail if you don't leave now." His eyes narrowed. "On second thought, I smell alcohol. Get out of the vehicle."

"If you smell alcohol, it's coming off of that pitiful excuse for a mustache."

She took her foot off the brake and shifted it to the right. There was plenty of room to get around the patrol vehicle, and she made sure not to brush the officer. Looking in her rearview mirror, the stunned deputy was trying to pull his pistol from its holster. An approaching firetruck came into view. She hoped the cop wasn't so stupid that he'd shoot at her with witnesses approaching.

An orange glow came from the direction of the lake. She followed it, driving like she was pursuing a fleeing suspect as a cop in Boston. The last street required her to make a hard right-hand turn. Firetrucks blocked both entrances of the driveway leading to the dream homes for her and Steve.

Heather parked in a driveway on the far side of the street. With heart already pounding, she sprinted toward the clogged driveway. A fireman tried to stop her, but she sidestepped him, still running at top speed. She moved up the street until she found a man wearing the white helmet of a supervisor. "Why aren't you putting water on the fire?"

"And who are you?"

"Heather McBlythe. I own this entire project, including the two homes I'm watching burn."

"Oh. Well, Ms. McBlythe, both sides of the duplex were fully involved when the first truck arrived. They put the water they carry on the right half and ran hoses to the nearest hydrant. That takes time. The fire was too advanced to fight it from inside. A second truck arrived, and it was the same story. As you can see, we've run multiple lines to the street and the nearest water. The sides of the structures facing the lake have already collapsed. We'll be lucky to save enough of the structure for arson investigators to gather any useful evidence."

Heather stared at the flames licking the sky, crackling and hissing with sadistic joy. Years of planning and untold hours of early mornings and late nights rose with the white smoke as water poured onto the conflagration. The garages that separated the two structures collapsed and threw a dazzling display of sparks into the night sky.

Darkness consumed all sound and light for Heather.

Her eyes fluttered open and she blinked at the overly bright lights. She tried to rise, but a firm hand held her down. A woman's kind voice said, "Take your time. There's no need to rush."

Heather whispered in a voice that didn't sound like hers, "What happened?"

"You fainted. You're in an ambulance."

"I've never fainted in my life."

"Don't worry. Your vitals are normal. So far, there doesn't appear to be a reason to take you to the hospital unless you want to get checked out by a doctor. The fire chief for this area of the county saw you wobbling and caught you when your knees buckled. When you're up to it, the sheriff wants to speak to you."

"I'm all right now."

Skepticism flashed across the attendant's face. "I'll help you sit up and give you a bottle of water. If that goes all right, we'll see how you do standing. I'll send someone to get the sheriff. There's also someone here you might like to see."

The walls seemed to move when the EMT left and Jack climbed into the ambulance. She held on to him with a ferocity that she'd never experienced. Words and tears tumble out. "They're gone. Everything's gone."

Jack said something that made no sense. It was like the fire's smoke had invaded her brain. She wouldn't and couldn't let him go. All she could do was repeat a lament. "I failed."

The sheriff joined them in the ambulance. He asked the EMTs to leave and close the doors. Jack pried her arms away from his neck but held on to her hands. The sheriff spoke in short sentences. "Steve called me. He said this sounds like something Bucky Franklin would do. And I agree. Steve also called Leo Vega. We're not waiting for confirmation from the fire marshal to tell us this is arson. I've already put out a BOLO on Bucky."

She stammered out something that sounded like thank you.

"By the way, I've spoken with the knucklehead who gave you a hard time at the entrance to your development. He now knows better than to pull that old, *I smell alcohol* stunt."

Heather swung her feet off the gurney. "Help me up," she said to Jack.

The next snippet of memory lasted only a few seconds. It involved a noisy ride in the ambulance.

"I'M SURE GLAD I CAME HOME EARLY FROM HUNTING. I'D HATE to have been hours away when this happened. Heather's not herself. They're taking her to the hospital. I'm following the ambulance."

Steve took in the information from Jack. "Is she hurt?"

"Not a scratch. She had two fainting spells, has a blank stare, and is rambling on about being a failure. It's spooky. I've never seen her like this. Heather's the most solid-thinking woman I've ever met."

Steve recognized the symptoms but kept his psychological diagnosis to himself. "She's in for a long morning of tests. You need to plan for them to admit her. They won't tell you anything because you're not family."

Jack blew out a breath of frustration. "What do you suggest?"

"I'm calling Heather's father as soon as I hang up. His plane has the same communication abilities as Heather's. He'll keep us posted on what the doctors say, but I'm sure they won't call him until they know more."

"That may take all day."

"Don't expect to hear anything of substance until this afternoon."

"I know you're right, but I don't like it."

"I don't blame you," said Steve.

"I'll make sure they have all the information they need to check her in, then wait until I hear from you or Allister."

The phone went silent and Steve made the call to Heather's father. Allister gathered the facts and spoke in a firm voice. "I knew she was pushing too hard. It's my fault."

Steve interrupted him. "This is something she had to learn on her own."

"I'm flying there as soon as my pilots can file a flight plan."

Steve told Allister which hospital to call and that Jack was making sure admission went without complications.

"I'll call him from my car."

Steve knew Allister's chauffeur did the driving, which brought a measure of relief. The entire call to Heather's father might have lasted a minute and a half.

The next call went to Rasheed. "Are you driving yet?"

"No, my friend. I'm fortifying myself with coffee and Krispy Kreme donuts. Your American food may shorten my life, but it is simple pleasures that I have trouble resisting."

"Can you be my driver for the day?"

"You sound as if you're in a hurry."

"I am. How soon can you get here?"

"The door to the donut shop has already closed behind me."

"Good. We have much to do today."

"Will Le Roi be my passenger, too?"

"Yes."

"Very good. I'll arrive with his blanket covering the back seat and his chew toy at the ready."

Steve retrieved his electric razor and went from his bedroom to the kitchenette. Le Roi matched his every step.

"You know something isn't right, don't you, *mon ami*?"

The dog's tail slapped against a kitchen cabinet.

"You're going to help me this morning."

More slaps.

"First, you need breakfast, and I need coffee." Steve scratched Le Roi's head. "You know the rules. My coffee is more important than your steak."

A snort came from Le Roi.

"Rules are rules." Steve had already filled the water reservoir the night before and placed a pod of dark roast coffee in the single-serve device. He pushed a button and moved to the refrigerator. It wasn't long before Steve set the dog's bowl on the floor beside a self-filling water bowl.

The razor buzzed while the coffeemaker gurgled and then hissed.

"Rasheed is on his way. Let me know when you hear him drive up."

"Woof."

"You and I both need to get dressed. Me in jeans and boots, while you need your vest."

Rasheed arrived a few minutes before Steve estimated. Once man and dog were in the car, Steve asked, "Did you speed getting here?"

"You know I rarely speed. It's too costly in so many ways. Traffic is lighter traveling away from the city and it is earlier in the day than when I was taking you to your training sessions. Where are we going?"

"To Heather's property development. A fire destroyed two structures."

"That grieves me greatly."

"Me, too. Heather and I won't be moving to our new homes for the foreseeable future."

"Where is Miss Heather?"

"In the hospital. She sort of burned herself out."

"Ah. Not a burn, but what you call burnout. It is a real and dangerous thing. I wish her a speedy recovery."

"I'll settle for the recovery to be slow and steady."

"Yes. That would be best."

Rasheed made smooth, careful turns as he wove his way out of the subdivision. Steve knew by the sound of tires on pavement and traffic noises when they reached busier streets.

Steve took out his phone and called Jack, who answered on the second ring. "Heather's father called me. He'll be here this afternoon."

"I didn't think he'd waste any time. Did you get her admitted with no problems?"

"I don't know who her father called or what he said, but I'm receiving text messages every thirty minutes with updates. So far, she's had blood tests and X-rays. A CT scan is next. A psychiatrist will see her once they're through poking, prodding, and taking pictures." Jack took a breath. "Are you in a cab? I hear highway noises."

"Rasheed is driving me and Le Roi to the lake."

"Why? There's nothing out there but smoldering ashes."

"I have a mental picture of the peninsula that Heather chose for our homes. There are roving security guards who patrol the development both night and day, mainly at night. It would be risky for the person, or persons, responsible for the fire to park anywhere near the property. If you were going to burn our homes, where would you park to hide a vehicle?"

"I noticed that some of the garage doors of the homes across the street were open. I'd pull into a garage and shut the overhead door."

"That makes sense. I'll put Le Roi's nose to the test and see if he can pick up a fresh scent that leads to what's left of our homes."

"Do you have something belonging to Bucky to match it to?"

"There's plenty in Houston PD's property room. He left town in a hurry and didn't bother to pack."

"Can you get Leo to bring it to you?"

"No need. I already trained Le Roi to react to Bucky's scent. When I say react, I mean attack."

A mechanical tone sounded, and Jack said, "There's the next text message. I'll call you back if it says anything of consequence."

"We're almost at the entrance," said Rasheed after the call ended. "You are a very clever man."

"So is the man I'm after."

After a few more minutes of driving and a couple of sharp turns, Rasheed announced. "We've arrived. I've parked in the first driveway on the opposite side of the street from the peninsula. Puffs of smoke are still rising from the rubble. It reminds me of scenes from my home country."

"Let's work our way down the street, one home at a time."

Once released from his jail cell, Le Roi received the command to search in French. His nose went to the ground. From driveway to driveway, they walked. Steve asked, "Are you sure there are no footprints in the yards?"

"No, my friend. They would be easy to spot in the soft soil."

Minutes passed without results. Steve let out a huff of frustration. "What are we missing? I thought for sure Jack was right about Bucky parking in a garage."

"Logic tells me to question the premise of this search," said Rasheed.

"What do you mean?"

"You assume this fugitive named Bucky parked a vehicle in a garage. Correct?"

Steve slapped his forehead. "Of course. My head is hard as concrete. We need to go back to the property line where Heather's peninsula begins. We'll walk along the bank. You look for tracks and Le Roi will search for a fresh scent."

"Yes. Coming by boat would be unexpected."

They returned to the property line and Rasheed said, "Our trek along the bank requires me to take off my shoes and roll up the legs of my pants. You were wise to wear rubber boots. No worries. I lived more years without shoes than with them."

Steve gave Le Roi the command to search again and dropped the handle attached to his vest. Steve noted the sound of squishing mud as the dog crossed back and forth in front of them. Rasheed placed Steve's hand on his bicep and warned him about obstacles.

They traversed what seemed like a long distance before Rasheed announced, "He's stopped, and he's sitting."

"He caught a scent. Do you see footprints?"

"Patience, my friend. We must catch up to him."

Excitement filled Rasheed's voice. "There's a depression in

the mud that looks like the bow of a boat made it. Footprints lead toward the place of the fire and back again."

Steve pulled out his phone but didn't activate it. "We need to go back the way we came." He spoke into his phone. "Call Jack."

It took Jack three rings to answer. "Still nothing new. What about you?"

"Call the sheriff. Tell him whoever set the fire arrived in a boat. They came ashore directly behind the homes. They'll find footprints leading up the hill. I'm wearing size eleven rubber boots, Rasheed is barefoot, and they'll find Le Roi's paw prints. The footprints leading to and from the fire belong to the arsonist."

"I'll get right on it," said Jack.

Steve told Le Roi to heel, and the dog returned to his side. *"Formidable, mon ami."* Steve grabbed the harness and took a step. "Rasheed, I made another assumption."

"Oh?"

"I assumed Bucky Franklin burned our future homes."

"Are you sure he didn't?"

"Not completely."

20

———

The woman wore a white lab coat with the name Dr. Tammy Scott stitched in blue letters. She had reddish-blond hair, nice teeth, and a soft voice. "Hello, Ms. McBlythe. I'm Doctor Scott. You're in the emergency room of the hospital in Conroe. How are you feeling?"

"Fire and smoke." Heather didn't know why she said that. Where had the woman said she was?

"I understand you've been under a lot of stress lately."

Heather wanted to say it wasn't anything she couldn't handle, but the words wouldn't come. She closed her eyes. It seemed like someone else was inside her saying, "It's all gone. I failed."

"Do you know where you are?"

"Fire. Smoke. I failed."

"I'm going to give you a shot that will help you sleep."

She wanted to tell her no but couldn't. Nothing mattered now.

———

THE NEXT DAY, STEVE OPENED THE BACK DOOR FOR LE ROI TO patrol the backyard in the stillness of a brisk, pre-dawn morning.

The dog loved to run with his vest and harness on and took full advantage of sprinting from one fence to the opposite.

A man's voice greeted him when he walked into the kitchen. "Good morning."

"Good morning, Allister. Have you had coffee yet?"

"Only one cup. Thanks for setting the timer last night. What about you?"

"The one I'm about to pour will be my third. Heather bought me a small, single serve coffee maker for my kitchenette. The plastic pods make it easy to clean, but I'm still looking for a blend that tastes as good as what I get by brewing a whole pot."

Steve changed the subject. "You returned late from the hospital. Did Heather ever wake up?"

"For a little while. The psychiatrist wants her brain and body fully rested before she does an assessment. When she left, I spoke to a nurse who seemed to know more than the doctor. He has a lifetime of experience. Judging by his looks, he probably could have retired five years ago."

Steve knew the type, but didn't want to slow the flow of words from Heather's father.

"The nurse explained her condition so I could understand. He said what's wrong with her is mental and emotional burnout. He likened her to a truck that was caught in a riot and set ablaze. Hence the burned-out analogy."

"What's the prognosis?"

"He thinks it's very good. First, she needs complete rest, and he gave the psychiatrist good marks for forcing sleep to allow her mind to reset. He says it like turning off a computer and restarting it later."

"How much later?"

"This evening will be the last dose of strong medication. A psychologist will administer a battery of tests on her tomorrow afternoon. What she doesn't need is to receive a report saying the project is falling even more behind."

Steve took his turn. "I spoke with Heather's personal

assistant yesterday and told her to have all the department heads in her office by eight o'clock." Steve cleared his throat. "I had no right to do that, but I know that when a leader can't perform, there's no shortage of people who believe they should be the one to fill the void. Heather doesn't need a turf war. Would you mind addressing her executives? Instructions coming from you will carry much more weight than if they came from a broken-down former detective."

Steve felt Allister's hand on his shoulder. "You, my friend, would have made an excellent CEO."

"I'm having a hard enough time trying to solve two murders. Running a company would have me looking like a burned-out car in less than a week."

"That reminds me," said Allister. "How do you intend to proceed without Heather?"

"I hired a driver. He'll get me where I need to go to continue the investigations without Heather until she can get back on the hunt. You'll like him. His name is Rasheed. He's not your average driver."

"Perhaps he should stay on full time. He could drive Heather, giving her time to think or rest. There are many days when my chauffeur listens to me snore."

"That's not a bad idea. Let's try him out this morning. He can drive Heather's car and you can sit up front and chat with him. He'll be here in about half an hour."

"Will you need your driver today?"

"I'll need him to take me to the county jail for an interview with Jack and his client this morning. After that, I'll return to the office and interview a woman who might be a suspect. Will that disrupt your day?"

"Not at all. I'd like to stay in Heather's office until the doctor gives me permission to see her. Do you want me to see if I can get you in to see her?"

"I'll go when she's better. She was supposed to be with me today for both interviews. When she comes out of the brain fog, she'll want an update on the case. She needs to hear I'm making progress."

"Are you?"

Steve chuckled. "I learned a long time ago that optimism opens many doors, even some that are locked. Perhaps I'll find a key or two today."

Steve's phone pinged to signal a text, followed by an AI voice informing him that Rasheed was waiting in the driveway.

"Let me grab my computer bag," said Allister.

"I need to get mine, too," said Steve. "It's going to be a busy day."

Allister and Rasheed hit it off better than Steve could have hoped for. It wasn't long before the businessman and the philosopher were locked in a deep discussion concerning time and how to use it wisely. Steve tuned them out and practiced his latest conversational French lesson on Le Roi. The Texas accent didn't impress the dog, as evidenced by frequent whimpers.

Steve unloaded Le Roi as the two men riding up front continued their lively conversation. Neither raised their voice or cut short a point the other was making.

They traveled up the elevator with Steve and Le Roi listening to two men thoroughly engrossed in minutia. Allister reverted to a Boston brogue, while Rasheed reclaimed the full measure of a Mid-Eastern accent.

The two paused briefly to say hello to Heather's personal assistant. Pam was always the first to arrive and often the last to leave. Allister made sure she would be present at the eight o'clock meeting.

He also told her to seat Heather's department heads as soon as they arrived. "I prefer employees waiting on me, and not the other way around, when possible."

"It's always possible when you're the leader."

"What do you mean?"

"It shows you to be in control. Your refusal to start a meeting on time because of an employee's tardiness puts them in control of your time and the time of others. Research has shown that meetings starting on time yield the best results."

Allister considered the suggestion. "That gives me an idea." He turned to face the P.A. "I'll be on my computer, making calls to my office in Boston. Please tell the receptionist that unless it's the hospital or Jack, I don't want to be disturbed for the next thirty minutes. Rasheed and I will be in Heather's apartment at ten minutes before eight. Heather's managers may come into the office then, but not before. Come get us at precisely fifteen seconds before eight. This meeting will start on time."

"Yes, Mr. McBlythe."

Steve and Le Roi went to their assigned places behind and beside Steve's desk. Noise reducing headphones with a microphone attached hooked to his laptop. Leo's call came a few minutes later.

"How's Heather?"

"No change yet. She's still in lullaby land. Any news on Bucky?"

"Not a peep," said Leo. "If he was anywhere near your new homes, he's disappeared like a shadow in thick fog."

Steve picked up something. "You said, if he was anywhere near our new homes. Don't you think he made good on a promise to harm me? What better way to do it than to come after Heather?"

Leo countered with, "You taught me not to jump to conclusions, but something isn't right. It looks to me like someone didn't like the questions you've been asking. Have you considered—"

Steve cut him off. "Of course I've considered it could be someone we interviewed. It could also be someone Heather offended or one of the contractors she had to fire, or some random jerk who likes to watch almost completed homes burn." He paused and heaved a sigh. "Sorry, Leo. Heather being in the hospital has me twisted tight. Hospitals and Christmas are two things that don't sit well with me."

Leo waited quite a while before asking, "Did that make you feel better?"

"Yeah. A little. Thanks for listening."

"It's a beautiful day. Why don't you and that German dog who thinks he's French take a long walk? It will do you both good."

"I'm booked this morning, but that's a great idea for this afternoon."

The call ended and the first three of Heather's executives came in and settled at the table. They spoke in hushed tones, the way people do at a funeral.

"She's not dead," said Steve. "She'll be back before you know it, cracking the whip again."

A man's voice came from across the room. "Are both condos a complete loss?"

"They burned all the way to the foundation."

"Good," said a second man. "Now you and Heather can make any changes you want to the original plans. She was having second thoughts about the configuration of the kitchens. I told her we could make the changes, but it would delay getting in by Christmas."

Steve looked at the situation from a different angle. "We'll be in by Christmas. It just won't be this Christmas."

More people filed into the room. Steve waited until one minute before the appointed time for the meeting to start before he asked Heather's PA to seat him at the far end of the table from Allister. She walked from where she'd placed him. Knocks sounded on the door to Heather's apartment.

The room grew quiet before Allister spoke in a strong, confident voice. "By now you should know that my daughter is in the hospital following what the authorities believe is the intentional burning of two homes at her lakeside development. No one was physically injured. For that, we are thankful.

"The gentleman with me is Rasheed. I'll let him pronounce his last name, as I'd mangle it beyond all recognition. Dr.

Rasheed is a time management expert who will coach me, and you, in maximizing the efficiency of the time we spend until Heather returns. We're all working toward the goal of completing the development in less time and bringing it in under budget with no compromises in quality."

Rasheed didn't hesitate to speak. "The principle of effective time management is amazingly simple. You spend the vast majority of your time doing what you do best. Other things, you pass them off to others with strengths in the areas of your weakness. There are various tests I will administer to you and your staff that will inform me of your strengths."

Allister took over again. "For the immediate future, I expect everyone in this room to rise to the occasion. Heather chose each of you because she believes in you. I'll split my time between here and Boston until she's able to resume her duties. I don't know how long that will be."

The words seemed to settle upon, and into, those gathered.

"Steve, do you have anything to add?"

"Only one thing. Who's responsible for the disposal of scrap?"

A voice spoke out. "I supervise all the sub-contractors."

"The sheriff and arson investigators will finish their work at the site tomorrow. You have two days to have every trace of the fire removed from the property. That includes the home's slabs."

"Consider it done."

Steve rose from his chair. "If you'll excuse us, Rasheed and I have an appointment."

21

———————

S teve spoke with teasing in his voice as he, Rasheed, and Le Roi traveled in Heather's Mercedes. "You and Allister seemed to hit it off. Is he a long-lost cousin?"

Rasheed gave a serious response to what Steve thought was a throwaway line. "He's a man in transition with many worries. The most pressing is his daughter. His perception of time is changing."

Steve wasn't expecting the level of concern in Rasheed's voice. "I'm a simple former cop. I understand and share his concern for Heather." He shifted in his seat. "You'll need to explain what you mean by Allister's perception of time."

"Steve, you are many things. Simple isn't among them. As for time, first world countries think of it in terms of strict chronology. Seconds add up to minutes. With enough minutes, you get an hour. With the addition of more and more counting units, you have years, decades, and centuries. Your lives revolve around the smaller units of time. Everything is carefully measured, especially time. You believe you can waste time or save time, and there comes a point when what you most want is to extend it.

"The Eastern mind thinks in terms of much looser associations. Birth to death is one continuous slide of a trombone, not jarring stops along the way."

Steve scratched his chin. "I see your point, but how does that apply to Allister?"

"He's jerking from adulthood into old age and confronting his own mortality. Until now, he's avoided the inevitability of his death. Business is the numbing agent he uses."

"So does Heather."

"You are correct, my friend, but she is young. She may yet learn the joy that comes with moderation."

Rasheed asked, "Shall I continue with Allister?"

"Please. This is fascinating."

"When Allister lost his wife a relatively brief time ago, it started the process of him having to face his own death and what to do with the limited time he has left. From our conversations, I learned that he's softened his heart toward Heather. Now, his seemingly indestructible daughter is in the hospital with a problem that baffles him. It's accelerating his perception of time. He's wanting it to slow down so he'll have more of it to spend with Heather."

"And time has now slowed to a crawl for Heather?" asked Steve.

"Correct. The trombone slide will need to go back into its new, proper position."

"Back to the way she was?"

"No, my friend. Not back that far. Time will have progressed and things will be different for her. All attempts to turn back time or rush it are futile. You must not allow her to make things as they were. She'll only harm herself again."

Rasheed made a couple of sharp turns and brought the car to a halt. "The man you described to me as Jack is approaching."

Steve absentmindedly reached for the door latch. He had to force his thoughts out of the discussion and return to the tasks at hand. "Do you want me to see if Jack can get you approved to sit in on the interview?"

"My fear of dogs still haunts me, but it pales compared to my fear of jails. I prefer to stay in this amazing car and listen to a book on my phone."

Jack met Steve with a question. "Any news about Heather?"

"I was going to ask you the same thing."

Jack released a sigh. "They told us she'd sleep late and be busy all afternoon. Not knowing and not being able to help is driving me nuts. I hope they don't knock her out again tonight."

Steve wanted to say he only wanted what was best for Heather, but those words might not come out right. Instead, he played it safe. "I'll get Le Roi out of his cell. We don't want to be late."

The words sounded silly after listening to Rasheed.

The slight tug forward on the harness showed Steve that Le Roi recognized where they were. "You recognize the smell of burned food and prison-made soap, don't you, *mon ami*?"

The same trustee stood at the front door, this time without a mop or bucket. "I see Ms. McBlythe isn't with you today. That's such a shame about the fire on that fancy property of hers. I hope she has insurance."

Steve came to a halt. "What's the word going around the cell block about the fire?"

"The young bucks don't have a clue. Some of the older cons think it's tied to the two women that pill-pusher killed."

"Is anyone covering bets that he didn't kill them?"

"Not anyone with any sense." The man lowered his voice. "That's an interesting question you asked, Detective Smiley. Inside information like that could sure make an old convict's life a little easier."

"If you're looking for a tip, I'll make an exception and give you one. When you get out, put five one-dollar bills in your front pocket. The rest of your cash goes into your shoes, which you don't take off until you're home at night. All you'll ever lose is five bucks."

The old man rocked with laughter. "If I'd a' done that fifty years ago, I'd have a closet full of shoes stuffed with money."

An officer took them to the visiting room, where they didn't have to wait for Luke to come. His voice carried a measure of relief. "I wasn't sure you'd come after what happened at Ms. McBlythe's property. I heard she's in the hospital. Was she burned?"

Steve saved Jack from saying more than he should by speaking first. "She's fine, but there was a fire. Don't believe everything you hear on the cell block. All information has already passed through at least three or four sets of ears and mouths. Most of the ears don't have many brains to slow the rumors down."

"I'm learning that the hard way. Everyone has a theory in this place. That includes the officers, at least the ones who like to talk."

Steve interlaced his fingers in front of him. "I'm meeting with Erin Stoops later today. I want to go over what you told me about your relationship with her again. Have you remembered anything about her you need to tell us?"

"Nothing new, but I want to emphasize how hard she took the breakup."

"That's understandable," said Steve. "If she had her heart set on marriage, I see how two people with so much in common would be a good match. Would you describe her as stable or impulsive?"

"Both. What I mean is she's very caring most of the time. In fact, almost all the time. Then, out of the blue, she'd turn into someone I didn't recognize. I've already told you and the police how she acted the night she pulled the pistol on me and my mother."

"Yes, you both told us about that. Could you go over that again?"

"I'll be glad to," said Luke. He then spent fifteen minutes recounting the story. He ended the detailed report with, "I hope what I've told you is enough to have my bail reduced to something more reasonable. The thought of not being home for Christmas is wearing on me."

Jack joined the conversation. "Our interview with Erin may well be a make-or-break moment in getting you in front of a judge. I'll do all I can."

Steve was more optimistic. "There's an interesting phenomenon that takes place close to Christmas. Judges like to clear out the jails. There's no guarantee, but I believe Jack can make a convincing argument that you deserve a break."

"Timing is important," said Jack. "If I file a motion tomorrow, I should be able to get a court date before the judge takes off for Christmas. Like Steve said, that 'good will toward men' thing seems to come alive, even for judges."

"Can't you file the motion today?" asked Luke.

Steve didn't give Jack time to answer. "Luke, I don't think you understand. You're looking at a prison sentence that won't end until you're a very old man or you die behind bars. Asking Jack to rush is beyond foolish. The best thing you can do for yourself is keep your mouth shut and stay out of trouble." Steve released a huff. "Go back to your cell and let us do our jobs."

Jack didn't speak until they were in the parking lot. "You came down on him pretty hard. Was there a reason for it?"

"Two reasons. The first was to remind him how serious the charge is that he's facing. We both know there's enough circumstantial and real evidence against him to get a conviction."

"True. What's the second reason?"

"I still don't like Christmas, and it always bothered me that judges get soft this time of year."

Jack chuckled. "Has anyone ever told you there's a bit of Ebenezer Scrooge in you?"

"Bah. Humbug. Let's go back to the office and interview Erin Stoops. I want to know if she's been naughty or nice."

22

———————

"Everyone's staring at us again," whispered Jack.

Steve whispered back. "I don't think they're looking at me, you, or Rasheed. It's amazing how much attention Le Roi draws. It's rare that someone doesn't ask me what breed of dog he is or if they can pet him. I may need to enlarge the DO NOT PET lettering on his vest."

Rasheed had another idea. "Perhaps blinking colored lights like what people wear on Christmas sweaters would help."

Jack joined in. "Go all the way and get emergency lights like they have on police cars. He's big enough to carry several and a car battery to power them."

They reached the elevator. Steve waited until the door shut before addressing his companions. "Go ahead, you two. Make fun of my dog if you want, but he's produced more evidence than the three of us combined."

"Steve has a point," said Jack.

The levity stopped once they stepped out of the elevator. Allister's voice came down the hallway from the direction of Heather's office. "There you are. Have any of you had an update on Heather?"

Steve said, "I thought you and Jack were getting regular updates."

Jack and Allister spoke over each other. Jack's voice was louder. "They're coming as promised, but say little."

Allister continued, "There's a maddening lack of details."

"The last text said, 'No change.'"

"Mine did, too," said Allister.

Rasheed said, "Sometimes proximity brings a measure of comfort. Would you like me to drive you to the hospital, Mr. McBlythe?"

Allister delayed a few seconds. "I've spent the last hour and a half roaming from department to department, making a pest of myself. Heather has done a stellar job of hiring competent people. She chose team members with a diversity of skills and personalities in mind. Her company is a model of efficient productivity. But what impresses me most is they're all genuinely concerned about her. I'm confident she could be gone for an extended period and this company would continue to run with minimal assistance from me."

Rasheed said, "I perceive Heather patterned her organization after yours, sir."

Heather's father took his time responding, and when he did, it wasn't what Steve expected. "Rasheed, I want to hire you as Heather and Steve's chauffeur."

"I'm honored," said Rasheed.

"Don't you want to know the details?"

"You are a fair man, and your daughter is a chip off the old stump."

Steve made a note to correct the mangled expression later. No need to embarrass Rasheed during an impromptu job interview.

"I'll increase your current earnings, provide an apartment nearby, and you'll drive a car identical to the one Heather's driving now. You'll also receive health care and dental coverage at no charge."

"And my duties?"

"Take Heather and Steve wherever they need to go whenever they need you."

"I am your humble servant."

"Not exactly. You'll report to Heather and Steve. My daughter needs the wisdom you possess. You'll be her driver and teacher. She never got around to studying philosophy."

"Then I am Heather and Steve's humble servant."

"Good. It's settled. Your first assignment is to take me to the hospital. We'll talk more on the way."

Rasheed gave a slight bow. "Steve, it seems I must leave you without transportation."

"That's not a problem. Jack and I will come to the hospital after we finish our interview. Jack will be my driver, and we'll have plenty to talk about. I doubt we'll discuss philosophy, but I always learn something from Jack."

Once inside Heather's office, Steve spoke to his phone, which gave him the time. "Fifteen minutes before Erin Stoops arrives. Are you ready with questions for her?"

"I have several. What about you?"

"I like to let people ramble. I'll start and you break in whenever you want."

"Let's hope she's talkative."

"Most people are, once you find what's important to them."

The sound of Jack sitting at the conference table where he usually sat reached Steve at his desk. Le Roi yawned and settled onto his bed.

Fifteen minutes passed, then twenty, and Erin still hadn't arrived. Le Roi sat up, and Steve said, "I hear her, too. Good boy."

A knock on the door came and the latch clicked. "Your guest is here, Mr. Smiley."

Steve allowed Jack to rise and introduce himself. Erin sat in the chair directly across from Jack and on Steve's right side. He sat at the head of the long table.

"Good morning, Erin. I'm Steve Smiley, Heather's business partner and Jack is an attorney. Heather won't be joining us today. It seems the rain and flooding have thrown everyone's schedules off."

"Tell me about it," said Erin in a soft, yet confident voice. "Road repairs are why I'm late, despite leaving in what I thought was plenty of time."

He asked, "Boy or girl?"

"What?"

"Your sister. Heather told me you were called upon to be a stand-in midwife?"

"Oh, my goodness. I've never been so afraid in my life. The contractions kept getting harder and closer. The midwife was stuck in traffic and there I was, trying to remember what to do if she didn't make it in time. I like to come prepared, so I brought masks, a gown, sterile gloves and scissors, and an umbilical cord clamp. I wasn't expecting to see the head crown. The midwife arrived with less than a minute to spare. She barely got on gloves before Andrew made his grand appearance. A full head of dark hair, and the ability to scream loud enough to wake the dead."

Her voice lost its lightheartedness. "Considering why I'm here, that was a terrible choice of words."

Jack asked, "Why do you think you're here?"

"Ms. McBlythe said it's because I used to see Luke Bains. I know they arrested him for killing Connie Petrovitch. Are you Luke's attorney?"

"Yes, I'm representing him. The police believe he killed her. What's your opinion?"

"I find it hard to believe."

Steve cut in before she could continue. "We'll discuss that later. For now, we want to ask you about your relationship with Luke. We're getting conflicting reports on how serious it was. If you don't mind, start with how you met Luke."

"That's difficult to pinpoint. I probably met him at the University of Houston's pharmacy school. He was ahead of me, and I spent most of my time with my head in books." She paused. "I should say with my eyes on the screen of my laptop."

Jack took a turn again. "Are we to understand that you rarely dated in college or pharmacy school?"

"Rarely? I didn't date at all. I don't date."

Steve was on the verge of asking for clarification when Erin kept talking. "I was part of a movement that's not as popular today as it once was. I believe in courting, not dating."

Jack asked, "Isn't that a matter of semantics?"

"Not at all." Erin's voice remained soft, but there was conviction underlying it. "Dating can mean anything, but the common understanding is that a girl or woman either entertains at her home, or goes somewhere unsupervised, with a man. There's no expectation at the onset of a lasting commitment. With courtship, the couple is supervised so to speak. There is always someone else with them on the outing or nearby if they are in the home. The expectation is marriage, then sex. Not the other way around."

Steve asked, "Do your parents live with you?"

"I'm almost thirty. That would be weird."

Confusion salted Jack's words. "Are you saying you and Luke were betrothed?"

"That comes later, after the courtship progresses. Then, if both agree that they're compatible, and the Lord desires them to take the next step, they become engaged, or as you said, betrothed." She paused. "Luke and I never made it past courtship."

"How did that make you feel?" asked Steve.

"Hurt at first, but now I'm super relieved. The wisdom of courtship instead of dating played out before my eyes. Luke proved himself to be unfaithful to the rules of the courtship and I have no regrets. I'll someday go into my marriage with a clear conscience."

Steve rubbed his chin. "You said the courtship stage involved supervision. How did you and Luke manage that when he came to see you?"

"Most of the time, we had friends join us. If no one was available, I'd do a teleconference with my parents."

Jack's voice held a blush of skepticism as he asked, "Are you currently courting anyone?"

Her voice dropped. "There's a seminary student I have my eye on. He used to be a corporate executive until his wife died. They practiced courtship before they married."

"How long have you known him?"

"I've known both of them for years. I was one of her bridesmaids."

Steve took his turn. "Can you tell us how she died?"

"A robber entered their home, killed her, and ransacked their home. Ray was in Silicon Valley at a tech meeting when it took place."

"Did they live in Houston?" asked Steve.

"Uh-huh. Did you hear about it?"

Steve answered with a nod of his head. It wasn't his case to work, and it went unsolved. He'd tell Jack about it later.

"Do you own a pistol?" asked Jack.

"Yes."

"What kind?"

"A nine-millimeter Glock, but not one like cops carry. Mine's a small-frame lady's gun. I have it with me if you want to see it."

"Sure," said Steve. "Jack's quite the hunter. He spent most of Thanksgiving weekend shooting trees instead of deer."

"That's not fair. My scope was so far off I couldn't hit anything."

Erin issued three tsks. "Always sight your scope in before the season starts and transport it in a hard-sided case."

"You sound like you're speaking from experience."

"My father taught me right."

Steve heard Jack manipulating the slide of a pistol. Then, the clip fell onto the table. "Nice little weapon," said Jack. "Perfect for that concealed-carry purse. Do you sometimes forget it's there when you go into a bank?"

"I haven't yet. My father insists I have a weapon because there are so many desperate drug addicts. Being a woman pharmacist has its risks."

Steve placed his palms on the table. "We have a report that you threatened Luke with either this pistol or one like it. What's your side of the story?"

"I showed it to them, but there was no threat. Luke knew I carried it and the pharmacy I work at doesn't prohibit me."

Jack asked, "Did you ever fight with Luke?"

"It depends on how you define fight. We disagreed on things."

"Like what?"

"Some of my stands on religion. We also had our own opinions on the efficacy of certain drugs. Otherwise, normal stuff like how to raise children and the role of women in churches."

Steve quipped, "Leaders start wars over lesser subjects." He then asked Jack if he had any further questions. He did not.

While Jack escorted Erin to the door, Steve took off his sunglasses and rubbed his sightless eyes. Erin said something important during the interview that he couldn't remember. He hoped the audio recording picked it up.

Jack returned and said, "I got what I needed, or at least it will be enough for the judge. If I can convince him that Erin has out-of-step beliefs, he might look at her as a viable suspect. Her carrying a gun won't hurt. Luke and his mother will both testify that she threatened them with the pistol we now know she carries."

Steve said, "Erin didn't threaten them."

"I know that, and you know that, but the judge doesn't. I'm not trying to get the case dismissed, only get the bail reduced."

Steve pushed back from the table. "Let's go to the hospital."

23
____

Jack wheeled his pickup into a parking space at the hospital. The truck had a back seat, and Le Roi didn't like Steve telling him to lie down for the trip from Heather's office building. Every so often, Jack would snicker.

Steve opened the back door and Le Roi jumped down. "Good boy for obeying."

Jack snickered again. "Well, almost."

"What did he do?"

"He sat up most of the time and looked out the window."

"He's obviously learning bad habits from Max."

"Yeah, I'm sure that's what it is."

The doors to the hospital whooshed open and Steve said, "I'll wait here while you find Rasheed. Tell him to come to me. I need to put a dog in jail."

Jack returned in less than a minute with Rasheed. The newly hired driver spoke with his usual accent. It reminded Steve of the staff at a restaurant where Heather loved to order takeout.

"How may I be of service?"

"I need you to take Le Roi and put him in the back of Heather's car. It's a cool day, so he'll be fine if you leave a couple of windows down an inch or two. Be sure to put some water in his bowl."

Rasheed took a step back. "Would it be permissible for me to ask Jack to perform this task?"

"It will be good for both you and Le Roi," said Steve. "The dog needs a refresher in obedience and you have fears to overcome."

"I will comply, but it is under protest."

"Peaceful protest is a cherished right in this country, but a heart that's willing to serve is more precious than many diamonds."

"I do not recognize that parable and I question its validity."

Steve flashed a smile. "I just made it up. I'll wait for you here and you can lead me in."

Steve had never heard grumbling in whatever language Rasheed spoke, but there was no mistaking the tone of his words.

Looking down at Le Roi, Steve gave a curt command. "*Voiture. Allez avec Rasheed.*"

"Do I have to grasp his harness?"

"He should walk with you. If he doesn't, or he balks about getting put into his jail cell, holler at me."

"What if he runs away or becomes aggressive?"

"Then you can help me look for a different dog, one that obeys."

"That is little comfort in the near term."

Rasheed mustered his courage. "Come, my four-legged friend. You heard your master. He said, 'Car. Go with Rasheed.' Complaining will do no good. Accept your fate as I must."

Steve wasn't surprised when Rasheed returned in a much better mood and said, "Le Roi and I came to an agreement. He'll not bite me if I improve my French."

"I thought you were fluent."

"It isn't the words, it's the accent. I have much practice to do."

They walked into the emergency room with Rasheed narrating for Steve. "It is very crowded, but I see Jack and Mr. McBlythe near a hallway. Jack is motioning for us to come to them."

The sound of multiple crying children and adults with wracking coughs made hearing almost impossible. Rasheed came to a stop, and Allister was the first to speak. "Let's find a place besides here to talk. They've taken Heather to a room, but we can't see her until she's fully settled."

Steve spoke before anyone took a step. "I don't know about the rest of you, but I haven't eaten all day. I vote for going to the cafeteria."

Jack quickly chimed in. "I've been here. The food isn't that bad, and I've not eaten today either."

"Nor I," said Rasheed.

Allister made the vote unanimous. "It must be quieter than this place, and a bite of something is what the doctor ordered for me. Literally. The doctor in the ER told me to eat several small, high-protein meals today. Something about blood sugar spiking up and down during times of high stress."

Allister and Jack led the way, with Steve and Rasheed following behind. Jack spoke as their footfalls sounded on the hard flooring. "Going to a room sounds positive for Heather."

"She tried to check herself out," said Allister. "The ER doctor and I had to threaten her with forced psychiatric commitment if she didn't agree."

Jack threw on the proverbial brakes. All four stood still as Jack let out a low whistle. "It doesn't surprise me she wanted out, but isn't an involuntary commitment excessive?"

"The head of the psychiatric department recommended it if she didn't agree. Heather's breakdown is nothing to take lightly."

Steve spoke up. "They didn't give me a choice when Maggie died. It took me months before I climbed out of the well. It didn't help that the well was pitch black because I'd lost my sight."

The group walked on to the cafeteria with no further delays. They made their selections and sat at a table as far away from anyone as they could. Each person seemed to wait for someone else to speak.

Jack broke the silence. "Not bad for hospital cafeteria food."

Steve was in mid-bite, so he couldn't respond.

Rasheed spoke in his sing-song cadence. "I've had limited interactions with Heather, but she impressed me as a strong woman. I believe her recovery will be short."

"Strong doesn't begin to describe her," said Jack.

The sound of two text messages arrived within nanoseconds of each other. Steve heard Jack and Allister moving at the same time. Allister made the announcement. "We're to go to the top floor and meet with Dr. Brandywine."

Jack added, "That's all it says."

Steve pushed back his chair. "I'm not sure if Rasheed and I should go, but I learned a long time ago that it's easier to ask for forgiveness than permission."

They traveled at a quick pace until stopping at an elevator. The ding of a bell announced its arrival. Good fortune was on their side as they rode to the top floor with no interruptions from passengers joining them. Allister and Jack did the navigating from there. They were all whisked into an office that Rasheed described as looking like a well-appointed living room. Steve found his chair to be exceptionally comfortable.

Dr. Joy Brandywine seated them in what sounded like an oval pattern. "If you didn't catch my name the first time, it's Joy Brandywine. I go by Dr. Joy. I'm the hospital's lead psychologist."

"Not a psychiatrist?" asked Jack.

"No. I'll explain more about that once we get to know each other a little better. Let's start with Heather's father, Mr. Allister McBlythe."

Steve listened as Allister gave a cryptic biography. Dr. Joy allowed him to finish before she said, "The brevity of your words shows a high level of concern for your daughter. You don't want to talk about yourself, and that's understandable. I've taken the time to do a cursory Internet search on you and Heather. I recommend a longer meeting with me, preferably today, immediately following your visit to her room."

"Of course. How is she?"

"She's safe, comfortable, and sedated. She'll be non-responsive. We're allowing her brain to rest by limiting her awake time to only a few hours a day."

Dr. Joy moved on. "Which one of you is Jack Blackstock?"

"I'm Jack."

"I thought so. I know you're a local defense attorney. Are you romantically involved with Heather?"

"Not as much as I want to be."

She paused. "I'd like to speak with you privately, too. I sense you'd be more comfortable speaking about affairs of the heart without an audience."

"I'll be uncomfortable either way. I've never spoken to a psychologist in my life, except the ones I cross-examined in court."

Joy had a nice, soft laugh. "Perhaps I'm the one who should feel uncomfortable. I'll take a chance. How does tomorrow morning sound?"

"I'll practice being vulnerable."

"I doubt that." She allowed the words to hang in the air.

"Moving on, you must be Steve Smiley. Heather mentioned your name when I briefly spoke to her. She wasn't making much sense, so you'll need to tell me about yourself."

"Steve Smiley, former homicide detective in Houston. Widower. Medically retired after an injury that took my sight. Heather and I are business partners and platonic temporary housemates. We occasionally try to solve murders."

Jack interrupted. "They don't try. They solve them. The cops call them when they're stumped."

"Fascinating. Were you and Heather working on a murder case when she had this episode?"

"Two murders. Possibly related," said Steve. "In the past, working a case always seemed to help her mentally. It revived her."

"Why do you think it didn't work this time?"

"Our agreement was for her to stop working on her business interests when a case came our way. This time, she tried to do both. I believe a combination of pressures built up until..." He allowed the words to taper off.

"Do you blame yourself?"

"Some." He spoke before she could. "Unlike Jack, I've seen plenty of psychologists. I still do, but the sessions are online and monthly."

"Thank you for being so open."

Rasheed spoke after several seconds. "That leaves only me, Dr. Joy. I am Rasheed. My last name is an alphabet soup of letters. Like you, I am a doctor, but not certified in this country."

"What discipline?"

"Philosophy. I am a guest in this country after war made paupers out of princes and drivers out of doctors."

"Were you a prince?"

"Only a college professor. Starting today, I drive for Heather and Steve." He took a breath. "I am not that familiar with current treatment techniques for what you call burnout. Those two words had a much different meaning in my country. It usually involved a building and a bomb or rocket. I have much study to do."

Allister added, "I believe Rasheed can aid in Heather's recovery and future well-being."

"Fate has smiled upon me again," said Rasheed.

"Speaking of treatment for Heather," said Jack. "What can we expect?"

"Several days in the hospital. After that, no stress. I can't force her to comply, but a long, uninterrupted break through

Christmas and beyond may be all she needs. I'll know more after she's well enough to take a full battery of tests."

"I thought she had those today."

"Those were all to rule out medical problems. A team of specialists did that and turned her over to a psychiatrist. She made a diagnosis and ordered medicine to make sure Heather sleeps much more than she'll be awake. In layman's terms, her brain is overloaded and needs to reboot and declutter the files on her hard drive."

Steve asked, "Does the time off work apply to her helping me solve these murders?"

Dr. Joy didn't rush an answer. "I'll need to think about that. If it's been therapeutic for her in the past, it could be again, but it could also be detrimental. Time will give us the answer."

She stood. "Thank you for coming. Heather's extremely lucky to have a team like you to support her."

24

———————

Heather took a deep breath with her eyes closed. "Do you have any idea how good it is to be outside, with Max on my lap?"

"I didn't have a cat, but I remember going outside and feeling the sun. It was nice."

Steve's voice had the same effect as the fleece blanket she'd wrapped around herself. He asked, "How do you like the new patio furniture your father bought for you?"

Heather felt the fabric. "It's like sitting on a cloud. Did you help him pick it out?"

"It was a group decision. Le Roi and Max were the only ones who didn't give their opinion."

"I'm surprised Father allowed discussion."

"He got his way in the end. I liked the way another set felt. Jack's priority was durability, and Rasheed didn't think arms would be a good idea because they might block the flow of energy if you were sitting in a lotus position."

"I like Rasheed. He's a gentle soul." She took another deep breath and opened her eyes. "What about my father? What were his criteria?"

"He let everyone talk and then told the sales clerk he wanted the most expensive set of lawn furniture made. He had to pay extra for a rush delivery."

"One of his favorite sayings is, 'Always buy quality. You'll save money in the long run.'"

"Maggie had a better idea. She'd look for premium brand-name clothes at thrift stores, especially those with original price tags on them. Someone paid top dollar and never wore them. You'd think it was Christmas if she found a new designer dress or jeans that fit her."

"Speaking of Christmas," said Heather. "I'm sorry we won't be in our new homes like we planned."

"It's for the best."

Heather turned to him. "How could that be?"

Steve rubbed his chin. "It will give me a chance to practice decorating. I'm turning over a new leaf and embracing the joyful spirit of the season."

"Christmas is your least favorite time of year."

"I'm changing."

"Why? What's the use?"

Steve tilted his head. "Those are two very interesting questions. In fact, they're such good questions that I don't know the answers. Perhaps our driver can help you discover the answers."

"Forget I asked."

"Yeah, you're right. A lot of things I say make little sense, like me wanting to decorate for Christmas. All I know is having holly on the mantelpiece, greenery on the stairway banister, a tree with lights and decorations galore, and a bunch of presents under the tree is the right thing to do this year."

Heather yawned. "I don't think I'll help you. All I want to do is sleep."

"Your chair reclines. See how it works for taking a nap."

"Will you stay here with me?"

"If I'm not here when you wake up, your father or Jack will be."

She yawned again. "That sounds nice."

WITH HER BELOVED CAT ON HER LAP ACTING LIKE A HEATING pad, it didn't take long for Heather's breathing to become deep and regular. Steve whispered to Le Roi, "Stay here. Let me know if anyone comes into the yard. She needs her rest."

He rose from his chair and went inside and followed the smell of coffee to the kitchen. Allister made his presence known by asking, "How is she?"

"Peacefully sleeping, which is a huge blessing. I was afraid she'd relive visions of the fire."

Allister interrupted. "Dr. Joy and Rasheed both warned us about nightmares. Was she coherent?"

"Much more than yesterday when she came home. I think she faked it enough to get Dr. Joy to release her after only four days."

"How could she do that?"

Steve wondered if he'd said too much. "It's a trick inmates use in jails and prisons. They display symptoms consistent with some form of illness, sometimes physical, but most of the time mental. The medical staff prescribes medication, but the inmate only pretends to take it."

"Why?"

"They sell or barter the pills for things they want. You can let your imagination run wild with what those things are."

"Don't the guards or nurses make sure they take them?"

"First, they have to make sure the pill made it into their mouth. If a person can slide a wallet out of a back pocket or do a sleight-of-hand card trick without getting caught, palming a pill is simple.

"Next, even if they put the pill in their mouth, that doesn't mean they swallow it. Most of the time they push it down or up into the gum-line, take a swallow of water, and open their mouth for a very brief inspection."

"And you believe Heather did this?"

"She did it to get her mind clear enough to come home."

"Are you saying she doesn't need the medication?"

Steve shook his head with vigor. "No, but she may not need as much as they're giving her, especially as time passes. I know I was over-medicated for months. It was like living in a zombie apocalypse movie and I was the head zombie."

"Should I take her to a different team of doctors?"

Steve had considered this question many times. "The short answer to your question is no. Dr. Joy already got the psychiatrist to reduce the dosage. She knew Heather wasn't taking all her pills."

Allister drummed his fingers on the marble bar. "I must have a dozen half-empty pill bottles in my bathroom cabinet. Heather's just like me in so many respects. We both believe the body needs a helping hand, but once we're out of deep water, we like to swim to shore."

"Good analogy, even if medical personnel hate patients to think independently."

Steve kept talking. "We need to monitor the quantity and quality of Heather's sleep. Rasheed believes two more days on her current dosage, and she'll start palming pills again. As long as it's only one a day, he says that's a sign she's getting better. The key is a slow, gentle reduction."

"For how long?"

"He said Dr. Joy was right on target. She's not to think about her businesses until after the new year."

"What about the murder cases?"

"Dr. Joy and Rasheed are of the same mind concerning that. Another week or two of observation before we bring up the subject to her."

Allister spoke with absolute conviction. "One week, and she'll be going stir-crazy. She's always been a fast healer." He paused. "I need to get outside."

"Take a blanket. It's another cool, overcast day with a gentle breeze. Perfect for taking a nap. Le Roi is on guard duty, and Max has Heather pinned to her chair."

"I may take you up on that offer. I don't remember the last outdoor nap I took."

"They're therapeutic. Helps activate the brain, and the Lord knows I need it."

Mild concern came into Allister's voice. "Are the two cases not progressing well?"

"Except for one interview that yielded little, the cases are like two boats run aground on a sand flat. Everything came to a sudden stop except Jack's motion for a bond reduction hearing."

"Is it scheduled yet?"

"He got it put on the judge's calendar for the last Friday afternoon before Christmas. If there's any delay, Luke will have Christmas dinner behind bars."

"That doesn't sound very appealing."

"Unless they find a better cook," said Steve, "it may be another burnt sacrifice."

Allister was walking toward the door leading to the back patio when he stopped. "I don't know why I'm saying this, but sometimes I have trouble choosing between two people for a promotion. When I do, I interview them again. Does that mean anything to you?"

"It certainly does, and I'm kicking myself for not having already done what I know to do."

"Worry has affected all of us."

Steve thought about the words. Once again, it was a throwaway line at the end of a conversation. As he sat sipping coffee, he silently repeated it. By the time he finished a cup, he had a fresh idea of how to proceed.

He knew how, but not when. It would be best if Heather were with him to describe what he could not see. But would she be up to it?

It then occurred to him that he had something else to do that would occupy much of his time for the next week. He had an entire five-bedroom home with a separate apartment to decorate for Christmas. That didn't count the front and back yards. Perhaps he was the one who needed therapy for coming up with such a crazy idea.

He went to his apartment and closed the door. "This may work out for the best. Heather can help decorate if she's up to it, and after a week maybe she can ease into the case. If not, I'll do what I can alone."

25

Heather looked on as a small army of employees from her office descended upon her home. Her personal assistant led the parade of tacky Christmas sweater wearers and gave her a hug that lasted much longer than expected. In fact, it was the first hug Heather had ever received from Pam.

The demure woman had literally and figuratively let her hair down. "It's so good to see you." She put extra emphasis on the word, *so*. "Don't worry about us staying late. We're under strict instructions to get in, set up, and get out. Your father hired a professional decorator named Hillary to make your home look like something you'd see in a magazine. She's half drill sergeant and half Santa's lead elf. There she is now, carrying in a box of holly. It's the real thing, not plastic."

The woman came to Heather and spoke like she'd known her all her life. "Hello, Heather. I'm Hillary. Your job tonight is to hang the holly on the mantle and tell Pam what other decorations you want. The fireplace is the focal point of the entire home. You may have keepsakes you put out every year. If not, we brought plenty of others to choose from."

Hillary gulped a breath. "Make sure the holly is thick and tumbles down both sides." She looked down. "Oh, my goodness, the dog and cat beds on each side of the fireplace are scrumptious. That will make a perfect photo setting." She set the box on the floor and brushed her hands. "I'm so excited to see how everything looks when we're finished. I'm going outside now to supervise the lawn decorations. Holler if you need me, but I can tell you have exceptional taste and need little coaching from me."

Heather looked at Pam when Hillary was gone. "Was that a woman or a tornado? I haven't heard that many words crammed into thirty seconds in a long time. She reminds me of a wind-up toy set at the wrong speed. She'd better slow down or she'll end up like me."

"She takes long breaks after each holiday and has a standing rule of a month off after decorating for New Year's Eve parties."

Heather heard the words and wondered who in her inner circle had coached Pam to plant a seed of how she could change her schedule. She smelled a conspiracy. She and Steve would have a talk after everyone left.

Pam handed her a sprig of holly. "We're to make garlands by tying them together with these green things that look like bread ties. Let's get started.

Heather gave Pam a look that communicated suspicion. "Is this Dr. Joy's idea of craft therapy?"

The answer came, but it wasn't from Pam. Heather turned around and looked down at the petite psychologist who wore a bright red sweater with a cartoon drawing of an elderly couple on the front. They sat in matching recliners with a Christmas tree and fireplace in the background. The man's eyes bugged out, and his mouth gaped open. The bubble of monologue above the woman's head, read: "We've been nice for over sixty years. Let's try naughty this Christmas."

A hearty laugh spurted from Heather's mouth.

Dr. Joy gave her a hug. "That was the reaction I hoped you'd have."

"Are you saying I'm cured?"

"Psychologists never say that. It's bad for business." She took a step back. "How are you feeling right now?"

Heather considered the question. "Mostly happy, but a little confused. Who arranged all this?"

"The usual suspects. Steve had the idea, and the other men in your life took it from there. I don't know if you realize what a big step this is for Steve."

Heather looked around. "I don't see him. Where is he?"

"In his apartment. He said hello to everyone and made his escape to his own little world."

Heather puffed out her cheeks. "I have a confession to make to you."

"Would you rather do it in private?"

"Pam knows almost everything there is to know about me. What's one more thing?" She took a deep breath. "I haven't been taking all the medication you prescribed me. Also, I palmed pills in the hospital. I was desperate to come home and didn't think you'd let me if I was all drugged up."

Joy pursed her lips together before smiling. "Steve told me to expect that type of behavior from you. You were compliant enough that I knew you were getting a large enough dose to do you some good. The wonderful and maddening thing about my line of work is how different people are. They each react differently to medications. One size doesn't fit all."

She lowered her voice. "You had an acute episode brought on by stress and extreme fatigue. You're making excellent progress, but you can't go back to pushing yourself so hard."

"When can I stop taking medication?"

"That depends. You're already down to the minimum effective dose because of your continued palming of pills."

"One at night helps me sleep. Any more than that and everything is fuzzy."

"Here's your new plan. I want you to continue taking one pill at night. Stay home for the next week. Let's keep your outside stimulus to a minimum. No work, especially anything to do with your businesses."

"Can I read?"

"Yes, but nothing dealing with business. That includes the *Wall Street Journal* and any other business-related publications. This prohibition of business includes television, YouTube, and the Internet."

Dr. Joy turned to Pam. "No emails, texts, or phone calls from the office. Pretend Heather is on a spaceship headed to Mars and her communication system is out. Pass the word to everyone at the office."

Pam responded. "Heather's father made that abundantly clear, but I'll have him put out a new memo."

"What about helping Steve with the murder cases?" asked Heather.

"I've consulted with several experts on that. The opinions varied from absolutely not to it would be a good interim step in the healing process." She hesitated before saying, "Since you've already shown non-compliance, I'm confident there's a good chance that you'll help Steve, no matter what I say."

Heather dipped her head. "You're right, but I know he won't allow me to help him without your permission."

"I've already given it, but with restrictions."

"And those are?"

"You're to stay home for a full week. He'll pass on all the information he gathers to you. You can study and have discussions about it only during the day and for a maximum of four hours. You must take regular breaks. Not more than one hour of study at a time and take your nightly dose of medication."

Joy put her hand on Heather's arm. "You're an amazing woman, but the biggest enemy to your mental health is the woman you see in the mirror every morning."

"I understand."

"Good." Joy's voice changed to a brighter pitch. "The smell of spiced apple cider and Christmas cookies is wafting through your home. I'm taking the hint from the woman on my shirt and I'm on my way to be naughty. I hear there's even a fruitcake from Collin Street Bakery."

Heather smiled. "You're one of the few people I know who likes fruitcake. Eat all you want and take some home with you."

Joy giggled like a child. "Ooh, that would be naughty."

The therapist moved on, leaving Heather alone with Pam, who turned to her. "It sounds like you're making significant progress."

"What she said about me being my own worst enemy is true. There's so much I want to accomplish and time ticks away so fast. But I don't want to end up in the hospital ever again."

Pam pursed her lips together and twirled a sprig of holly.

Heather reached for two sprigs of holly and a tie. "Spit it out, Pam. You're holding something back that's important."

"I can't. At least not yet. You heard the doctor. And besides, your father will fire me."

"There was a time when he would have told you to do whatever it took to toughen me up. He's changed so much since Mother died. I'm still your boss and I promise I won't fire you."

Pam leaned into her, a sheepish smile on her face. "There's one thing going on at work that I need to tell you about."

"Remember what Dr. Joy said. No bad news, If it's bad, tell my father and let him handle it."

Sparkling eyes met Heather's stare. "There's a genuine office romance going on."

A wave of relief spread over Heather. Despite the doctor's orders, she'd been expecting the worst. "Do they work in the same department?"

"They don't even work on the same floor. Completely different supervisors."

"Then there's no problem. I wish them well."

"Thank you."

Heather's head jerked to the left and she searched Pam's face. "You sneaky thing. How long has it been going on?"

"About six months."

Heather shook her head. "One more reason to follow Dr. Joy's orders. I need a break if I can't see my own assistant is involved in a romance."

Steve and Le Roi picked that moment to walk up. "I understand my business partner is coming back to help me part-time."

"Sir, I'd like to discuss business with you, but my craft therapy is more important. I have an opening in my schedule tomorrow morning at ten o'clock."

"I didn't think it possible," said Steve. "You can teach an old dog new tricks."

"I'm not sure I appreciate being referred to as an old dog, but otherwise, you're accurate in your assessment. Change is possible."

"Good to have you back." He sniffed the air. "The smell of hot apple cider lured me out of my room."

Pam added, "All kinds of goodies are in the kitchen, even a Christmas fruitcake."

"Maggie made me eat one slice of fruitcake every year. I've sworn off it since she's been gone, but I might as well face my fears tonight and choke down a thin sliver."

"I'll go with you," said Heather. "It may taste better than I remember. Sometimes we need to go back in order to move forward." She hooked her hand through Steve's arm and whispered. "How's the investigation going?"

"I could use some help."

"Good. I don't like craft therapy."

"I didn't either," said Steve. "Let's solve a couple of murders."

"Send me your latest files and we will."

"You're not on the clock until tomorrow morning at ten."

Jack's voice sounded from behind them. "Who's not on the clock until tomorrow?"

Heather said, "Me," at the same moment Steve said, "Heather." She released Steve and grabbed Jack by the lapels of his jacket, pulled him toward her and planted a loud kiss on his lips.

"Someone's feeling better," said Jack. "I wasn't expecting such a warm reception."

"Look up," said Heather.

Jack did. "Someone hung mistletoe over the doorway."

Steve explained. "It's part of my therapy. Maggie put mistletoe over every door in the house, including the one leading to the pantry. I told the decorator to do the same. Even an old curmudgeon like me enjoys a peck on the cheek now and then."

Heather obliged him while Jack asked, "Is it safe to talk about the case yet?"

She had a quick reply. "Not until tomorrow morning at ten. I'm changing my ways and following doctor's orders."

Jack announced, "It's a Christmas miracle." He paused. "I'm hoping for another. Mary Jo Bains is one of the pushiest people I've ever had the misfortune to know. I'm not sure it's worth what she's paying me to represent Luke."

Heather wagged her finger at him. "That's too close to discussing the case. We're on our way to score some Christmas goodies. How about a nice, thick slice of fruitcake?"

"Yuk."

26

Heather heard the door to Steve's rooms open at precisely ten o'clock in the morning, the day after the decorating tornado struck. He joined her in the home office. "Good morning," she said.

"And the same to you. Are you well rested?"

"That pill I take at night is small but potent. Nine hours of sleep leaves me groggy."

Steve issued a quick, "Uh-huh," and changed the subject. "How do the decorations look?"

"Excessive. Did you know they put a full-size version of Santa's sleigh and all the reindeer on the roof? That doesn't count the inflatables and the manger scene in the front yard."

"Did you see the dog-and-cat themed decorations in the backyard?"

"Who's going to see them?"

Steve shrugged. "Your father told me Le Roi lifted his leg on the inflatable cat dressed in an elf costume." Steve kept talking. "The sleigh and reindeer on the roof were my idea." He paused. "It was really Maggie's, but I put my foot down when she wanted to do it. I could see myself in the hospital with multiple broken bones. There was also a good chance I'd electrocute myself with all the lights she wanted on it."

Heather gave him a hard stare. "I don't know if you're joking or not."

He held up three fingers. "Scouts honor. The roof decorations are my tribute to Maggie. When I say she went overboard at Christmas, I'm not exaggerating."

Heather spoke without thinking. "I can learn a lot from Maggie, even though she's been gone for years. Somewhere along the way, I forgot how to have fun." She thought for another moment. "I never learned how to rest, either. It always seemed like I was wasting time if I wasn't moving."

"Jack can help you with that. He works hard but knows when to stop. Weekends, holidays, and vacations are his times to unwind and recharge."

Heather glanced at him. "Have you been talking to Rasheed again?"

"Does it show?"

"Uh-huh. You're changing."

"I introduced Rasheed to the joy of shopping at second-hand, and consignment stores. He's like a kid opening presents. A crushed velvet purple couch in his new apartment is his biggest score to date."

"If I had somewhere to go, I'd like to talk to him."

"He'll be by this afternoon. You're going for a walk with us."

"Where?"

"A short drive north of here in Sam Houston National Forest. Your dad, Le Roi, and I are going too. Dr. Joy recommended it."

"That sounds nice."

"We'll leave after lunch." He paused for a moment. "But first, you ease into the day. Your father thought the sketch of the banquet table in Houston needed more detail. He reworked it."

"Dad's a stickler for details."

"Depending on how the day goes, I may send you a recording that contains a second interview that Jack and I did with Luke.

It isn't much, but I need your opinion about it. For the next hour, you and Max are going to the backyard and rest."

"Rest doesn't sound very appealing."

"I didn't say you had to sleep. Dr. Joy is concerned about the amount of information you put into that computer between your ears. She likened it to taking small bites and chewing them thoroughly. Tomorrow, I may send you the interview Jack and I did with Erin Stoops. In the week to come, if you make good progress, you and I will go back to the beginning and review everything. We're in no rush to solve these cases. In fact, we're in no rush to do anything. That's why you're not getting the interview Jack and I did with Erin until tomorrow."

"Do you have any idea how hard it is to do nothing?"

"As a matter of fact, I do. It took months of practice, but once I got the hang of it, I wondered why I'd pushed myself so hard."

RASHEED TIED HIS HIKING BOOTS WITH FIRM TUGS ON THE laces. Heather asked, "Are those boots new?"

"The store clerk told me they were gently worn, perhaps only one or two short walks. They are my latest bargain. The price was so reasonable, I didn't haggle. The way people conduct business in this country seems so strange. People challenge prices in my home country. To accept the first price is proof you are a fool."

Heather understood. "I once spent thirty minutes in Algiers getting the price of a rug down to where I knew it should cost."

"How many times did you walk away?"

"Twice."

Rasheed held up his hand with five fingers splayed. "Five times minimum in my country. People in the West scroll on their phones for entertainment. My countrymen find great joy in testing their prowess in the marketplace. My mother was the best I ever knew in monetary negotiations. Some vendors would close their stalls when they saw her coming."

Heather looked at a sign that pointed to a trail. "Let's get started. I know you two didn't drag me out here without some sort of agenda. What subject do you want to start with?"

Rasheed turned to look at her and said, "I have no agenda other than to identify as much flora and fauna as I can. I picked up a book on plants and trees in the same store where I purchased my hiking boots. The book cost me a quarter."

"Our agenda is to take a long walk," said Steve. "In fact, my agenda is to have no agenda other than to pay attention to the smells and sounds. Le Roi may have something else on his mind, but he's keeping it to himself."

"I thought we were going to discuss the cases."

"Not today. I told you I'd send the interview that Jack and I did with Erin, but first, we're all going to practice patience."

Heather didn't believe them. "Aren't we going to talk?"

"Not me," said Rasheed. "I've only visited city parks since I came to this country. Nothing to date has prepared me for the beauty of the forest. It is beyond my wildest dream. Being in a forest for the first time is something I want to experience without words." He looked up at the tops of towering pine trees. "This is like seeing a cathedral for the first time. It's somehow holy and worthy of reverence."

Rasheed took a deep breath. "There's so much clean air with the scent of pine." He reached down and picked up a handful of soil and pine needles. "The earth smells so... earthy. I'm leaving my book in the car."

"Good choice," said Steve.

Heather asked, "How long is the trail?"

Rasheed seemed to be talking to himself. "It starts and ends here. I won't go far before I sit, look, touch, and listen."

Steve said, "We'll walk as far as we like. You can turn around and retrace your steps or keep going until you end up back here."

"When will we leave?"

Rasheed said, "The forest doesn't have a watch, but it speaks. It's calling to me. Enjoy your walks."

Heather waited for Rasheed to disappear until she turned to Steve. "I didn't know he was going off by himself. Do you think he'll be all right?"

"He survived much more than losing his way in a forest. Le Roi will find him if he's not back before dark."

"I had no idea we were staying that long."

"Does it matter?"

"Not really."

"Now you're catching on."

LATE THAT AFTERNOON, HEATHER OPENED THE EMAIL attachment from Steve. She listened to the audio recording of Steve and Jack interviewing Erin Stoops three times, making notes and adding to them with each replay.

She didn't know if the walk in the forest had dulled her mind, or if her lack of concentration came from something wrong with her brain. Whatever the origin, she didn't like the feeling. One thing was certain, the long walk had awakened her appetite. It occurred to her that she'd been eating without tasting food since the fire.

She strode into the kitchen where Steve sat on a barstool. "I don't know about you," she said, "...but I'm starving."

"Walking five miles will do that to you. What sounds good?"

"Everything sounds good, but I'd really like barbecue ribs, coleslaw, and an order of fries."

"That's brain food, or at least it is for me. I'll see what Rasheed wants and call it in."

"Thanks. I'll take Max on the back porch with me." It didn't occur to her until later that there was a pet door that allowed Max to get out any time he wanted to. The same couldn't be said for Le Roi. Too much dog for the small door.

She remembered to grab a blanket which was Max's signal to join her. Once again, the chair seemed to swallow her, especially with the tubby cat pushing her into the cushion. How could she be so tired when all she did was walk a few miles before taking a nap while leaning against a monster pine tree?

Rasheed's voice awakened her from a dream that included scenes of fire—not the fire that took her new home, but flames that were chasing her.

"Heather. Heather! Wake up Miss Heather."

"Huh? What?" She sat up straight. "Where's Max?"

"Inside. You were thrashing," said Rasheed.

"Take your time getting up," said Steve. "Everything's fine. Max is safe and parked in his bed by the fireplace. Supper is in the oven keeping warm."

Heather focused her gaze on Steve, then looked beyond him. "It's dark. How long have I been asleep?"

"It doesn't matter. Did you dream about the fire?"

"Uh-huh. It's the first time."

Rasheed spoke with confidence. "That is a very good sign. It shows your brain is learning to cope with the terrible memory. You're making excellent progress."

"It doesn't seem that way to me."

Steve took his turn. "It's been a good day."

The sound of the patio door sliding open reached her ears. Her father took her hand. "How are you, dear?"

"Hungry."

"Your wish is my command. A feast fit for cowpunchers on a trail drive awaits us."

"If you turn up wearing boots and a cowboy hat, I'll start to worry about you."

27

———————

Days passed with long walks in the forest. Times for beginning the outings varied, as did the locations, or at least the trails they explored. Heather's father surprised her by wanting to go. He even bought hiking boots and a full ensemble of outdoor wear from a high-priced store in The Woodlands that specialized in top-name merchandise. Rasheed didn't understand why Allister wouldn't look at thrift stores first.

Heather kept her word and took her nightly dose of medication, which gave her eight to nine hours of uninterrupted sleep. Dr. Joy reduced the dosage by half again the previous week. Heather took the first steps toward understanding what Dr. Joy, Rasheed, and Steve were teaching her about time. Some things take the time they take. At first, the sentence made no sense, but the more she meditated on it, the more the murky waters cleared. Hard work and drive had their place, but the world sometimes threw curve balls. In her case, it was a downgraded hurricane that hit the coast and settled over the area north of Houston. The depravity of mankind showed itself when someone burned her and Steve's dream homes.

She believed she could control time and so much more. The revelation came slowly, but it came. Nature and the actions of people conspired to reveal much about this hard-driving executive named Heather McBlythe. She came to realize that how she reacted made all the difference in her mental health. Steve took everything in stride. She considered setbacks as personal attacks and fought them with impotent verbal jabs and swings. All she did was exhaust herself until she burned so hot only a shell of herself remained.

Heather left her bedroom and went to a chair in the living room. Sleet peppered against the windows. There would be no walk in the forest today, and she had a decision to make. Would she complain about the weather, make an alternate plan to go to a gym for a vigorous workout, or would she sneak a call to the office to get a quick report on how things were going? Max leaped into her lap and settled himself there. "Good choice, Max. Let's stay here and let the day reveal itself to us."

Steve joined her and brought a cup of coffee with him. She sniffed. "That smells good."

"It's yours. I've been up a while."

"Thanks." She took the mug from him and settled it on the table next to her. "It's sleeting. I can't remember the last time we had sleet."

"Last year in February. It's a good thing your father flew out yesterday instead of today."

"He called me this morning, just to ask how I'm doing. He wants me to go on another cruise with him this spring."

"Are you going?"

"I told him I would if we weren't working on a murder case."

"Let's finish this one first."

"I agree. It's already halfway through the month. We're talking daily about what we've done so far, but it seems like we need to interview everyone again."

"Do you think that's necessary?"

Heather shot him a glance and a smile that he couldn't see. "You're not fooling me, Steve. You've held back on the investigations until I could join you. It's been almost a week since Dr. Joy discontinued my medication. It's all out of my system and the gray cells are talking in full sentences to each other again. We need to interview everyone at least once more, and you know it."

"We'll not do more than one interview a day. How does that sound?"

"Like I need to think like a tortoise and not a hare."

Steve chuckled. "Who do you want to start with?"

"I was telling Max that we should wait and let the day come to us."

"It already has."

"What do you mean?"

"Mary Jo Bains filed a complaint against Jack with the State Bar Association. She's claiming Jack purposefully delayed filing the reduction in bail hearing so he could milk more money out of her."

"That claim will go nowhere. Jack acted strategically. He filed the motion after you two interviewed Erin Stoops and found another legitimate suspect. He doesn't control the court's calendar. She's an overbearing mother who can't let go of her son."

Steve raised his palms. "That's why I scheduled us to see Mary Jo tomorrow morning. We're going to speak to her and see what happens. If we do it right, Jack won't have to spend his time answering a frivolous complaint."

"I'll review the files and make sure there's nothing I missed."

"Four hours of work for both of us today. We're to be at Mary Jo's at nine in the morning."

"I'll have to find my watch. I stopped wearing it the first day we walked in the forest."

"Leave it off. Your phone has all anyone needs."

"What about counting my steps?"

"Do you weigh the same now as you did before you went into the hospital?"

"A few pounds less."

"Do you get out of breath when you walk?"

"No, but I walk slower than I used to."

"Is taking a walk in the forest a competitive sport?"

Heather let out a puff. "All right, you've made your point. I'll leave the watch off for now, but if I gain ten pounds over Christmas, the watch goes back on."

"If I gain ten pounds over Christmas, I'm buying a watch. Five is my limit."

A minute of silence passed without words. Steve broke into the quiet. "I thought you'd spring from the chair and rush to review the files."

Heather listened to and watched half-frozen rain splatter against the windows and slide down. "I'm practicing patience. Besides, Max wouldn't appreciate me moving. I have the rest of the day to review files I've already memorized."

"Memorizing is good, but it doesn't solve murders. There's so much more that we need to do."

"Like what?" Exasperation filled her voice. "My brain feels a little mushy right now."

"I'll give you help with the first question tomorrow if it doesn't come back to you. Remember, small bites, and chew them well."

THE NEXT MORNING AT BREAKFAST, STEVE TESTED HER. "What's one thing to remember when interviewing?"

She placed a pan of brown-and-serve biscuits into the oven. "Verify what someone tells you. Use reliable sources when possible."

"Very good," said Steve. "What else do you remember about interviewing people or suspects?"

Heather retrieved a carton of eggs from the refrigerator. "You're getting scrambled eggs this morning."

"Perfect. I'm wearing a clean shirt and yoke stains don't make a good impression. By the way, that's another rule I made up for conducting professional interviews. Don't look like a slob. You don't have to worry about that, but not being able to see makes me dependent on someone to tell me when I'm wearing part of my meal."

Steve hadn't forgotten the question asked before she went off topic. "Expand on what you said about verifying information."

She drew a breath and took a stab at an answer. "This speaks to why people give misleading information. The first is that they remember things differently than they happened. Talk to ten people about what they saw during a bank robbery, and you'll get multiple versions of what happened. This may not be intentional lying."

"Excellent," said Steve. "Tomorrow you can add something else to the list."

"I have another now."

"Good. Save it and we'll talk about it tomorrow." Steve then asked, "Any more dreams about fire?"

"Don't you mean nightmares?"

"Whatever you want to call them is fine with me."

Heather thought about the night's sleep. "As a matter of fact, I did. Someone tied a burning stick to Max's tail. I chased him but couldn't catch him."

"Hmm," said Steve. "Did you journal that for Dr. Joy?"

"I'm journaling my nighttime sleep and if I dream during naps."

"That's good. I stopped after three years."

Heather tilted her head as she used a fork to scramble the eggs. "Why did you stop?"

"I thought I was cured. When Bucky attacked me and burned our old condos, the night sweats and crazy dreams came back. I record what I dreamed about every morning now."

"I don't get it," said Heather. "You're fully functioning and have the sharpest mind of anyone I know."

Steve said, "Check the biscuits. They smell like they're a perfect golden brown."

Heather glanced through the stove's window. "You're right again. Nothing gets past you."

"Not compared to Le Roi."

Steve changed the subject. "Do we still have some of those pre-cooked sausage patties?"

"How many do you want?"

"Two. One for each biscuit."

He then changed the subject again. "Did you make up questions you want to ask Mary Jo this morning?"

"I came up with a short list, but in the light of day they all sound lame. If it's all the same to you, I'll stick with follow-up questions."

"That's fine. You'll need to put some heat under the skillet unless you want raw eggs."

Heather let out a groan. "Will I ever be the same again?"

"You'll be better, but different in a thousand little ways."

"Name one."

"You'll never forget to butter biscuits while they're still hot."

Heather rolled her eyes. "That's not important."

"It is to me. Hot biscuits with butter and honey dripping from them are one of the simple joys of life. You'll be surprised how many little things will bring you pleasure. Yours may not come from food, but you now enjoy walks in the forest and engaging in philosophical discussions with Rasheed. You also appreciate Max more than you did. Slowing down has done you a world of good."

Heather dabbed her eyes. Facing away from him, she said, "If you're planning on slopping butter and honey on that clean shirt, I suggest you change."

"Good idea. Breakfast and our first interview since the fire. I get my partner back. It's going to be a great day."

28

———————

The double garage of Heather's home now held two identical black Mercedes SUV's. The engine of the closest and newest made crackling noises as it cooled. Her father was adamant that Rasheed perform his duties as her chauffeur, and that she refrain from driving until further notice. It made sense to give Rasheed a garage door opener to access the garage. No need for any of them to fight the weather while coming or going.

It didn't take long for Le Roi to enter his jail cell and Steve to slide into the back seat. Heather took her place in the front passenger's seat while Rasheed closed the door behind her.

"I put the address of Mary Jo Bains into the car's computer. It estimates we have a twelve-minute drive before we arrive."

Steve waited until they were moving forward before speaking. "Rasheed, I think it would be best if you waited in the car while Heather and I go in and speak to Mary Jo."

"I purchased several books for this very reason. I couldn't wait to read one last night. It teaches the proper etiquette for a chauffeur." He gave her a hopeful look. "I don't mind wearing a dark suit, but the hat of a chauffeur doesn't suit my face."

Heather smiled. "The hat is optional. So is the suit. Wear what you normally wear."

No one spoke until a mechanical voice sounded. "You have arrived at your destination."

"Not yet," said Rasheed. "The book says I'm to park as close to the front door as possible, making sure not to brush or run up onto the curb." He brought the car to a whisper-smooth stop and said, "I'll find a parking spot that gives me a clear view of your return. The book prohibits me from leaning on the car or smoking cigarettes while I wait. That will be no problem as the sleet has turned to rain and I no longer smoke."

Heather unbuckled and reached for the door latch before she realized Rasheed was out of and scurrying around the car. He had an umbrella open and held it over her as she slid out. His expression was impassive, like a highly trained English butler from a century ago. Steve didn't give him a chance to open his door. She guessed the prospect of getting back to investigating the two cases had Steve thinking about more important things than waiting for the chauffeur to open the car door.

Heather went to Steve and shared her over-sized black umbrella. "Are we taking Le Roi?"

"Of course," said Steve. "He's part of our team. Besides, Luke's mother is afraid of him. He may distract her enough that she doesn't realize what she's saying."

The sound of the back of the car opening caught Heather's ear. Rasheed gave Le Roi the command in French for him to get out of jail and go to Steve. The dog did as instructed and stood at Steve's side.

"Do you see the apartment?" asked Steve.

Heather looked in time to see curtains fall back into place. "Our hostess is inquisitive. She watched us get out of the car."

"Let's not keep her waiting," said Steve. "Punctuality is the number one priority of a chauffeur."

"Precisely," said Rasheed. "It shows you value your employer's time."

Making Steve and her wait for over thirty seconds on a dinky front porch after Heather knocked on the door was Mary Jo's first play for control over what would transpire. She took one look at Le Roi and said, "No one said anything about that dog coming. Go put him in your car."

Steve gave his widest smile. "We're a package deal. It's all or nothing and I think what we have to tell you will be well worth your while. Besides, you already have a dog, so I know you're not allergic to them. I have a firm grip on him, and like I told you last time, he's a trained police dog and a certified service dog."

Heather asked, "What breed of dog do you have?"

"A cross between a Heinz 57 and a junkyard. Luke thought I needed a companion when he moved to his own apartment. I wish he'd asked me before he got him from the animal shelter and put a big red bow on him for Christmas two years ago. The idiot ate the bow."

Heather watched drops of water trickle off the umbrella. "We have important news. May we come in?"

Mary Jo flashed a look of suspicion coupled with a reluctant, "I guess so, since Mr. Smiley was good enough to ask for an appointment."

Heather led the way across the threshold. Steve was taking off his boots when Mary Jo said, "Don't worry about the carpet. It's cheap and needed replacing when I moved in. The manager and I lock horns every month about this ugly brown stain catcher. They advertise this floor-blanket as plush and luxurious carpet. What a joke."

Heather had seen carpets of far lesser quality than this and surmised its condition had more to do with Mary Jo's house-keeping than anything else. She scanned the room and noticed a new couch and chair. She also noticed that Mary Jo was wearing designer jeans, a mock turtleneck top, and a puffy vest. A new pair of Uggs covered her feet. It was a marked improvement in her appearance from the first time she saw her in Jack's office. Had Mary Jo dipped into her son's savings and given herself retail therapy while Luke was behind bars?

Steve got down to business. "I can't go into details, but we've found someone that we believe had the motive, means, and opportunity to kill Connie Petrovitch."

"Then why is my Luke still in jail? Lawyers aren't anything but thieves in suits. I told him he'd better not try to milk more money out of me. What does it take to get lawyers and judges to do what's right?"

"Jack has a bond reduction hearing scheduled," said Heather. She sensed her face flushing and stopped. This was not a good sign. Steve would need to do the talking.

"Like Heather said, there's a bond hearing scheduled." He paused and lowered his voice. "There's only one thing that could throw a monkey wrench into Luke being home for Christmas."

"There better not be."

Steve ignored the implied threat. "Do you remember the murder in Houston back in the summer?"

"How could I forget it? Luke was at the same table when some gal from France died."

"Exactly," said Steve. "Luke was in Houston when one woman died and was also present when another woman died. The district attorney in Houston may file additional charges against Luke just to keep him in jail."

"That ain't right," shouted Mary Jo.

"No, it's not, but it's a possibility. We thought you should know." Steve paused a moment. "On the other hand, that list of suspects you gave me might keep the police busy for months."

"I don't understand. Is that good or bad? There must have been two or three hundred names on those lists."

"That's hard to say," said Steve, as he rubbed his chin. "If the police take it seriously, the district attorneys might ask for a delay in the bond reduction hearing so they can investigate."

The hand-wringing began. It was this gesture that brought Heather's eyes to Mary Jo's manicured nails. Not just manicured, but fake, long nails with extravagant decorations on each nail. How could she grip a bowling ball with claws like that? Steve would need to hear about this and the other changes in Mary Jo's appearance. She wouldn't be the first parent to dip into an adult son or daughter's bank account while the wayward child waited for the wheels of justice to slowly turn.

Fatigue settled on Heather like a cloud. She mostly tuned out the conversation, but heard enough to remember Steve telling Mary Jo she might want to revise her list and delete all but a few names of people who had legitimate grievances against Luke.

The interview ended, and she led Steve out the door and into more rain. Sleep overtook Heather on the way home with the phrase *small bites and chew well* ringing in her ears. Perhaps, instead of another interview, tomorrow should be a day of rest and reflection.

29

Steve wondered if the interview had been too much for Heather to handle. She slept all afternoon, woke up in time to eat a few bites of supper, then settled into a recliner close to the fireplace in the living room. He needed her help, but not at the cost of a serious relapse.

The logs crackled as Steve settled into a chair near enough to hers that she could see him when she woke up. It was approaching ten o'clock when she roused and he asked, "How was your nap?"

Her voice had a hint of hopelessness in it. "I'm discouraged. The only thing I accomplished today was to type my notes of the meeting with Mary Jo."

"That's good."

"No, it's not. They were just words on a computer screen. I couldn't see how they related to anything she said before or statements from any of the others."

Her response thrilled him. "Do you realize what you just said?"

"Yes, and I'm not pleased about it. My mind used to be sharp and clear. Now it's muddy as the lake after the flood. It's not just muddy, the words are like debris floating on the surface."

"You're not seeing the bigger picture. This is the first time you've looked for similarities and discrepancies in any of Mary Jo's statements. What about her appearance?"

"It was much improved. From the way she was dressed, I'd say she ran up the bill on her son's credit card. There was also new furniture in her apartment."

Steve sensed Heather hadn't finished, so he stayed silent.

"The oddest thing about her was her hands, especially her fingernails. They were fake, done in a salon. I remember thinking that it would be impossible for her to bowl with them."

"Do you remember her shoes?"

"Uggs."

"What do you mean, *ugh*?"

Heather chuckled. "Uggs is the name of the company. They're best known for making sheepskin lined boots that keep your tootsies toasty. They make a full line of footwear and other products."

He wasn't expecting Heather to hand him a boot with the top half almost the height of a leather cowboy boot. He ran his fingers over the outside, inside, and across the sole. "These are nifty. I bet your feet never get cold."

"It surprised me to see Mary Jo wearing them. They're not exactly cheap, at least the branded ones aren't. You can get knock-offs, but they're made of fake sheepskin."

"What size do you think Mary Jo wears?"

"Small. Everything about her is stubby. Size five, maybe a six."

"Do they make Uggs in men's?"

"A full line."

"I may have to raid my piggy bank and order a pair. My house shoes are on their last leg, or would it be their last foot?"

Heather gasped. "Not only did I lose my memory, I've lost my mind. You hate to pay the suggested retail price for shoes or clothes."

"Don't worry," said Steve. "I'll check the thrift stores first. Retail is an option I reserve as a last resort."

Heather retrieved her boot and slipped it on. She bent over and gave Steve a hug. "Thank you."

"For what?"

"Coaching me back into the land of the living."

"Do you want to do another interview tomorrow?"

She considered the offer as she walked back to her chair. "Today showed me I'm not where I need to be yet. If it's all right with you, I'd like to stay here. Tomorrow is Saturday. That means football. I think I'll ask Jack and Briann over. He'll watch the games while Briann and I make Christmas cookies."

"Good choices, especially the cookies."

"In case you're wondering," said Steve, "Rasheed and I will speak to Marjorie Hicks tomorrow."

Heather thought for a few seconds. "You knew I wouldn't be up to sitting through another interview tomorrow."

"I considered the possibility. If you insist on going with us, I won't stop you."

After weighing the pros and cons, she swallowed a large lump of pride. "I don't want to go back to the twilight zone. Baking cookies sounds better than trying to winnow out truth from lies."

Steve rose from his chair. "Let's compromise. You'll get a copy of the interview. If you feel energetic enough, you can transcribe it into print after Jack and Briann leave."

STEVE'S SEATBELT CLICKED INTO PLACE. "CHANGE OF PLANS, Rasheed. We're meeting Marjorie at a coffee shop. When we get there, I want you to find us a place to sit that's away from anyone who might hear our conversation."

"The choice of words and tone of your voice resemble those used by film noir gangsters. I never thought I'd be in the middle of a real American detective movie. There's even a beautiful woman who received harm and may still be in peril."

"Are you talking about Heather?"

"Of course. She was never in physical danger, but the attack on her property has certainly thrown her for a lasso."

"Thrown her for a loop," Steve corrected.

"Neither loop nor lasso makes sense if taken literally."

Steve didn't want to debate a master of logic, so he changed the subject. "Do you want the address, or will you use telepathy to extract it from the thoughts circling my head?"

"Ah-hah. I have hit an undercooked nerve."

Steve sighed but didn't correct him.

Rasheed must have realized he'd been too verbal. "I apologize. Please give me the address so I may speak to the voice that lives inside the computer."

The minor dust-up between the two served one beneficial purpose. It was a quiet ride to the coffee shop, which gave Steve time to collect his thoughts.

As they pulled to a stop, Rasheed announced, "The gracious lady in the computer is right again. We have indeed arrived at our destination."

Steve unlatched the seat belt but turned to face Rasheed instead of climbing out of the car. "It will be best if you remain in the character of a chauffeur and say little. You're playing the role of a driver, not a Doctor of Philosophy."

"May I take notes?"

Steve wasn't expecting this question, but he had an answer to give. "I'll be recording everything on my phone."

"That will give a record of words, but not expressions."

"That's a valid point. Do you have a blank sheet of paper?"

"Only a small notebook that fits in the pocket of my shirt."

"That will work. Did you bring a book with you?"

"Several."

"Take one of average size. Act like you're reading it and

taking notes on points that stand out to you. Pretend you have no interest at all in what Marjorie and I are discussing."

"I'll write in my native language so she won't know what I'm doing."

"Excellent."

"Thank you. Knowing multiple languages will come in handy, especially if you give the dame the third degree."

Steve released a louder sigh than the previous one. Introducing Rasheed to the world of detectives was trying at times.

Once inside, Rasheed led Steve past multiple people having muted conversations, and one with a woman whose laugh sounded eerily like the bray of a donkey. They walked on until his guide announced, "We have good fortune. The room is long and narrow and the woman with the unusual laugh is far away. It seems the customers prefer the front end of the shop."

"Do you see Marjorie?"

"I studied the photo of her and the description you provided. That looks like her coming into the shop now. Shall I retrieve her?"

"Yes and ask what she would like to drink. Then order it, get me a small cup of regular coffee and get yourself something. I'll pay you back when we get home."

"You are most generous."

Steve waited until he caught a whiff of Marjorie's perfume. He stood. "Good morning. Thanks for meeting me."

"Who's the man?"

"My driver. His name is Rasheed. Heather couldn't make it this morning but sends her regards."

"I heard about some fires at her development. Was anyone injured?"

"Not a soul, and none of the new homes flooded during the storm. The golf courses acted as a buffer, but she expected minor flooding there."

"What about the condominiums and the garden homes?"

Steve thought the question unusual. He tilted his head. "If I were a salesman, I'd say you're interested in moving to the lake."

"I'm considering it, if I can swing it financially."

His curiosity got the best of him. "Are you looking at downsizing?"

The muted laugh surprised him.

"You're very diplomatic, Mr. Smiley, and your choice of words is better than you can imagine. To be perfectly honest, I'm ridding myself of three-hundred pounds of useless husband. I've already spoken with an attorney. Claude will receive papers after the holidays."

This news brought with it mixed emotions in Steve. He never liked to hear about long-running marriages crumbling, but Marjorie seemed to have a heavy burden lifted from her shoulders. Relief seasoned her words, so he asked, "Does Claude know of your intentions?"

She shot back, "He quit paying attention to me a hundred pounds ago, and that's been decades. It would be easier and cheaper if he'd died of a heart attack, but it looks like he'll live forever. I won't change my mind. He'll receive divorce papers in January, even if they have to serve him in jail."

Rasheed picked that moment to return to the table. "Coffee for three. The decaf latte is for Mrs. Hicks."

It sounded like Marjorie spoke through gritted teeth. "It won't be Mrs. Hicks for long."

30

Steve heard the crinkle of a book opening. In his imagination, he saw Rasheed take a small notebook and a pen from his shirt pocket. Jarring candor had marked the meeting with Marjorie up to this point. Would it continue?

Before Steve delivered a follow-up question, Rasheed said, "My apologies for the delay. The line was very long, and the baristas lacked experience. Pardon my interruption to your conversation. Please don't think me rude if I read my book and take notes on what the author is saying."

The words came out forced, like Rasheed was reading a bad script for the first time.

"Think nothing of it, and thank you for the coffee."

Steve thought Marjorie might stop talking, but Rasheed's arrival seemed to invigorate her. "You seem like a level-headed man who likes dogs."

Steve stifled a groan. If she only knew of Rasheed's struggle to overcome his fear.

"Tell me, Rasheed; what would you do if you were a woman like me? Let's say you're a professional woman from an above-average family. Raising show dogs is a family tradition, and it's your passion. You marry a handsome man of average height and weight. He's also a well-educated professional, and he promises to support your love of raising and showing dogs in prestigious competitions. Ten years into the marriage, he gains over a hundred pounds, invests in every get-poor scheme he can find, and prohibits you from not only raising show dogs, but having any animals in the home."

Rasheed's voice changed to that of a university professor. "I'll process what you say after I have more information. I also need to mentally dress myself in a niqab and try to think like a woman."

"Yes. You do that. By the way, what's a niqab?"

"A long headscarf to cover hair, forehead, and shoulders. A veil hides all the face but the eyes."

"Thank you."

"You're welcome."

Steve hoped Rasheed was having a good time because his career as a silent partner was in jeopardy.

Marjorie kept talking. "My Prince Charming turned into an ugly toad before my eyes."

"And a very large toad, at that," said Rasheed.

"Exactly. Not only did his appearance change, so did his personality. His passion for his petite wife melted like snow in the desert. He replaced her with gourmet food and schemes of unearned wealth to fund his gluttonous habit of rare wine matched with choice fare. The coup de grâce came when he took up gambling, trying to fix the financial shortfalls. The woman transformed from a wife into an indentured servant, good for only bringing home money to support his habit and growing vegetables and herbs to satisfy his pleasures."

"No meat?" asked Rasheed, who seemed fully immersed in the story.

"Rabbits and chickens. He made her raise rabbits and chickens until the police evicted them from their home and they lived in a shack in a seedy part of the county. Almost all the money both earn goes toward food, drink and gambling."

Steve sensed she was running out of complaints. He was wrong.

"Not only did he habitually lose money, he also stole it."

This caught Steve's attention, so he let her ramble on. Rasheed proved he was listening better than expected by saying, "Tell me more about stealing. Who did he steal from?"

"Anyone foolish enough to loan money to him." She sucked in another full breath and continued. "He was smart about it though. Usually not over five thousand dollars, but there were so many loans that he never intended to repay."

With air left, Marjorie changed direction. "Remember, you're an American woman, faced with this untenable position, and you're miserable. Life is slipping past you. What would you do?"

"Please allow me a few moments to consider." Time dragged on like pouring cold molasses. Rasheed finally asked, "Did you say I'm to respond like an American woman?"

"Respond however you want."

"A woman from my country would find a teenage girl for him to marry as a second or third wife. This would give her someone to share the burden with. An American woman would act differently. A well-educated, professional woman, like the one in your hypothetical example, would likely divorce him. A poor woman would leave him and move in with a relative or friend."

"What if she thought he might harm her if she left him?" asked Marjorie.

"Ah. That is a different pan of fish. This woman would devise a way to rid herself of the man forever."

"Like kill him?"

"That's one way, but not the only way. The man you described will die soon enough from the many ailments related to obesity. She could simply wait for death to take him."

"But she can't wait. She senses danger."

"There is yet another course of action she could take. All a smart woman must do is devise a plan for him to go somewhere he is not a threat."

"Where? How?"

"Prison, of course. She could make it appear he committed a crime and allow American justice to remove him."

Steve cleared his throat. "On that cheerful note, let me ask you something, Marjorie. Did you try to poison your husband at the banquet in Houston?"

"No, but someone tried to poison me. If you remember, Claude moved the place cards on the table. He said he did it so he could sit next to that French pastry disguised as a pharmacist. That should have been my seat. If you're looking for the killer, I'd talk to my future ex-husband."

Steve challenged her. "Why would he want to kill you?"

"He discovered I was hiding money from him. A year ago, I started going to church and set up an automatic draft of ten percent of my gross pay. I told him the money was my tithe, and that God would smite him if he tried to take it. I lied to him, and I don't regret it. It really went into an investment fund. It's grown enough so I can now afford to leave him."

Steve realized that's why she asked about Heather's apartments and condos.

Rasheed took his turn again. "You are a very strategic thinker. I commend your resourcefulness."

"Thank you, Rasheed. It's so refreshing to be appreciated."

The proverbial train seemed to be in danger of slipping off the tracks again, so Steve raised his voice enough to make it clear he was conducting the interview. "Let's focus on the death in Houston. It makes no sense to me that Claude would go to all the trouble of placing Michelle next to him so he could discuss food and then forget he put poison in a dish intended for you."

Marjorie came back with, "Remember how single-minded he is with food? If he and Michelle were discussing the best chefs in Paris, he likely forgot which plate of chicken confit he put the poison in. Don't hand him a prescription to fill any time near lunch. There's no telling what he'll put in the bottle."

Steve shook his head. "That's too far of a stretch,"

He heard Marjorie lean back. "All right, let's pretend Claude didn't poison Michelle by mistake. There's someone else at the table who has a longstanding grudge against him. Claude borrowed ten grand from Luke Bains and never repaid it. My husband may have wanted to get rid of me as much as Luke wanted to be done with him."

Rasheed chimed in again. "Your logic is sound, but the delivery of the poisoned food confuses me. Could you explain?"

The same question had gnawed on Steve's mind.

"That is a head-scratcher," admitted Marjorie. "Our server wasn't the sharpest knife in the drawer, and you know how banquets are. People get absorbed in conversations. Plates come and go. That's not a problem with identical salads, but with the main course and desserts, there's a fifty-fifty chance that you'll get what you order. It's easier to swap dishes than try to stop a hit-and-run server and tell them to give people what they ordered."

Steve sat up straight. "Did that happen on the night Michelle died?"

"Of course."

"Did you notice if the server mixed up the entreés?"

"Michelle and I both ordered chicken *confit*, but she received Claude's *beef bourguignon*. They traded plates."

Steve closed the interview by telling Marjorie that the sales of condos were going fast, and prices would rise soon. She stated she'd try to get a showing that afternoon.

Once in the car, Rasheed apologized. "I failed you. Words tumbled off my tongue like I was an American teenage girl. Please forgive me."

"You did no harm this time. In fact, you did well. Marjorie was comfortable talking to you. Did you notice she was more at ease with you than with me?"

A hint of pride came into Rasheed's reply. "I noticed, but I don't know why it was so."

"Heather described you to me. She said your hair and beard

are a mixture of black and gray. Your bearing reflects confidence, but there's a boyish charm about you. Your build is appropriate for someone from your country. For a woman who's been married to a toad in a loveless marriage, speaking to an attentive man with a sultry accent was a refreshing change."

"Are you saying that this woman has an attraction towards me?"

"Why not? You're handsome, extremely well educated and you drive a new Mercedes."

"But it is not my car."

Steve wanted to teach him a lesson for taking over his interview. "She doesn't know this isn't your car. She may think you're the Persian version of Sam Spade or Dick Tracy. Let's go to the thrift store and see if they have a trench coat and hat that makes you look like a film noir movie star. You'll have women chasing you like sharks after an injured seal. You could have your own harem in no time."

Rasheed held up a hand. "Enough. You jerk my leg one too many times."

Steve's belly jiggled with each laugh. "Are you sure you don't want to catch Marjorie on the rebound?"

"Too many miles on that car," said Rasheed.

Both men erupted in laughter that lasted more than a minute. Rasheed finally started the engine, and the car gained speed.

"It's just as well," said Steve after they'd driven for several minutes. "Marjorie admitted to having a motive for killing her husband. She was there and could have slipped the poison into his food."

"This is true," said Rasheed. "I reached the same conclusion regarding her husband."

"Don't forget Luke Bains. It's possible the police already have the killer in jail."

"I'd forgotten about him."

Steve hadn't. "The switching of the place cards and the plates adds another level of complexity to the case."

Another mile passed before Rasheed asked, "What is your next step?"

"Heather and I will have a visit with Claude tomorrow."

"Do you believe his version of the events will vary from what Marjorie told us?"

"I can almost guarantee it."

31

Heather knocked on the door to Steve's suite of rooms and opened it enough to announce her intention to enter. "Are you decent?"

"Come in but avert your gaze from Le Roi. He's not wearing his vest."

Heather took three steps and entered the living area. If she took two more steps to the left, she'd be in the kitchenette. "Are you making wise cracks so early in the morning?"

"Eight o'clock isn't early."

"It is to me. Nine hours of sleep last night has me feeling restless. Let's go out for breakfast."

"I'll call Rasheed and tell him to come get us now." Steve completed the task then said, "He'll be here in ten minutes." His attention turned to Le Roi and he spoke a command in French for the dog to fetch his vest.

The dog sprang from his bed with tail in motion, his paws sliding on the slick tile floor. It wasn't long before he came back with his vest gripped in his mouth.

"Good boy," said Heather. "Have you trained him how to put it on with no help?"

"The Velcro straps make it easy for me, but not having

opposable thumbs limits him." A sly smile pulled at the corners of Steve's mouth. "Since you're in a good mood, how would you like to hear a joke?"

"Not if it's one that takes more than a minute to tell."

"You're in luck," said Steve with an impish grin. "It's only four words."

"I know I'm going to regret this but hit me with your best shot."

He allowed tension to build before saying, "Velcro. What a rip-off."

It turned out that clamping her mouth shut to blunt a laugh wasn't a good idea. The only thing it did was force the explosion of air to come out of her nose. She walked out of his room without saying another word.

Once in the living room, Heather realized she was moving her lips to repeat Steve's joke. Silly or not, it stuck in her brain like a song from her early days at Princeton, or like... She laughed out loud. Like Velcro.

A short time later, Heather heard the overhead garage door opening. She slipped on a jacket, dropped her phone into a crossbody purse, gave Max a scratch behind his ears, and followed Steve and Le Roi out the door leading into the garage.

Steve and Heather had come to an unspoken agreement years ago. Lunch and supper were negotiable, but Steve chose where they ate breakfast. This worked out well since she could get by with toast or a bagel.

Right on cue, Steve told Rasheed where to go.

He replied with a toothy smile. "I perceive you desire the Lumberjack Special for breakfast this morning. The Lumberjill is sufficient for me."

Heather had no intention of filling her stomach to the point she couldn't think straight. She'd transcribed Steve's notes but wanted additional clarity on a couple of things. "This question goes to whoever wants to answer it first. Based on what you observed yesterday, do you believe Marjorie Hicks is a legitimate suspect?"

Steve said, "Rasheed, you go first."

"I hesitate to do so. I am a simple chauffeur, not a famous detective."

"Baloney, and double baloney," said Steve. "You're still mad because I teased you about Marjorie being interested in you. Detectives giving each other a hard time is part of the game. Develop a thick skin to that sort of thing."

Heather looked to her left. "What Steve did yesterday by teasing you is an enormous compliment. You excelled in getting information out of Marjorie. He teased you so your ego wouldn't get out of hand. It's how cops and detectives sometimes treat each other so they don't get overconfident."

Rasheed pushed out his lips as he processed the information. His face brightened. "Is this practice of teasing something like hazing in college fraternities?"

"Very similar," said Steve. "Expect to be on the receiving end of a practical joke now and then."

Heather glanced out the window. "Now that we're a happy family again, is Marjorie a legitimate suspect or not?"

"Yes!" said Rasheed. "She testified against herself. Motive, method, and opportunity are all present. Her husband treats her as someone in the lowest caste and she seemed genuinely fearful of physical harm if he discovers her actions to divorce him."

Heather saw Steve as he nodded with each point Rasheed made, and said, "Well done, Rasheed, but how will you prove she killed Michelle?"

"Me? I'm only a humble—"

Steve didn't give him a chance to finish the sentence. "We know, Rasheed. You're only a humble chauffeur."

Heather raised her voice. "What about you, Detective Smiley? Is Marjorie still a murder suspect?"

Steve dodged the question. "Did I tell you Marjorie wants to buy one of your condos or rent an apartment? I called your sales team and gave them her name and number. They said sales are going like gangbusters. Word is out that your property can withstand a hundred-year flood."

She shot a glance at Rasheed. "Get used to Steve not answering questions, especially when he's getting close to the end of an investigation."

Rasheed's eyelids widened. "He knows who's playing fast and baggy with poison?"

"Fast and loose," came the words from the back seat.

Rasheed slapped his knee. "It is my turn to tease you. I purposefully misspoke that expression to see if you would correct me. You fell into my trap."

Steve let out a low growl.

"By the way," said Rasheed. "Since I did the most work yesterday, I should get the Lumberjack breakfast and you, the Lumberjill."

Heather kept a straight face. "He has a point, Steve."

From the back seat came the lament, "I've created a monster."

"A hungry monster," said Rasheed.

Heather summarized her feelings. "First breakfast with three of my favorite monsters, and then we'll interview Claude." She paused. "Notice that I included Le Roi in the trio. This has the makings of a wonderful day."

Steve leaned forward. "Do you realize that's your first attempt at humor since this summer?"

"No," she said with incredulity. "Have I been that much of a stick in the mud?"

Steve didn't directly answer the question, but said, "You're getting back to your old self, and your timing couldn't be better. One more interview, and it will be time to put the pieces together."

"Are you sure?"

"Unless something unforeseen pops up, like another person being poisoned."

Rasheed ended the conversation with, "Must we speak of poison with the restaurant in sight?"

THE ELEVATOR DOOR CLOSED BEHIND HEATHER AS STEVE continued his thought. "No wonder Rasheed wanted to stay in the car and read. From what you've told me, he's thin as a rope. How did he eat everything on the Lumberjack special?"

"It defied at least one law of physics. He won't read two pages before he slips into a food coma." They entered Heather's outer office and greeted her receptionist and personal assistant.

"Your father and Jack want you to call them when you get a chance," said Pam.

"Anything else going on here or at the jobsite?"

"I'm under strict instructions not to tell you if there is."

"That's the correct answer," said Steve. "I need her mind clear of anything related to her project for the next couple of weeks."

Heather didn't grumble. She wouldn't say it too loud, but she was enjoying the break from the treadmill of work that had put her in the hospital. They walked into her office and waited for Claude to arrive.

Heather glanced at Le Roi when Claude Hicks came through the door to her office. The dog stayed at Steve's side, but his ears stood at attention and his nose wiggled as if he was having olfactory sensory overload. She shifted her gaze to their guest. "By the way Steve's dog is reacting, you must have had something delicious for breakfast."

"It was more of an early brunch, with a couple of chef friends I know. Nothing too fancy. We started with mimosas and a charcuterie board, fruit cups drizzled with wild honey and a squeeze of lemon, Bananas Foster French Toast casserole, venison and pork sausage, and thick-sliced mesquite-smoked bacon."

A brief wave of nausea swept over Heather as unchecked

gluttony seemed to surround her on all sides. That wasn't exactly true, as she and Steve had left over half of their breakfast on their plates.

She mentally regrouped. "Thank you for coming in. We have a few more questions for you, and this shouldn't take long."

"Always glad to help."

Steve had already made his way to the conference table. Heather sat with her back to the wall on Steve's right side while Claude squeezed into a chair opposite her and on Steve's left side. Without prompting, Le Roi left his bed, took quick steps toward the table, gave Claude a thorough sniff and sat beside him.

"If you don't mind," said Claude, "I forgot to take my allergy medication this morning. Could you send the dog back to the other side of the room?"

Heather explained. "Le Roi is reacting to something he smells."

This was all she needed to say for Steve to get a mental picture of what was going on. "I believe I told you before that Le Roi is a trained police dog. Part of his training involved detecting illegal drugs and various types of explosives. I'm sure there's a simple reason for him to react. Are any of the chefs you were with this morning avid sportsmen?'

"Not that I know of."

Heather asked, "Perhaps one of them smoked a joint before they came?"

"Not to my knowledge, but I wouldn't put it past any of them."

"That's probably it." Steve gave the command in French for Le Roi to return to his bed. The dog hesitated but did as instructed.

Heather wondered why Steve didn't follow up on what Le Roi might have smelled but trusted him enough to believe he had his reasons. Then she second-guessed herself. She was on the verge of saying something, but Steve asked, "Do you often have chefs over for breakfast?"

"Rarely for breakfast, but I've made friends with many people over the years who have a keen interest in food. I'll host a dinner party once or twice a week and attend at least one more."

"Do the gatherings include wine pairings?" asked Heather.

"Of course. After we receive the email announcing the menu, everyone selects a wine pairing and brings it. It's a friendly competition to see who can bring the wine that blends the best with the main dish. Decisions are sometimes controversial and we're not bashful about voicing our opinions."

Steve jumped back in before Claude could continue his discourse. "That sounds like an expensive hobby."

Claude lifted his chins. "Playing golf, painting with watercolors, or collecting shot glasses is a hobby. Being a serious epicurean is a way of life. It's a passion shared by the intellectual elite and royalty for centuries."

Heather asked, "Why doesn't your wife share your passion for food?"

Claude lowered his gaze to his thick hands. His voice took on a tone that hinted of conspiracy wrapped in regret. "It's clear to me that any love Marjorie had for me ended many years ago." He hesitated. "I believe my wife tried to kill me in Houston but killed Michelle instead."

"That's a serious accusation," said Steve. "What proof do you have?"

"Isn't the body of an innocent woman enough?"

Steve folded his hands in front of him. "It takes solid evidence, not suspicion."

Heather played the good cop. "If you know anything that could help clear an innocent man, now is the time to tell us. We've been told you and Luke have had your differences, but that's no reason to keep vital information to yourself."

Claude seemed to consider his options while Heather and Steve waited. The pharmacist finally said, "I ordered the boeuf bourguignon; Michelle ordered the chicken confit. But the server gave my dish to her, so we traded plates. We weren't the only ones with the wrong entrée; I saw people trading all over the room. The service was atrocious."

Steve pulled a hand down his cheek. "So, you have no solid proof your wife tried to poison you."

"None, other than what I just told you; but her hostility toward me has increased more and more this year."

"Thank you for coming in," said Steve. "You've been most helpful."

"I hope so. I'm not fond of Luke, but I'm convinced he didn't poison Michelle."

"But you believe Marjorie did?" asked Heather.

"Marjorie didn't mean to kill Michelle. She meant to kill me. Whoever she hired to poison my food, put it in the wrong entrée."

Steve reentered the conversation. "We know you and Marjorie are deep in debt. Why would she want to kill you?"

Claude hung his head. "She's been hiding money from me, and I know what she's been doing with some of it."

"And what's that?" asked Heather and Steve at the same time.

"A life insurance company contacted me and said I'd need to submit to a physical exam before they could give me the reduced rate they advertised. There's no telling how much Marjorie will collect if I die."

Steve held up a finger and said, "There's one other thing that's been bothering me, a stain on the tablecloth. I smelled paté de foie gras."

"You have a very discerning nose. I brought a small jar with me that I shared with Michelle."

"That explains it."

Heather stood. "You've been most helpful. Let me show you out, Claude."

Le Roi stood with his nose twitching as soon as Claude extricated himself from the chair. A low growl sounded until Steve snapped his fingers.

Heather returned to her chair at the table after thanking Claude again for his time. "Le Roi alerted to either drugs or explosives."

"I know," said Steve. "Do Claude and Marjorie live in the country?"

"Yes."

"Do you have their work schedules?"

"They both work this afternoon on the same shift."

"Good. Let's send Rasheed on a field trip with his book on plants."

"Is he looking for hemlock?"

"Your thinking is getting clearer by the minute."

32

Rasheed's accent seemed heavier than normal when Heather and Steve returned to the car. Steve wasted no time in giving their driver his assignment for the afternoon. "We want you to go to Claude and Marjorie Hicks's home. Does that book on plants found in Texas forests have a picture of hemlock?"

"Yes, and the photos are in color. It's a fern-like plant that has a green stalk with purple dots or splotches and white flowers that bloom in the spring and summer."

"What about in the fall and winter?"

"A mature hemlock will drop its seeds and the plant will die. It has a two-year life cycle, but the seeds all but ensure it will return. The plant prefers moist areas, like ditches and the banks of creeks."

"Could you recognize a plant this time of year?"

"The purple dots on the spindly stalk and bowed branches make it recognizable."

Heather took her turn. "I'll give you the address. It's off a country road in a low-lying, sparsely populated area of the county. The people living at the residence shouldn't be home this afternoon."

"Do you want me to bring you a sample of the plant?"

Steve had the answer. "Take a photo of one if you can find it. We'll also need to know the location and how close it is to their home."

"I will enjoy the walk in the woods. It's what I need to atone for my sin of eating like a goat."

Rasheed delivered them safely to Heather's home. "I'll pull into the garage, but I noticed a delivery on your front porch."

Heather shot a glance toward the front door but was too late to see what Rasheed had noticed. "Thanks. I'll get it as soon as we're inside." With phone in hand, she said, "I sent you a text with Claude and Marjorie Hicks's address. Good hunting."

"I'll search until dark if necessary. Will you have further need of me tonight?"

"Not tonight," said Steve, "but be here at eight thirty tomorrow morning."

"Why?" asked Heather.

"Have you spoken with Jack lately?"

"Every day, but we didn't talk about the case."

"Luke's bond reduction hearing is tomorrow afternoon. We have a meeting with Jack tomorrow morning at nine at his office. You and I will spend the rest of today putting together evidence and testimonies."

Surprise filled Heather's voice. "What's today's date?"

"December the eighteenth," said Rasheed.

"Holy smoke," said Heather. "That means there's only one week left before Christmas."

Steve chuckled. "Your math is also improving."

"I haven't thought about presents for anyone, let alone done any shopping."

Steve waved away the comment. "Under the circumstances, no one is expecting anything from you this year."

"That may be, but I couldn't live with myself if I don't do something. What do you want?"

"Nothing."

"Come on, help me out." She stuck out her bottom lip. "After all, I've been sick."

The hyper-pathetic plea produced a roaring laugh from Steve. "All right, I'll take pity on you. I want a fruitcake, but it has to be a Collin Street fruit cake."

Heather looked to her left. "What about you, Rasheed?"

"Me? It is not the place of a humble servant to presume to ask for anything."

Steve said, "You can drop the humble servant routine. She'll make your life miserable if you don't tell her what you want."

Heather gave her head a firm nod. "Steve's right."

Rasheed pinched his lips together, which gave him the appearance of a man deep in thought. "I'd like a book. Plato's *The Republic.* Tomes that discussed ethics and politics were some of the first burned when they closed the university."

"Excellent choice," said Heather. She didn't tell him he would receive a large bookcase filled with ancient classics.

Rasheed's departure left Steve and Heather alone to discuss the case. Steve retrieved his laptop while Heather grabbed her valise, with everything she needed to reference emails, conversations, and legal pads with notes. Steve sat at the dining room table, took off Le Roi's vest, and gave him instructions to take it to his room. The dog then returned to sit by Steve's side. The obedience earned a pat on his head and an instruction to go to his bed by the fireplace.

"Who do you want to start with?" asked Heather.

"No one, until you make a pot of coffee. You know that deep thinking requires strong coffee. I can't remember ever solving a murder without it."

Heather rolled her eyes. "I wonder how long and how much coffee it's going to take before my brain fully kicks in."

"All things considered, you're making remarkable progress, but I can tell you're not there yet. You didn't get the package off the front porch."

She knew Steve was right. The old Heather wouldn't tolerate

things out of place, which included deliveries left outside. "Now that you've said something, it will drive me nuts if I don't bring it in and see what's inside. Are you expecting something?"

"No, but it's only a week before Christmas. It's that time of year when packages are supposed to come."

She gave Steve a long look. Something was different about him. "Be careful, Steve; you're getting dangerously close to losing your membership in the Ebenezer Scrooge club."

"Not yet, but I must admit I'm enjoying some of the old Christmas songs you have playing in the kitchen. Perhaps Maggie's Ghost of Christmas Past is growing tired of haunting me."

This confession struck Heather as being a profound admission. She wondered how many more Christmases he'd endure before he could fully enjoy the season.

They both seemed to snap out of the spirit of Christmas at the same time. "I'll get the package and start the coffee," she said.

"Do you want to take Le Roi with you?"

"Why would I do that?"

"To sniff for explosives. There's at least one person out there who isn't content with putting a lump of coal in my Christmas stocking."

"I'll bring it in but won't open it. Le Roi is snoring so loud, he must be dreaming of chasing bad guys. He can give it a good sniff after his nap."

"You know that won't work. He's trained to protect. You won't make it three steps into the hallway before he's in front of you. Make the coffee then try to beat him to the front door."

"You're probably right, but I'll put him to the test."

Le Roi was lying on his back with his head lolled to one side when Heather pushed the button on the coffee pot. After removing her shoes, she walked on the balls of her feet toward the front door. She turned the corner without the dog giving any sign he'd detected her destination. She picked up the pace and was reaching for the doorknob when he bumped her leg and looked at her.

If eyes could speak, Le Roi would have said, "Nobody goes in or out with me knowing about it."

Steve followed his laugh with, "I told you so."

She reached her hand straight out and gave Le Roi a good scratch behind his ears and opened the door. The dog took a couple of steps onto the front porch, went to the Christmas bag, sniffed, and sat.

Heather took two steps back into the home and shouted, "He alerted to something in this gift bag."

The tap of Steve's cane sounded on the tile floor as he hollered for Le Roi to come to him. After praising the dog and giving him a treat, he turned his attention to Heather. "Describe the delivery."

"It's a Christmas bag about sixteen inches tall. The base is about one foot by one foot."

"Can you see inside the bag?"

"The top seems to be gapped open. I'll take a quick look."

She walked to the bag, making sure she didn't jostle it. "It's a plain white box, about six to nine inches tall."

"Come back in and call the police. I'll call Leo. I think I know why Le Roi alerted, but the bomb squad needs to tell us for sure."

Heather half-mumbled, "If I have another house destroyed, somebody will pay dearly."

33

The first fire truck followed a patrol car. Both parked a good distance away from Heather's driveway. Their response was so quick that Heather, Steve, Le Roi, and Max had barely cleared the garage when they arrived. Heather stopped to confirm the reason for her call and told the officer they were leaving the immediate area. She also told him she'd left the home unlocked and clear of all humans and pets.

Heather chose a nearby convenience store parking lot to watch the onslaught of emergency vehicles. It reminded her of a gentle rain that morphed into a steady downpour which left her quiet subdivision saturated.

Steve said nothing as Max wailed, protesting the confinement of his carrier. Le Roi looked through the mesh wire on full alert. Sirens and emergency lights were some of his favorite things. It took a while, but the vehicle she was looking for passed in front of them. "There's the portable command center."

Steve broke his silence. "Get behind it and follow them in." Heather did and parked behind the headquarters-on-wheels about three blocks from her home.

After a flurry of activity related to setting up, the center was open for business. Heather's phone rang. The conversation didn't take long. She turned to Steve. "That was the chief of police. He wants us to join him in the command center."

Steve nodded, opened his door, and went to the back of the car to get Le Roi. Heather considered taking Max inside, but the idea of lugging such a heavy load didn't appeal to her. Besides, it was a nice, cool day and Max had finally stopped complaining. She opened the door to the mobile command center for Steve and Le Roi. Their four-legged partner looked right at home among the representatives of multiple emergency agencies.

A man Heather didn't recognize was the first to speak. "Half of my available personnel and equipment are here evacuating a three-block area around your home. This better not be a false alarm."

Steve spoke with confidence. "It's some sort of explosive or an attempt to poison me, Heather, or both of us. I'm betting on the latter, but we'll have to wait to find out."

Radios crackled and a woman monitoring them announced, "Houston bomb squad has an ETA of fifteen minutes."

Heather found a spot by the door where she settled Steve into a folding chair. Another report came over the radio from a K9 officer. His dog didn't alert to anything. Steve reacted by saying, "Just as I suspected."

The bomb squad had with them a portable X-ray machine which later verified the absence of anything mechanical in the package. Steve told them again it was much more likely they would find poison instead of a bomb. After an extensive discussion, the experts agreed with Steve, and officers took the box containing a Christmas fruitcake for analysis. From start to finish, it only took three hours to make the determination to lift the evacuation order.

With the crisis averted, Heather and Steve expressed their thanks to the supervisors and stepped down from the command center. Heather opened the back door of the SUV for Le Roi. Steve was buckling his seatbelt when Heather closed the car door and noticed her phone on the center console. She retrieved it and counted seven missed calls from Jack. "Let me make a quick call. I'm sure Jack's worried sick."

Jack answered on the second ring. "What in the world is going on? Are you all right?"

"Everyone's fine. We received a suspicious package on our doorstep and Le Roi alerted to it. Considering all that's happened, we weren't taking any chances."

Steve interjected. "Someone's trying hard to ruin our Christmas."

Heather took her turn. "I called the police and they sent a bomb squad. They've canceled the evacuation now, and we're going home."

"I'm coming over."

"Good," said Steve. "Bring Briann and we'll call out for pizza. Let's have the meeting we scheduled for tomorrow morning."

"Briann is doing a sleepover with a pack of her friends tonight so she won't be with me. Tomorrow they're going Christmas shopping. While she's doing fun holiday stuff, I have to represent Luke in court."

Heather broke in. "Stop whining. You hate Christmas shopping almost as much as Steve does. Your idea of holiday fun is going into the woods and killing something with fur or feathers."

"I plead guilty to both charges." He took a longer-than-normal pause. "Today's bomb scare may help me tomorrow. One thing is for sure, Luke had nothing to do with what happened today."

"I already thought of that," said Steve.

A note of hope filled Jack's next question. "Have you added any new evidence or testimonies that I don't know about?"

"Heather, Rasheed, and I have been busy. You'll have too much if you use it all. I don't want to play all my cards."

"I'll wait until I'm there to ask you to explain, but you need to give me enough to convince the judge to reduce Luke's bail. His mother is making me rethink my choice of careers. I'm leaving my office now before she calls again."

"We'll be home," said Heather.

After the short trip home, Heather eased her car into the garage. Steve was out his door before she could unlatch her seatbelt. She released Max from his carrier and allowed him to flee from the car on his own.

Steve and Le Roi walked past her to the door leading into the house where Steve cracked open the door and gave Le Roi the command for him to clear the dwelling of any intruders. In he went, on full alert. With no regard for danger, Max followed.

Before Heather could respond, the cat's hissing screech came from somewhere in the house, followed by the yelp of an injured dog.

Steve chuckled, "Serves him right. That dog should know by now that no one messes with Max's kitty treats."

Heather marched into the house. "Le Roi better not smear blood on my chair again."

The dog was upstairs by the time Heather made it to where Max crouched, crunching on his pre-supper treats. She looked behind her. "There's no blood trail."

Steve cleared the hallway. "You'd better put on a fresh pot of coffee. We have a lot of ground to cover tonight."

The words and the way he said them caused a tingle to run down Heather's spine. "You have everything figured out, don't you?"

"Most of it."

"Both murders?"

"Uh-huh, but there's a couple of loose ends that need tying up."

"Do you want Jack to hear all you have to say?"

Steve surprised her by answering her question with one of his own. "Has he been a good boy all year?"

She fought off the desire to laugh and matched the serious tone of his words. "Jack's been a much better little boy than I've been a good little girl."

"Then he deserves something special. I'll tell him almost everything."

"Almost everything?"

"Maggie taught me Christmas was the season for secrets and surprises."

Heather turned to go make coffee and mumbled, "Good surprises I can handle. I'm asking Santa for no more bad ones."

Steve shuffled off to his room and came back with his computer and a set of headphones with a microphone attached. He looked like an airplane pilot, but the gear allowed him to perform all kinds of activities by himself.

Heather retrieved her valise but waited for him to dictate his notes of the morning's interview with Claude Hicks uninterrupted. The sound of the garage door opening drew her attention away from listening to Steve. She didn't need to announce Rasheed's return as Le Roi thundered down the stairs and sprinted to the garage door.

Rasheed's habit was to knock three times, wait precisely ten seconds, then enter. Le Roi was used to the routine and their driver never pressed his luck with a premature entrance.

"Come in," shouted Heather.

"Thank you, and blessings upon this home," said Rasheed.

"Steve's in the dining room waiting for your report. Don't tell him what you found until we each have a cup of coffee in front of us."

"You bring back memories of being many years younger in my home country. Business is never discussed until a hot drink is served and halfway consumed."

She joined the men as they sat talking about the weather forecast for Christmas Day. Neither seemed in any hurry to discuss Rasheed's hunt for hemlock. Heather made it through half of her cup of scalding coffee before her curiosity got the better of her. "Well, did you find any hemlock?"

"Yes, and yes, again," said Rasheed, and quickly explained. "I found a stream." He paused. "It wasn't really a stream. More like a seep. It was very slick and muddy. The book said this was a likely place for hemlock to grow. I also walked down a fence line and found what might have been some, but I couldn't tell for sure."

Rasheed then gave a detailed account of his foray into the woods. Steve finally interrupted when the philosopher-turned-botanist took a breath. "Did you take photos?"

"Of course. I'll show them to Heather." He manipulated his phone and placed it in front of her. She examined the photos. "The stem has purple splotches, just like the photos in Rasheed's book."

She dragged her finger across the screen. "Where did you take this photo? This looks like a greenhouse of some sort."

"Yes, but don't worry," said Rasheed. "I wore gloves, and the property has no close neighbors. There was no lock on the door, so I walked in with no trouble."

"Did you check to see if there were security cameras on the property?"

"Ah... It was an unfortunate oversight on my part. Am I in trouble?"

Steve sat up straight. "It's too late to worry about that now. What does the photo show?"

Heather gave the answer. "It's a mason jar containing some sort of liquid. The label on the bottle reads, DANGER, POISON! It's sitting next to a much larger jar of what looks like hemlock stems and wilted flowers."

"And seeds," said Rasheed with excitement.

"And illegally found," said Heather.

Steve smiled. "Let's not quibble over a legal detail. Claude spends all his time, energy, and money on food. I doubt he'd waste any of those things on security cameras for this greenhouse."

"We still need to tell Jack," said Heather.

Steve lifted his head. "There he is now. He'll never sneak up on anyone as long as he's driving that old truck."

Heather greeted Jack at the front door with a sprig of mistletoe in her hand. She made sure he saw it and raised it above his head. A soft smile preceded a smoldering kiss. He spoke after they came up for air. "That's one Christmas tradition I vote we keep all year round."

She took him by the hand and led him to the dining room table where Steve and Rasheed sat. Steve took the lead. "Since Briann didn't come, I make a motion that we order Indian food instead of pizza."

Heather rushed into the next sentence. "Hearing no objections, the motion passes. I'll surprise you with what we eat."

"Good choice," said Steve. "I want to begin by summarizing what I believe will happen tonight, tomorrow, and the next day." He held up his index finger. "Tonight, we'll all share what our investigations have revealed."

Jack spoke up. "Is Rasheed part of the team now?"

Steve gave his head a firm nod. "He helped us immensely today and has an interesting story to tell you."

"What about tomorrow?" asked Heather.

"Jack's going to earn his wages tomorrow." Steve turned his head to face the attorney. "Tomorrow morning you'll need to meet with detectives and someone in the district attorney's office who can make a big decision."

"What kind of decision?" asked Jack.

"To be in favor of reducing the bail on Luke Bains."

Jack puffed out his cheeks and blew out full breath. "I'll need something equally big to convince them of that."

Steve smiled. "There are multiple people with the motive, means, and opportunity to give the police and D.A. You'll see what I'm talking about later but keep this in mind: All you promised your client was a reduction in bail, and that's all we're after tomorrow afternoon."

"I don't understand" said Jack and Rasheed at the same time.

"You will the day after tomorrow when the police gather all the suspects from both murders in Jack's office."

Heather wrapped up the brief outline by saying. "I can tell by the sound of his voice that he knows who killed Michelle Le Blanc and Connie Petrovitch and he can prove it." She stared at Steve with admiration and frustration. "We need to prepare for a Christmas surprise."

Jack asked, "You don't know who the killer is?"

Heather gave her head a slow shake. "Not this time. It's going to be a Christmas surprise for everyone."

34

Twinkling Christmas lights, a forty-foot tall fully decorated tree, and a massive holly wreath comprised the exterior decorations of the county courthouse. Once inside, Heather, Steve, and Le Roi met Jack in the hallway outside the courtroom. For the occasion, she wore a midnight blue skirt with a matching blazer covering a white, collared blouse, and black high heels. She'd corralled her long, auburn hair into a tight bun at the back of her head. This was her go-to style when appearing in court. Her acknowledgment of the holiday season was a bejeweled broach of a snowman, a gift from her mother years ago.

She and Jack had a long-standing agreement to minimize public displays of affection when they were working. It wasn't unheard of for one of them to break the agreement, but they kept the violations to a minimum. Heather started the conversation. "Rasheed is parking the car; in case you were wondering. He and Steve will sit at the back of the courtroom and listen."

Steve joined in. "Did you have much trouble convincing the D.A. to agree to a reduced bond?"

"The D.A. let the chief of police do most of the talking. He didn't like it, but that's because he realized the case wasn't as airtight as his detectives led him to believe. I had to tell them more than I wanted to in order to make the deal."

"Did you give them anyone but Claude Hicks as a viable suspect?"

"Only his wife, Marjorie. The chief thinks they were working together to harvest hemlock. He obtained a warrant to search their property and greenhouse this morning."

Steve asked, "What about tomorrow? Is the chief agreeable to bringing everyone to your office?"

"He wasn't in the mood to hear anything else from me last night. I think you and Heather will have better luck talking to him."

Heather thought this unexpected news might upset Steve, but he surprised her. "Leo and I will take care of the chief. I should have known he'd react like he did. The chief is under pressure to put someone in prison for killing Connie Petrovitch. His detectives didn't keep an open mind and stopped fishing when they reeled in the first fish that swam by."

Jack asked, "What will you do if the chief arrests Claude and Marjorie Hicks?"

"He'll be in no hurry to do that today."

"Why not?"

"He already has egg on his face for making a rush judgment about Luke killing Connie. Neither Marjorie nor Claude are flight risks, so he'll chew out his detectives and tell them to make sure they have enough evidence to convict before they arrest anyone else. He'll probably also say the arrest and incarceration of Luke could mean a lawsuit." Steve finished his remarks with, "All we need is one more day and to get Luke out of jail."

Rasheed arrived and said, "I love all the decorations and everyone wishing me a Merry Christmas, but I am confused about how a fat man in a red suit can bring presents to every qualified person in the world. It defies logic and logistics."

Heather answered. "Santa has lots of helpers."

"Do you mean the elves in his workshop at the North Pole?"

"He has other helpers besides them. Are you familiar with the Latin words *in loco?*"

"It means in the place of."

"Correct. Everyone can act *in loco Santa*, regardless of age or nationality."

"Now the custom makes sense."

Jack broke in. "It also makes sense to not keep the judge waiting. It's time to get Luke out of jail in time for Christmas, or his mother will fill my socks with lumps of burning coal with me wearing them."

On the way to the half wall that separated the gallery from the official proceedings, Heather noticed Mary Jo Bains staring at them. Luke's mother rose and blocked Jack's path. "This will be your only chance to show you're worth the money I'm paying you."

The statement didn't deserve a response. Jack and Heather passed through the swinging half-door and settled at the defense table, while Steve, Rasheed, and Le Roi took seats at the rear of the courtroom. A young attorney from the D.A.'s office sat at an identical table, looking over notes. Jack leaned toward Heather and whispered, "They sent a new-hire, fresh out of law school."

Heather replied, "She looks scared. I hope she has sense enough not to mess this up."

Luke, dressed in an orange jumpsuit, appeared through a side door, escorted by two deputies. They placed him in a chair at Jack's table and stood behind him. As expected, handcuffs and a belly chain limited the movements of his arms.

Before Luke could ask a question, a third deputy called out, "All rise!" The normal announcement of the judge's name, title, official data concerning the court, and warnings opened the proceedings.

As soon as the judge settled into her high-backed chair, she announced, "Be seated." The rustle of people following her instruction preceded her saying, "Prosecution and defense attorneys, approach the bench."

Jack, Heather, and the Assistant D.A. did so.

The black-robed woman covered her microphone with her hand. "It's my understanding that you have come to an agreement to reduce bail from two and a half million dollars to one-hundred thousand. Is this correct?"

"Yes, Your Honor," said Jack.

"Uh... that's correct, Your Honor. The district attorney feels the subject is not a flight risk, and..."

The judge interrupted. "A simple yes is sufficient."

"Yes, Ma'am. I mean, yes, Your Honor."

This brought a smile from the judge.

"Let's not drag this out. I have ten things to do today and none of them involve dispensing justice. I've read the proposal submitted by the defense, and the response from the District Attorney's office. Stand back."

What followed was the shortest bond reduction hearing Heather had ever witnessed.

Mary Jo blocked the aisle again as she and Jack approached her. "Do you mean to tell me I had to pay forty-thousand dollars for fifteen minutes' work?"

Jack lifted his chin. "I explained my fee, and you agreed in writing that the charges were reasonable. In fact, I'm not finished because the murder charge is still pending. I'll need to see you and Luke in my office tomorrow morning at ten o'clock, and I'll tell you what to expect next. This was just round one of a long fight."

Mary Jo's eyelids narrowed. "We'll be there, but it won't be to talk about what happens next. I want a detailed accounting of every charge. If you think you can get by with robbing me, you have another think coming."

Jack's neck turned a lovely shade of pink as he walked around Mary Jo. Heather lingered with Luke's mother. "It will take a while before the paperwork is ready. Once that happens, you'll go to the detention facility where they'll release him."

"I want him to come with me now."

"You haven't posted bond yet." Heather stepped around her and rejoined Jack and Steve at the back of the courtroom.

Steve asked, "Where are we going for lunch?"

Jack had the answer. "Anywhere that serves good food and old whiskey. I need a shot of something strong to get a bad taste out of my mouth."

"Only one drink," said Heather. "It won't be time to celebrate until after tomorrow's meeting."

35

Heather began her day at 6:00 a.m. with deep breathing exercises and stretching on her yoga mat. It wasn't a full workout because there was much to do. She needed to shower, wash and dry her hair, and prepare herself mentally for the meeting in Jack's office. Hot water pounded her back as she washed her hair before she realized she hadn't thought about her construction project in over a day. She put her head under the water and spoke out loud. "Steve was right. The world didn't stop spinning when I didn't show up for work."

The tile floor of the bathroom felt like a block of ice. She looked forward to the day when she rebuilt her new home because it would have in-floor radiant heat. She slipped into a warm fleece robe and wrapped her hair turban style with a towel. The addition of winter house shoes was all it took before she went on her morning search for coffee.

As expected, Steve sat on a barstool with his dog sitting beside him. She spoke two sentences of morning greetings in French, which set Le Roi's tail swinging back and forth. It was then that she heard the strains of Christmas music playing softly.

"You sound like you're back to your old self," said Steve.

"I feel better than that," said Heather. "And speaking of being better, I like the music you have playing. It's good to see you enjoying yourself."

"Same to you. Between yesterday's shopping spree, your father arriving this afternoon, and you getting your mind off the project by working a couple of murders, this holiday season is turning out much better than I imagined. I can't wait until you see the presents Jack and your father have for you."

Heather held up her hand. "Teasing me like that is against the rules. No hints or I'll tell you what you're getting and ruin the surprise."

Steve slipped off his barstool. "The only thing I want today is for nothing to go wrong at the meeting."

Heather asked, "Did you make your list, and check it twice?"

Steve grinned. "Some were naughty, and some were nice." The smile left his face. "It's a shame people have to go to jail this close to Christmas, but it's more of a shame that two women aren't celebrating Christmas this year."

His voice went up a step. "You'd better dry your hair and dress for the day. Wear something festive. We need to be at Jack's office by nine-thirty. All the suspects except Mary Jo and Luke will arrive at nine-forty-five."

"And we'll have a full house at ten o'clock," said Heather. "It promises to be a stimulating meeting."

"Let's hope it's not too stimulating."

Leo waited in the parking lot outside of Jack's office for Heather, Steve, Rasheed, and Le Roi's arrival. A blustery north wind blew Heather's hair into her face as soon as she opened the front passenger door of the newest car. Steve and Rasheed met at the back and unloaded Le Roi, who sniffed the air with extra intensity.

Leo approached Steve and said, "This feels like old times."

"The characters change, but the basics remain the same. People kill other people; we find out who and why." Steve gave his former partner a toothy grin. "There are two big differences now. I don't arrest them, and you get stuck with the paperwork."

"You're only half right. You always stuck me with the paperwork."

Heather tugged on Steve's arm. "Come along, boys. This wind is wreaking havoc on my hair."

Steve turned toward Leo. "Rule number twenty-two in the book How to Have a Happy Life: Never respond to a woman when she mentions anything about her looks, especially her weight, or hair."

"I learned that the hard way," said Leo. "Let's get inside."

Heather led the way. Jack stood in front of the receptionist's desk, looking relaxed in jeans, boots, and a red and black plaid flannel shirt. The manly, relaxed, winter look took her mind off business. Without words, she approached him and broke their agreement concerning public displays of affection.

He received the gift and returned the kiss with one of his own.

Leo cleared his throat while Steve, who must have guessed what was happening, said, "You're not supposed to do that unless you're under mistletoe."

Briann spoke from behind her desk. "Thank you, Mr. Smiley. It's not right that they use Christmas to break rules they want me to follow."

Jack said, "I have a sprig in my pocket. Does that count?"

"It's close," said Steve, "but it might be best if we keep our minds on business. Are the detectives here yet?"

"They're running a little late but promised to be here by ten o'clock."

Steve's grin told Heather he'd expected this. It was passive-aggressive behavior, likely the result of being chewed out by the chief of police. He turned his attention back to Briann. "Did your dad tell you what to do?"

"Yes, sir. Rasheed is to help me this morning. We're to send everyone on the list he gave me to his office as soon as they arrive. The only exceptions are Luke Bains and his mother."

"Excellent," said Steve. He turned to face Jack. "Lead the way, counselor. There's work to do this morning."

Chairs, most of them retrieved from a conference room, formed a semi-circle in front of Jack's over-sized desk. Steve told Heather to place him and Le Roi on the far end of the line, close to Jack. Her assigned seat was at the other end of the crescent-shaped row.

Once seated, Steve said, "Leo, you have the seating chart. Be sure people are in the chair I assigned them to be in. You and the other detectives will either sit beside or stand behind our guests. I'm not expecting any trouble, but you and Heather both know what to do."

Jack's phone buzzed. He picked up the receiver and listened, then returned it to its place. "Erin Stoops and Marjorie Hicks are here."

Heather asked, "Did they come together?"

Steve shrugged. "Ask them after they're settled."

Rasheed led the women into the office, where Steve stood and gave instructions. "Good morning, Erin and Marjorie. Leo, would you show these ladies to their seats?"

"Of course. Erin, sit beside me. Marjorie, please sit beside Steve."

Jack spoke before the women could ask questions. "Welcome, and thank you for coming, ladies. As soon as the others join us, we'll get started. We know you have questions, but to save time, we'll wait for everyone to arrive before we answer them."

Heather fixed her gaze on Marjorie. "I have a question for you since you live some distance from town. Was there any sleet falling at your home this morning?"

"A little. It's always a few degrees colder in the country. I left early to make sure I wasn't late."

"What about you, Erin?"

"Wind and mist, but no sleet. I hate to be late. Marjorie and I arrive early to work nearly every day."

"Do you know each other well?"

Marjorie answered for both of them. "Even though there's an age difference, we've developed a friendship over the last few months." She looked directly at Heather. "I've convinced Erin to share an apartment with me in your development. Your team is helping us work out the details."

Erin quickly added, "I love the idea of having three bedrooms and a home office instead of a two-bedroom with no office. Splitting the rent will allow both of us to save money for a future home or town home."

Heather looked at Leo. His face had suspicion etched into it. She shifted her gaze to Steve, who took in the news without a reaction.

A knock on the door sounded. Rasheed appeared in the doorway and announced, "Mr. Hicks is here." The driver stood to one side and Claude waddled in while scanning the room. A scowl appeared on his face when his gaze rested on his wife. "What's this about, Marjorie? Why did the police tell me to come here this morning?"

Leo rose from his chair and identified himself. "Good morning, Mr. Hicks. Please take a seat next to your wife. We'll get started as soon as our last two guests arrive."

"I'll do no such thing."

"Yes, you will."

Heather tilted her head and gave him her most innocent, confused look. "What is it you don't want to do—sit beside your wife, or wait for the other guests to arrive?"

The question must have caught him off guard, as he couldn't form a sentence. Leo spoke again. "In case you don't remember me, I'm Detective Leo Vega with Houston Homicide. You have your choice of sitting beside your wife or sitting by Erin Stoops. Which will it be?"

Steve spoke up. "I understand a constable served you with divorce papers yesterday. Perhaps you'd feel more comfortable sitting beside Erin."

"I'd feel more comfortable in my kitchen."

"This meeting will determine if you'll be cooking at home or in jail for the foreseeable future," said Leo. "I strongly suggest you sit and be quiet."

Steve added, "We know the police searched your greenhouse yesterday. Other detectives will be here soon. Detective Vega will detain you if necessary, but that won't be necessary if you cooperate."

Claude lifted his double chin. "Very well, but I'll not sit next to the woman who betrayed me."

Heather directed him to the empty chair next to Erin, who smiled at him then said, "There's only two chairs left. I wonder who we're missing?"

Claude spoke as if he were omniscient. "Isn't it obvious? One of them is Luke Bains. The other must be for one of the out-of-town pharmacists who left the conference at the last minute. These people want to reenact the murder in Houston."

No one corrected or disputed his words. Five minutes passed before another knock sounded on the door.

36

Rasheed replayed his actions of guiding two more guests into Jack's office. He stood aside as Luke and his mother entered, with Mary Jo leading the way.

Jack stood. "Please come in and have a seat."

"Why are all these people here?"

"I'll explain after you sit down."

Steve added, "Good morning, Mary Jo. Luke, how was it to sleep in your own bed last night?"

"Wonderful. Sleeping on a two-inch thick plastic-covered mattress on a steel bunk is torture. Mom cooked a steak last night with all the trimmings. I thought I'd died and gone to heaven."

"What did you season it with?" asked Claude.

"None of your business," snapped Mary Jo.

A triplet of knocks sounded on the door. A man and a woman that Heather recognized as detectives walked in. Rasheed and Briann followed them, with Jack's daughter announcing, "I'll put the cake on the table. Rasheed has coffee or hot chocolate for anyone that wants it."

Jack gave further instructions. "Serve everyone please. We'll talk while we celebrate."

"Celebrate what?" asked Mary Jo.

Steve answered, "One thing is Luke being released on a very low bond."

Claude spoke next. "That looks like a fruitcake."

"It is," said Steve. "My late wife insisted we celebrate Christmas properly with fruitcake. I know everyone doesn't care for it, but I'm asking you to honor her memory by having a few bites. Pick out the candied fruit and nuts if you don't like them."

Briann and Rasheed busied themselves serving the dense cake on paper plates. They took drink orders and delivered them as most of those assembled ate a few bites of the cake. It surprised Heather when Claude had only two bites of his cake.

The mood lightened as Steve eased into things pertaining to the real reason for assembling the group. He narrowed the conversation by saying. "It's of interest to everyone here that the police have eliminated two people as suspects for the murder of Michelle Le Blanc in Houston."

"Who would that be?" interjected Claude.

Leo took his turn. "The two pharmacists from out of state. Their alibis checked out as they had no motive or connections to anyone in Texas."

Marjorie asked, "Does that mean you suspect one of us seated here, from Montgomery County, to be Michelle's killer?"

Steve spoke in a soft tone. "I wouldn't use the term suspect. Think of it as being a person of interest. It's only natural for the police to question you in order to discover who killed her and why." Steve paused. "It didn't help your case that you kept important information from us and the police."

Marjorie stiffened. "I did no such thing."

Steve let out a huff. "Multiple people saw you drinking way too much the night of the meet-and-greet at the conference. You told us that Claude's drunken behavior was what drove you into the table covered with glasses of champagne. Based on witness statements, you were three sheets to the wind."

"Can you blame me? Claude is such a glutton he insisted we

arrive early. That meant he pulled his usual shenanigans to get us both off work that day. I felt bad for Luke and Constance. We knew they were dating and looked forward to going to the conference together." She took a breath and pointed. "There's no limit to what that man will do for food and wine."

Claude replied with, "I shouldn't have wasted my time. Both were substandard."

Steve asked, "Is that why you overindulged and lied, too?"

He shrugged. "We paid good money to attend the conference. I drink too much when the quality of the food is horrid. It's a weakness that I cannot always overcome."

Marjorie added to Claude's admission. "He also used that 'weakness' excuse to bankrupt us on two occasions."

"That's not true," said Claude. "It was the fault of others for taking us to court and getting judgments against us."

"You silly man," said Marjorie. "You never intended to pay them back."

He shot back, "And you betrayed our marriage by lying when you said you'd found religion and were giving ten percent of your income to the Lord's work instead of helping me pay things off."

Steve interrupted. "I hope you both realize that the detectives are listening to what you're saying, and it's making them wonder if one, or both of you, killed Michelle Le Blanc. Leo knows about the money you owed Luke and how you switched name cards and dinner plates until Michelle wound up with poisoned food."

Marjorie shook her head in disgust. "One more reason for me to divorce Claude. If I'm under suspicion, it's because of his gluttony. The only things bigger than his appetite are his ego and his sense of entitlement. He talked Luke into loaning money to him — money he knew Luke couldn't recover in court. I believe Claude poisoned Michelle, but he meant to kill Luke."

"I did no such thing," shouted Claude.

Steve took hold of Le Roi's halter and whispered to him. The dog lunged forward with teeth bared, barking in a way that sent a bolt of fear down Heather's spine. No one dared move. The two local detectives had their hands on their pistols until Steve gave a simple command and Le Roi settled by his side.

Jack took his turn. "I hope everyone now understands that it's not a good idea to raise your voices." He paused. "Steve, I don't think you finished."

"Not yet. I want to ask the two local detectives to tell us what they found this morning."

"I'm Detective Kimberly Sims from the Montgomery County Sheriff's Office."

"And I'm Detective Mitch Logan from the Conroe Police Department."

The female detective took the lead. "Based on a tip from a confidential informant, we secured a warrant to search the grounds and greenhouse of property currently occupied by Claude Hicks. In that pre-dawn search, we discovered plants identified as hemlock. We also found a quantity of a substance that we believe to be a liquid form of hemlock. We're awaiting results from the lab to confirm our suspicions."

"Thank you," said Steve. "Claude, you have some explaining to do."

He let out a snort from his nose. "It's simple. Hemlock is a common plant with medicinal benefits if properly administered. I'm prone to allergies that lead to congestion, drainage, and severe coughs. What you found is a well-known home remedy for severe coughs. People in rural areas have used it for centuries."

"That may be," said Detective Sims, "but it's not legal."

Detective Logan added, "It's also enough for me to take you in for further questioning."

Steve thanked them but added, "Before you reach for your handcuffs, let me ask Marjorie Hicks a few quick questions. Are you still living with your husband?"

"Not for long. Erin has a spare bedroom that isn't being used."

"Did you know Claude was adding hemlock to cough syrup?"

"No, but it doesn't surprise me. He loves to experiment with many things in the kitchen."

Beads of sweat appeared on Claude's forehead. He retrieved a handkerchief and wiped his face.

Heather shook her head from side to side. "Claude, you're going to need a lawyer."

Steve asked if anyone needed a break. No one responded except Mary Jo. "Let's get this over with."

"Good idea. There's something that occurred to me the minute I heard that Constance Petrovitch died from an overdose of hemlock." He let the words settle until Jack asked, "What was that?"

"What are the chances of two young, attractive female pharmacists from the same county in Texas being poisoned with hemlock in the span of a couple of months?"

Jack responded, "It's not likely."

Steve rubbed his chin. "Sometimes we get so involved in the details of a case that we don't ask simple questions."

Detective Sims asked, "Are you saying the two murders are linked?"

"I'm saying we should have backed away and looked harder for things that are similar or the same in both cases. Let me ask everyone, what are those things?"

"Same poison," said Heather.

"Pharmacists," said Detective Logan.

"Gender and age of victims," said Detective Sims.

"Both victims were from the same county," said Leo.

Steve waited, but no one else said anything. "Your answers are all correct. In my mind, that means there are way too many similarities for the two crimes not to be linked."

Mary Jo spoke up. "The answer to who killed both of them is clear as the nose on your face. Luke told Erin Stoops to take a hike because he was interested in Connie Petrovitch. He's a normal, red-blooded boy. What can I say? Women fall for him, including Michelle Le Blanc. Erin had to eliminate the competition. She poisoned both of them."

Erin gasped.

"I considered all those things, but they don't add up. Erin wasn't at the banquet in Houston."

Leo spoke up. "My partner and I watched every bit of hotel video three times. Erin didn't have much of an alibi, but she wasn't at the banquet, wasn't a server, nor did she attend the conference. We may not know where she was when Michelle died, but we know where she wasn't, at the hotel."

"Then she hired someone to put the poison in the food."

A sly smile crossed Steve's face, but it left as quickly as it appeared. "Let's change gears for a minute. Is everyone feeling all right? The fruitcake isn't setting well on my stomach."

Heather took over where Steve had left off. "Perhaps it's because of what happened yesterday."

"What was that?" asked Jack.

"You know. The bomb scare that turned out to be a harmless fruitcake."

Jack asked, "Where did you get the cake we ate a few minutes ago?"

Steve answered. "Heather's electrical contractor left it on our front porch in a Christmas bag and Rasheed brought it inside. I tried to sneak a slice, but Heather thought it would be nice to save it to celebrate Luke coming home for the holidays." He grimaced and held his hand to his midsection.

Luke spoke next with more urgency. "What about the bomb scare?"

Mary Jo asked, "Were there two fruitcakes?"

Heather shifted her gaze and said, "We've been extra diligent about packages since someone burned our new homes. We called to report a suspicious package on our doorstep and the first responders evacuated our neighborhood. Houston's bomb squad took it away and disposed of it."

She turned and looked at Jack. "How are you feeling?"

"Fine, but I have a confession to make. I can't stand fruit-cake. You'll find my piece in the trash can under my desk."

"I only took one bite," said Heather. "It tasted bitter, so I ate no more."

Mary Jo spoke next. "If you were suspicious, why didn't you have the police take the first cake away?"

Steve shrugged. "Heather's electrical contractor sends her a cake every year." He paused, then said, "Let's get back to something I forgot to mention about similarities and believing in coincidences."

"What's that?" asked Heather.

"Both murder victims were born in foreign countries."

Claude Hicks threw up his hands. "What difference does that make?"

"Not much, in itself," said Steve. "But when you add it to all the other coincidences, it's one more brick in the wall that will eventually build a jail cell for someone in this room."

Steve clutched his stomach and bent over.

Jack asked, "Are you sure you can go on, Steve?"

"There's something I have to do to protect everyone who ate the fruitcake."

He gave a command in French and Le Roi rose and sniffed around the chairs.

"What's he doing?" asked Marjorie.

Heather answered for Steve. "Le Roi had special training in detecting a variety of substances."

"Like what?" asked Luke.

"All kinds of illegal drugs, explosives, and even poisons, including hemlock. Look at him. He's alerting to something."

Detective Logan shot to his feet. ""That's exactly how police K9's react to drugs. He's alerting to Mary Jo Baines!"

37

L e Roi returned to Steve's side. Heather doubted if anyone else noticed Steve give his dog a treat for a job well done.

"It's over, Luke," said Steve. "Your mother has no control over you anymore. No one but you paid attention to the server who delivered the main course to Michelle Le Blanc in Houston. You recognized your mother, didn't you?"

Mary Jo sat silent, with a look of defiance in her eyes.

Luke's eyes shifted left to right, as if looking for an answer.

Detective Sims asked, "Are you saying Mary Jo Bains poisoned Constance Petrovitch, too?"

Steve didn't answer the question. Instead, he said, "Luke, how did you enjoy your stay in jail?"

Luke snorted. "It was horrible."

"That's what I thought. You have a choice to make. You can keep protecting your mother or be free to live your life without her directing your every move."

"But she's my mother."

Steve mixed sympathy with reality when he said, "That's true, and she always will be, but she has to answer for what she's done."

Steve paused, then took up where he left off. "Luke, what do you think about your mother's new look? She's been on a spending spree, getting a full makeover and a new wardrobe. That and new furniture for her apartment are what we've observed. Now that she's going to jail and you're out on bond, you can check your bank accounts and see how much her habits have changed."

Leo gave his head a firm nod. "I looked at your accounts today. It looks like she's enjoyed spending your money."

Jack jumped into the conversation. "As your attorney, it's my duty to give you sound legal advice. Say nothing. This is your chance to save yourself from a very long prison sentence. Now that the police know who killed Michelle and Connie, they'll work backwards and find evidence to prove your mother's guilt."

Mary Jo shot out of her chair. "What kind of lawyer are you? I'm the one paying, and you're trying to put me in prison?"

Le Roi surged toward her, teeth bared and barking, but Steve held tight to the halter. "*Couché*," he commanded, then said, "That was close, Mary Jo. I'd hate to see what he would do to you if I hadn't stopped him."

Jack folded his hands together on top of his desk. "Mary Jo, sit down and make no sudden moves. You're not my client, so you'll get no more free advice from me."

Steve spoke in a low, serious tone. "Luke, you have nothing to gain and everything to lose by not telling the truth. I sense you're ready to live as a free man."

A sudden stillness settled over the room as Luke seemed to look inward. He lifted his head and looked at his mother. "You killed both of them because you couldn't stand the thought of sharing me."

Mary Jo spoke through gritted teeth. "I sacrificed everything for you, and you were ready to betray me. I should have known you'd turn out like your father. What else could I expect from someone with foreign blood?"

Steve moaned again.

"What do you mean foreign blood?" asked Luke.

"Your father was a fast-talking Italian, with no intention of making an honest woman of me. Do a heredity test if you don't believe me."

Leo looked at Jack. "I'd like to stay and get a statement from Luke, if that's all right with you?"

Detective Sims spoke before Jack could answer. "We'll all take statements at the county detention center."

Logan said, "I'll call for a patrol officer to take Ms. Bains to jail and book her in." He stood behind Mary Jo. "Stand up and put your hands behind your back. You're under arrest for the murder of Constance Petrovitch."

Leo said, "And I'm arresting you for the murder of Michelle Le Blanc."

Heather looked up in time to see a malevolent smile part Mary Jo's lips. "At least the blind guy who ate the fruit cake won't live long enough to see me go to prison. You might as well charge me with another murder while you're at it."

Detective Sims asked, "So it was you who put the poisoned fruit cake on Heather's porch?"

She sneered. "For a detective, you're not very bright. I knew from my visits with Luke that they were getting close to discovering the truth."

Steve groaned while clutching his midsection. "Did you also burn our new homes?"

"Why would I do that? I'm not an arsonist, but I'd like to shake the hand of the person who did."

Steve straightened up. "Thanks for the information."

Mary Jo's eyes narrowed to angry slits as she realized she'd been tricked.

Heather said, "That reduces my list of arson suspects to one person, and it's not Mary Jo."

Steve took over. "For those of you who ate fruit cake, don't worry. It wasn't poisoned. I had two slices for breakfast this morning."

Detective Sims broke in. "That's two more charges of attempted murder for delivering a poisoned cake to your home."

Steve didn't contradict her.

Heather stood. "Unless there's something else you need from us in the next two hours, Steve and I are taking our team to a champagne brunch. Detectives, we'll send you and Jack a copy of the recording I made of this meeting, along with our formal statements."

38

———

After dressing, Heather made her way into the kitchen where Steve sat wearing a perfectly hideous Christmas sweater. She greeted him with a cheerful, "Good morning and merry Christmas to you."

"Are you wearing the sweater you received last night?"

"I haven't turned on its lights yet. The ornaments and sequins are all I could stand before my first cup of coffee."

"Rasheed and I had a blast picking them out. Waiting until the last minute paid off with a seventy-five percent discount. Rasheed insisted on speaking with the manager and bargained with her until she agreed to another ten percent off because we wanted so many."

Heather rested her mug of stimulant on the kitchen counter. "Perhaps I should hire Rasheed as a procurement specialist."

"You could do worse."

Heather heard nothing but Le Roi yawn until Steve said, "Your father's up and leaving his room." Lines of concentration etched Steve's forehead. "That second step from the top landing always squeaks."

She sipped her coffee until her father made his grand appearance wearing a bright green sweater emblazoned with a picture

238

of one of Santa's elves. Her intention was to pay him a compliment, but she knew she'd burst out laughing if she tried.

Steve asked, "Does your sweater fit?"

"The fit couldn't be better, and I'm looking forward to seeing what everyone else looks like. I'm so happy to be away from Boston for the holidays. It was a close call flying out ahead of winter's first major snowstorm."

Heather found the switch to her sweater's battery and clicked it on. She held her arms out to her side. "I won't be able to sneak up on anyone wearing this."

Allister kept a straight face. "I'm having light bulb envy."

"Rasheed and I will have to find you something with more bling next year."

Her father turned to Steve. "I wish I could have been here to see you and Heather solve another murder." He corrected himself. "Make that two murders, and more attempted murders by poisoned fruit cake."

Steve shifted on his barstool. "Mary Jo confessing to spiking the fruit cake she delivered to our door was an unexpected bonus. Luke didn't turn on her until he realized she'd grown used to solving perceived threats by killing people."

Allister asked, "What made her confess to anything?"

"Ah," said Steve. "That's an excellent question. Many criminologists will tell you that most people are hard-wired to unburden themselves of guilt. Skilled interrogators and therapists know this gives them opportunities to face what they've done."

"Does that apply to all people?" asked Allister.

Heather responded for Steve. "Not if the person is a sociopath or psychopath."

"Right," said Steve. "For others, their defenses and self-deception aren't usually so strong they can live with what they've done. It took pressure and a little trickery to squeeze the truth out of Luke and Mary Jo. That's where Le Roi proved his worth."

Her father's eyebrows narrowed with a look of confusion, so

Heather explained. "Jack went duck hunting a couple of days before the big meeting in his office. I took two spent shotgun shells out of the pocket of his hunting vest without him knowing and taped them to the bottom of the chair Mary Jo would sit in."

Steve sat up straight. "We allowed everyone in the room to believe Le Roi alerted to hemlock, even though he detected spent gunpowder."

"Isn't that entrapment?" asked Allister.

Steve shook his head. "The recording Heather made clearly shows we stated Le Roi could detect many things, including explosives."

Allister had one more question. "Why did you include the three other people in Jack's office?"

A sly smile pulled up one corner of Steve's mouth. "To give Mary Jo false hope. She worked hard to point the blame at Erin Stoops. Luke was under instructions from Jack to say nothing to the police, so he didn't contradict his mother until after he realized what a monster she'd become."

Heather took her turn. "That left us with Marjorie and Claude Hicks as possible suspects. They were suspects in the two murders because of the wild hemlock on their property and the distilled hemlock found in their greenhouse."

"Will the police arrest either of them?"

Steve raised his shoulders and let them fall. "It's possible for them to go after Claude, but not Marjorie. Neither of them were completely honest with us to begin with, but we're used to that."

The ringing of the doorbell put an end to the talk of poisons, murders, and all else except hot chocolate and Christmas presents. Heather ran to open the front door while Steve and Allister made their way into the living room. The locks clicked, and she threw open the door. Father and daughter, each wearing gaudy sweaters, escaped the frosty air.

Briann received a hug and instructions. "After you put your presents under the tree, go to the kitchen and stir the hot chocolate. Steve and my father are so deep in conversation, they won't realize anything's burning until the smoke detector goes off."

Jack kicked the door shut behind him as he carried a covered casserole dish in one hand and balanced presents in the other. Heather wanted to greet him with a kiss under the mistletoe, but didn't trust him to keep everything balanced. Instead, she looked at the closed door and asked, "Where's your mom?"

"She came down with a sore throat and sniffles."

"Oh, my goodness. I hope it's nothing serious."

Jack shook his head. "I tried to get her to come, but you know Mom. If anyone came down with a cold because of her, she'd feel terrible."

Heather stuck out her bottom lip. "You, Briann, and I will go by to check on her this afternoon."

"That's what I told her. She said to put this in the oven on low heat to keep it warm."

Heather took the dish from him as he smiled, turned, and pointed to the sprig of mistletoe hanging above the front door. She whispered a choice he could make. "Would you prefer a quick peck now, or something better after we open presents?"

"Both."

"I like the way you think. Bend down and don't drop the presents."

It was a plan, but not a good one. The peck turned out to be a toe-curler and presents crashed to the floor. Steve's voice sounded from the living room. "Would you two get out from under the mistletoe? I'd like two big marshmallows in my hot chocolate and I want to open presents."

Heather slipped out of Jack's grasp and took the casserole into the kitchen. She even remembered to slide it into the oven and turn on the heat. Briann was filling Christmas mugs with rich brown liquid with a marshmallow or two bobbing on top.

Heather delivered mugs to her father, Jack, and Steve. Rasheed announced his arrival from the hallway leading to the garage. He strolled into the living room, sporting a lime-green

Grinch sweater, complete with matching snood. The blazing fire was his first stop, where he warmed his hands. Looking up from the flames, he examined the mantle and asked, "Is it custom to open Christmas cards as they arrive, or wait until after Santa comes?"

"As they arrive," said Heather. It was then she noticed an envelope poking out from behind the bow on the holly. She retrieved it and said, "This is addressed to you, Steve."

He chuckled. "If it's not written in Braille, you'll have to read it to me."

Heather tore open the envelope. Her eyes scanned the short message, and her eyes narrowed to angry slits. "The card reads: 'Too bad about the fire and not being able to have Christmas in your new home. When you mess with the bull, you get the horns.' It's signed, Bucky Franklin."

Silence descended on the room until Steve broke it by saying, "Bucky doesn't realize it, but he couldn't have given me a better Christmas present."

Heather wondered if some of her mental problems had rubbed off on Steve. "How is this good news?"

"Now we have proof that Bucky torched our homes. We can add another charge to the list of things he'll be convicted of once we catch him. I'm thinking about how many years he'll eat Christmas turkey from a metal tray in prison." He inhaled a breath and continued, "Nothing's going to spoil our Christmas. Let's finish our hot chocolate and open presents."

Briann passed out gifts, one by one, as everyone sipped hot chocolate. She squealed when she opened a new laptop.

Clothes dominated most of the other gifts until Briann took a long, narrow, expertly wrapped gift to her father and said, "This is to you from Heather. Whatever it is, there's something similar under the tree with my name on it."

Heather said, "Let's make an exception to the rule and both of you open them at the same time."

Neither Jack nor Briann objected. They tore into the packages revealing hard plastic gun cases. Jack looked at Heather. "Is this what I think it is?"

Briann had already placed her gift on the floor and flipped open a series of latches. Jack did the same. Both sat with mouths hinged open. "I can't believe it."

"Me either," said Briann. "I never thought I'd own a shotgun like this. Look at the engraving."

"I'm looking," said Jack as he flipped the lever and broke open the shotgun. "I've always wanted this exact Benelli shotgun. I can't wait to down a mallard or two."

"You won't have long to wait, but it won't be ducks," said Heather. "Look at the cards inside the case."

They glanced at each other and thrust their hands into the gun cases. Briann tore open her card first and read it. Her chin quivered. "This can't be true."

Jack swallowed hard as he cast his gaze to Heather. "This says we're going the day after tomorrow. How is that possible?"

Allister had the answer. "Steve came up with the idea. All I did was make a few phone calls."

"Don't let him fool you," said Steve. "Allister gets most of the credit. We started talking about how much Jack and Briann like to hunt. Before I lost my sight, I always wanted to go on a dove hunt in Argentina. It's hands down the best dove hunting in the world. That's all it took for Allister to run with the idea."

Allister handed Heather a present that looked like Jack's and Briann's. "I hope you like it."

Paper, ribbon and bows rained down as she ripped open the wrapping. She took out her new shotgun and ran her fingers over the stock.

Allister continued as Heather tried to read the card through tears. She looked up and said, "The only way this could be better is if you and Steve were going with us."

"We are honey. My airplane is undergoing its annual inspection, so I called your pilots. I hope you don't mind if we take yours."

"Spending time with you is the best gift you could ever give me."

The ringing of the doorbell took Heather by surprise. "Someone else needs to get the door while I find a tissue."

Steve and Le Roi were already on their way. They arrived back in the living room at the same time as Heather. He announced, "Heather, I couldn't gift-wrap your next present, but we hope you like it."

Rasheed appeared with a sleek German shepherd.

Max hissed and ran from the room. Le Roi locked his gaze onto the newcomer with his tail swinging like a pendulum.

Heather gasped. "You got me a dog?"

Steve spoke with pride. "Me, your dad, Jack, and Briann went in together on her. She's not just any dog. She's a trained police and therapy dog. Doctor Joy thought you could use a full time four-legged companion."

"Her name is Princess," said Briann.

Allister came to Heather and gave her a hug. "Doctor Joy wants you to ease back into work, so Rasheed will take you and Princess to Houston five mornings a week for training. That should last about three months. After training sessions, you two can return to the office and work the second half of the day."

Heather allowed the tears to fall without trying to catch them. She looked up at her father. "Daddy, this is the best Christmas of my life."

Thank you for reading *Hemlock And Homicide*. Whatever the time of year, I hope you enjoyed your Christmas escape as you turned the pages to find out whodunit! If you loved it, please consider leaving a review at your favorite retailer, Bookbub or Goodreads. YOUR review could be the one that helps another mystery lover discover their next great book!

To stay abreast of Smiley and McBlythe's latest adventure, and all my book news, join my Mystery Insiders community. As a thank you, I'll send you a *reader exclusive* Smiley and McBlythe mystery novella!

You can also follow me on Amazon, Bookbub and Goodreads to receive notification of my latest release.

Happy reading!
Bruce

Scan the image to sign up or go to brucehammack.com/the-smiley-and-mcblythe-mysteries-reader-gift/

www.ingramcontent.com/pod-product-compliance
Lightning Source LLC
Chambersburg PA
CBHW061807190726
48289CB00007B/2107